WHAT TEARS US APART

Also by Deborah Cloyed

THE SUMMER WE CAME TO LIFE

DEBORAH CLOYED

WHAT TEARS US APART

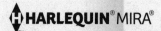

HARLEQUIN® MIRA®

Recycling programs
for this product may
not exist in your area.

ISBN-13: 978-0-7783-1379-3

WHAT TEARS US APART

For questions and comments about the quality of this book, please contact us at
CustomerService@Harlequin.com.

Printed in U.S.A.

First printing: April 2013
10 9 8 7 6 5 4 3 2 1

To debianca, and redbird.

Newswire America: December 31, 2007

NAIROBI, Kenya — Incumbent President Mwai Kibaki was hastily sworn in yesterday, beating out Raila Odinga in Kenya's heated election. Allegations of fraud sparked violence countrywide.

In Kibera, one of the world's largest slums and Raila Odinga's stronghold, thousands flooded the streets, bearing rocks and machetes, chanting, "No Raila, no peace!"

Members of Raila's Luo tribe lashed out at their Kikuyu neighbors—the tribe associated with Kibaki—setting shops and homes aflame. The Mungiki, Kenya's notorious Kikuyu mafia, retaliated, riots escalating into a rape and murder spree. By midnight, smoke blanketed Kibera, flames licked the sky, and mutilated bodies littered the roads as screams rang out from every corner of the slum....

PROLOGUE

December 30, 2007, Kibera—Leda

NO. PLEASE. PLEASE, WORLD, GOD, FATE, DON'T *let this happen.*

Each man's hands on Leda's skin are like desert sand. Hot. Gritty. Rough as splinters of glass.

She ricochets around their circle, a lotto ball in the air mix machine, fate holding its breath. Behind the lunging silhouettes of the men, the slum explodes—fire licking and climbing, spitting at the world. There's another sound, too, mixed with the whooshing sound of the inferno. Wood, metal, bodies—all crumbling, cracking, hissing and screaming in the flames. It is a symphony of loss.

The men, who are boys really, they yell incomprehensibly, but Leda knows their intentions.

They rip the buttons on her shirt.

They yank the hem of her skirt.

A cloud of reddish dust rises from their feet, as though trying to hide her. But the dust dashes away when Leda is flung to the ground.

For a moment nothing happens.

Then it's like vampires at the sight of a wound. The men converge—kicking, poking, laughing. They tug at all her protruding parts. Leda's a centipede in the dust, trying to fold in one hundred legs. Trying to protect the things that matter, things that cannot be undone.

Maybe they will just beat me and go away. This is not my fight. I came to help. Leda wants to shout in their faces. *I came to help.*

But then she hears it, jumbled with the clatter of their words. *Ita.* Another one says it. *Ita.*

So they know who she is.

She is a fish flopping, a tree fallen. A spider in the wind.

She is Ita's love.

For an instant, Leda thinks it will save her. But as their voices rise, she knows it has doomed her instead.

When the boy drops down on top of her, the force of it is like a metal roof pinning her in a hurricane.

Instantly, all Leda smells is him—sweat and dirt, but rancid, like musk and cheese rusted over with blood. He uses his trunk to flatten her into the ground, his rib bones stabbing into her sternum, her bare skin grinding into the rocks and trash. His legs and hands scramble for Leda's flailing limbs. The man-boys above laugh and holler.

All she can do is flail and scream.

Leda calls out for the man she loves, the only person who's ever really loved her.

But it's the devil who arrives instead.

Ita's beloved monster, Chege.

Chege's voice arrives first—a low growl, a familiar snarl. It is the battle cry of an unchained wolf, at home in the darkest of times.

Chege is above her. His dreads close over Leda and her attacker, a curtain of night.

"Help me," Leda says. *Did Ita send him?*

As Leda tries to decipher Chege's spitting words, he yanks the man off and her body takes a breath. The rancid smell, his clawing zipper, the pain in her lungs—it all disappears into the racket above and for one second Leda feels light as a sparrow in the sky. She allows herself to breathe. There is mercy in Chege's heart after all. He will save her. At least for Ita's sake.

But then Chege's eyes flicker, a flap of emotion like blinds shuttering daylight. His hand shoots down and wraps around her throat, a coiling python, and Leda's breath is lost. His other hand snaps the necklace from her neck. The gold necklace Ita gave her, the sacred chain that is everything to him.

This, Chege knows better than anyone.

He stares at the necklace in his fingers, his eyes bulging, and Leda knows the truth. Chege's heart isn't merciful, it's a furnace of coal that burns only with rage. When both his hands pull Leda up by the throat, the glint of the gold chain taunts her, the shiny sparrow charm a spark in her peripheral vision as the necklace drops to the dirt.

Up, up through the dust, Chege brandishes her like a chunk of meat.

He's claimed her. Head wolf gets the kill.

His eyes dart about. Leda sees it when he does—a door ajar. He smiles, baring his brown teeth.

Faster than she can scream, Chege kicks her feet to knock her off balance, then drags her across the alley, to the open door. The boys lap at their heels, eyes ravenous. Behind them, the fire rolls atop the mud shacks like a river of exploding stars.

Maybe they will burn for this. Maybe we all will.

Chege yanks her into the dark room, kicks the door shut, and all light goes out in the world.

CHAPTER 1

November 14, 2007, Topanga, CA—Leda

LEDA SAT IN THE SUN, FEELING JUDGED BY THE mountains.

Nearby trees wriggled their pom-poms of leaves, but Leda stared far off in the distance, where the scrubby canyon peaks took their turns in the sun and the rain, under the stars and the moon.

Everything in its place.

Except me.

A multicolored mutt entered the patio through a doggie door and hopped onto Leda's lap. He curled into a furry ball to be petted.

"I quit, Amadeus," Leda whispered.

The little dog looked up and sniffed.

"I know. Again." Leda nuzzled the dog's Mohawk. "Sorry, buddy, no more leftover filet mignon. I told François Vasseur to shove it."

Amadeus whined.

"Oh please, you won't starve." They wouldn't lose their cozy home in the canyon, either. Leda didn't have to be a chef, she didn't have to be anything. Not for money, anyway. But she'd really thought she'd finally found her calling.

Maybe I just don't have one. A calling. A purpose.

Leda sighed. On a table to her left sat her laptop, waiting smugly for her to start the process again, an all-too-familiar sequence of searching.

Maybe some more iced tea first. Leda went inside, past her bookshelf of cookbooks (culinary school), past the corner display case of cameras (photography school). She bumped the stack of *Discover* magazines atop the stack of the *New Yorker*s (double undergraduate majors in science and literature).

When Leda returned with tea, she battled the urge to procrastinate further and pulled the computer into her lap. Mentally, she ran through the various paths she'd tried, weighing them. The thought of starting school again was both exciting and exhausting, but if necessary, so be it. She didn't want a job, she wanted a career, something she cared about deeply. Something she could throw herself into.

Her fingers hovered, ready to fill the Google search box. She typed in *career*. Then she added *meaningful.*

When the search results loaded, she clicked on one after another. Social worker. Counselor. Teacher. An article about a nun in Canada.

The next one was a website listing volunteer opportunities.

Leda inhaled. Why not? She didn't need the salary, but she felt awful when she wasn't working. She should leave the paid positions open for people who needed them and help people for free.

Leda sat up straighter in her chair. She scrolled down the listings, each one a short link next to a picture. Teach English as a second language. Tutor troubled teens. Read to senior citizens...

On the third page, Leda saw a link titled *Triumph Orphanage,* with the tagline *We Need Your Help.* Next to it was a photograph of a man with a wide, strong, clear face, rich brown skin, and a smile written across like a welcome banner in a crowded airport. Leda leaned forward to stare into the picture. She clicked on the link and it opened a new page, with the picture enlarged within. The man's smile held no trace of mental chatter or self-consciousness behind it. It was free and complete, open. Leda felt a surging desire to touch it, the smile, an entirely unfamiliar urge.

Below the handsome man's picture was a snapshot of seven schoolchildren in an orphanage, smiling ear to ear. Leda looked closer at the photo, at the background. She scrolled down to the text. The man who ran the orphanage funded it by guiding safari tours—

Whoa. The orphanage was in Africa. In Kenya. In a slum called Kibera, outside Nairobi.

Leda exhaled and clicked the back button. *No way. Let's not get crazy,* thought the woman who got anxiety in crowded grocery stores. Leda looked down at Amadeus, then inside to her cozy little house, each piece of furniture and decoration meticulously chosen and arranged.

No way could she do something like that.

Automatically, she fingered her burn scar, the patch of skin near her jaw, so smooth and soft, it was like a stone in the ocean's break. She shut her eyes, felt her heart begin to race, heard the song humming the start of an awful memory.

When the phone rang, Leda nearly fell off her chair from startling.

She grabbed her phone from the table. *Estella.*

She hadn't spoken to her mother in months.

"Leda?" came the raspy voice on the other end of the line.

"Hello, Mother. Something wrong?"

There was a pause. Leda sank into her chair.

"You're the one who sounds like something's wrong." She sighed. "What is it?"

Leda frowned. Estella would get it out of her eventually. "I quit my job."

"Surprise, surprise. What was wrong with this one?"

Leda's teeth gritted together. Invisible armor clinked into place. "It was a sweatshop. My boss was abusive. But mainly it just wasn't what I thought it would be." Leda looked up. The mountain was still staring at her. She averted her eyes. "I wanted to find something meaningful to do with my life."

As soon as she said it, she regretted it. Naked emotion was nothing but ammunition for Estella.

Sure enough, Estella "hmphed" loudly. "Not sure you're the charitable type, dear."

Leda thought of the photo of the man with the smile. "Actually, I was just looking at a posting to volunteer in Kenya."

Estella's cackling laugh poured into Leda's ear like a bucket of wriggling maggots. "Leda, you are, what, thirty-two? Isn't that a little old to play the college kid off to save Africa?"

Choice words died on Leda's tongue. "Was there something else you called about, Mother?"

Estella's cackle snuffed short. A pause. "No. I think that's enough for today."

Leda listened to the call disconnect, her eyebrows knitted together. When she set the phone back on the table, she saw that her hands were shaking.

The laptop's face was in sleep mode. Leda swiped her finger across the mouse pad and the screen jumped back into view.

The picture was waiting.

She read the caption beneath the smile. His name was Ita, the man who ran the orphanage.

Ita, with a gaze fair and bright, surrounded by smiling children.

College kid, indeed.

Leda opened a new tab. Travelocity.

CHAPTER 2

December 9, 2007, Kibera—Leda

WHEN LEDA LOOKED OUT OVER KIBERA FOR the first time, she thought of the sea behind her mother's house, how it unfolded into infinity, unfathomable and chilling even on a sunny day. Leda stumbled at the top of the embankment, grabbed for the handle of her suitcase and stood tight until the rushing realization of smallness receded from her knees.

One million people, her guidebook claimed, crammed into a labyrinth of mud and metal shacks. It was a maze to make Daedalus proud. No Minotaur could escape from here. The slum *was* the Minotaur, gorging itself on fleeting youth and broken dreams.

Leda felt the dampness of her washed hair morph into sweat. She'd arrived the night before, had been ushered quickly into a cab and sped to her shiny white room at the Intercontinental in Nairobi. But now she stood on the edge of Nairobi's secret, two terse sentences in the hotel's welcome binder—the Kibera slum. Bounded by a golf course, towering suburban gates, a river, a railroad and a dam. Cordoned off. Now Leda saw what that meant—a place with no running water, no electricity, no sanitation system—the blank spot on the map of the city, officially unrecognized. A space smaller than her Topanga Canyon neighborhood, but thirty times the population density of New York City.

From where Leda stood, Kibera below was an undulating sea of rusted rooftops, ending at the horizon and the glaring morning sun.

Samuel, the guide Leda had hired to take her on a tour of Kibera and to the orphanage, stood likewise frozen, but unalarmed. More than likely he was used to the tourist gasp, had it penciled into his schedule.

Leda looked at him sideways, her eyes grabbing on to him like a buoy at high sea. Samuel was younger than her for sure, no more than twenty-five, but taller by a foot. His face was smooth, shiny in the heat. How did he feel? Awkward, as she did, embarrassed? Was he secretly seething?

Normally, Leda was good at discerning people's thoughts and moods, a skill learned early in her mother's house. It wasn't a talent that brought her any closer to people, however.

She closed her eyes to the miles of dirt and metal, shut her ears to the clanging roar before them and the gridlocked traffic behind them, and tried to sense any irritation or ill will coming from Samuel. But his stretched posture and his even stare gave nothing away. If nothing else, he seemed dutiful. This was another Sunday, another customer.

Samuel sensed Leda's searching, as people always did, and he turned. "Do you want to take a picture?"

Leda's hand went into her pocket, wrapped around her camera. Right. A photographer should want to take a picture. But when she saw the men down the embankment staring, her hand let go of the camera. These were the kinds of moments that confirmed for Leda she wasn't cut out to be a photojournalist.

"It's okay. Let's just go," she said.

Samuel nodded and stepped behind Leda to pick up her sixty-pound suitcase. He hoisted it onto his back heavily, as though it was a piano, and started down the dirt hill.

The sight gave Leda a queasy jolt. "Wait. There's no road?"

She'd looked at the pictures online, she'd seen the narrow alleys. But she'd also assumed there would be a way in, a way out. A road.

Samuel turned. He smiled.

Leda felt the sneer behind his smile. She looked down, her cheeks burning. She studied the orange dust under her boots. The color was due to the dearth of vegetation, she'd read. The iron turned the clay minerals orange.

Samuel was off and walking. Leda scrambled after him down the hill, feeling like a clown fish in a pond. She watched him start across a rickety footbridge arched over a brown swamp of trash, with sugarcane growing in thick clumps through the waste. Children waded in near the cane.

Leda followed, studying her shoes to avoid all the eyes on her.

The other side of the bridge landed Leda in a landscape that was more landfill than ground, and she nearly went down on the twisted path of plastic bags. She was grateful for her tennis shoes, but still furious at herself for the suitcase. Imagine if she'd brought her second one, instead of leaving it with the hotel. Underneath the ridiculous load, all she could see were Samuel's sandals traversing the winding path over rock and drainage creeks. And all she could do was follow along, like a princess after a porter, trying not to trip. Her mother's words blared in her head. *Off to save Africa?*

As doubt clogged her throat, Leda felt sure she would drown in the smell. Moldy cabbage, rotten fish, cooking smoke, but mostly it was the steaming scent of human waste that poured into Leda's nose and mouth, saturating her as if she could never be free of that smell again. She opened her mouth to breathe, and gagged on the sweat that dribbled in.

Now the view of the slum had disappeared and they were inside it, weaving through narrow spaces and crisscrossed paths like an ant farm in hyperdrive.

Men with hollowed cheeks and yellowed eyes stared at Leda. Women—in the midst of tending children and selling and trading and gossiping and cooking and cleaning—their eyes flickered warily as she passed.

The children, however, were a different story. Schoolkids flew up around Leda like clouds of sparrows, waving their arms and chirping *Howareyou? Howareyou?*

Leda was grateful to them for their acceptance and she answered with the Swahili words she'd only ever spoken to her iPod. "Jambo," she said, and they giggled.

"Present," one boy shouted amiably.

Samuel stopped suddenly, and motioned for Leda to stand beside him. He shooed away the children, not meanly but firmly, and set down the suitcase, ready, Leda supposed, to continue with the tour he'd begun when they met that morning in the café in Nairobi.

"So, you are here to volunteer. What is it you do in America? Are you a teacher?"

Avoiding his question, Leda looked away. "Yes, I'm a volunteer. Here to help."

Samuel nodded. "Do not give the children money. They do not understand it. In your country maybe you are a poor teacher, but here your money is a lot. This puts ideas in the children's heads."

Leda looked into Samuel's face, at the sheets of sweat soaking his T-shirt. She moved closer and released the handle on the suitcase, demonstrating that she would pull it.

Samuel smiled again, the smile Leda hated and that she felt hated her. She nodded toward the children playing nearby. "What ideas?"

"The idea that begging is a job. Or that robbing you would not be so bad since you give it so easily."

Samuel took a breath and walked a few steps. Now he resumed his script as he pointed here and there. "When the British left, they gave this land to the Nubians—Muslim Sudanese soldiers. But with no deeds. The Nubians became illegal landlords and the seeds of war were planted in this dirt. Muslim against Christian. Kikuyu against Luo. There have been many problems."

"But then, technically, the government owns the land? They could help."

They passed a beauty salon of women who stared at Leda struggling to wheel her suitcase through the trash. Samuel waited. Silently, he watched the trash pool around the suitcase wheels until Leda found herself dragging, not wheeling, the suitcase. His look more or less said *I told you so.*

"Yes, they could help," Samuel said. "But it is more convenient for them to do nothing. As long as the slum is illegal, they do not have to provide what the city people have rights to."

A man tripped over Leda then, for cosmic emphasis, sloshing water from a yellow jug. The dirt beneath her shoes turned to mud and the man looked at it and frowned. Leda's skin burned under the man's indignation. He huffed and walked on. How far had the man walked for that water? "Then how do they get the necessities?"

"Everything is for sale in Kibera. Water. Use of the latrine. A shower. People pay the person who steals electricity for them. They pay the watchmen, really paying them not to rob them. They pay thieves to steal back what other thieves stole in the night. Women who sell *changaa,* they pay the police a bribe. Women who sell themselves, they pay the bribes with their bodies. But still one must pay for charcoal and food and school. The hardest thing to justify is school."

"How do people pay for everything?"

"They don't." Samuel pointed at the ground.

Leda lifted her right foot and a sticky plastic bag dangled from it in the dusty air. She considered anew the blanket of trash bags.

"When you can't pay or it's unsafe to go, then you do your business in a bag and—" Samuel's hand carved an arc through the air that ended at her shoe. "Flying toilets." He took the suitcase, now soiled from her dragging it through the refuse.

"We're almost there." He pointed ahead.

Leda was in shock. But before they moved on, she had to ask a question she thought she knew the answer to. "Do you live in Kibera, Samuel?"

It was the first time emotion crossed his face unfettered. "Yes," he said, and heaved the suitcase onto his back as he turned away, a turtle putting his shell back on.

Leda followed him deeper into the slum, supplementing his practiced explanations about Kibera with the rushing things her eyes and ears told her. Kibera was an assault of objects, colors, smells and sounds, all suddenly appearing out of the dust inches from her face. As they ducked between mud/stick structures, colored laundry fluttered and dripped overhead. A volley of muffled chatter and music echoed from all directions.

Leda wondered what privacy meant in Kibera, if anything. How would any one of these people feel if they found themselves alone in a quiet house like the one she shared with Amadeus? Or in a mansion of marble, glass and sky, like her mother's? So much space all to themselves.

People passed each other the way cats do, touching, brushing skin, sliding off one another in the sweaty heat. Personal space was an oxymoron and as soon as Leda put words to the thought it made her recoil, dodging this way and that to avoid contact in the swarming crowds. She saw she would have to form new habits in Kibera, new ways of moving through space.

Women streamed by in bright dresses, in business attire, in jeans and flip-flops. Men streamed past in athletic jerseys and ragged South Park T-shirts and button-downs. All on a mission, edging doggedly in one direction or the other.

Chickens and stray dogs darted through the two-way parade with a bravado Leda wanted to admire. But the smoke searing her eyes and the jagged rays of sunlight darting through the metal turned the path ahead, behind the bobbing suitcase, into an obstacle course of certain peril.

Eventually, the suitcase stopped.

It dropped to the ground and revealed Samuel heaving to catch his breath so he could announce the obvious.

"We're here," he said, and pointed at a small, hand-painted sign tacked to a towering wall of corrugated metal. *Triumph Orphanage.*

Most of the maze of houses and shops were single-roomed, and could be seen right into if the bedsheet doors weren't drawn. But they'd passed several tall metal partitions, walled-off spaces, which the orphanage seemed to have, as well. Leda tried to get a sense of how big the structure was and poked her head around the corner.

The metal wall spoke to her. Rather, it laughed.

The hair on Leda's arms stood up. The laugh was a sound like midnight thunder rolling across the sea. Leda shut her eyes. From the moment she'd entered Kibera with Samuel, winding through the dust, through the throngs of smiling children and scowling mothers, through the smells and jolting clamor, whenever it seemed too much to bear, Leda had blinked her eyes long enough to see the smile from the website. A smile full of calm and certainty.

Leda would bet her soul that the laugh on the other side of that wall and the smile were one and the same.

When Samuel banged on the door with his fist, the laugh snuffed out. Leda's eyes shot open.

A section of the metal wall slid open.

And there it was—the smile that belonged to the laugh.

"Leda," the smile said, wide and shining.

"Ita," she said, feeling the grin tug at her lips, a sensation as rare as it was delicious. For once, she wasn't politely mimicking—the smile sprang from inside, as though freed from a cage.

Samuel looked back and forth with a curious expression. "Have you met before?"

Ita smiled wider, shaking his head. "We have now."

Leda laughed, enchanted by the simple confidence he radiated like a lightbulb. Feeling breathless, she looked down at her dusty feet and had another vision of standing by the sea—watching in wonder as the sand, the shells, her whole body was drawn in by the tide, magically pulled by the moon. Leda looked up and took another gulp of seeing Ita's lit-up face.

Then she turned to Samuel and held out her hand. "Thank you, Samuel. I wish you well."

Samuel snapped free of the moment and nodded. "Good luck, Leda. Good luck in Kibera."

Ita held out his hand, too. "Samuel. *Asante sana.*"

Samuel shook Ita's hand, craning to peek inside the orphanage with the same urgent curiosity Leda felt. Ita stood firm with his smile, blocking the view. Samuel nodded once more. *"Karibu. Kwaheri."*

Leda watched her guide disappear around a corner and then turned back, which left her and Ita alone across the divide of the entrance. She found herself close enough to be struck by the smoothness of his skin. It was flawless, reminding Leda of a hand-dipped cone. Imagining that it would feel like velvet to the touch, Leda lurched forward for her suitcase handle, letting her hair swish over her face.

"Please, let me help you," Ita said. He took the suitcase from her and swung it through the doorway in one fell swoop, opening a new world to Leda. The orphanage.

Leda got a two-second glimpse at a horseshoe of shadowy rooms around a dirt courtyard, before the view filled with children, bumping like bees as they swarmed past Ita to greet her. Six boys, Leda counted—toddler to preteen—as they tugged her inside, chattering competitively in Swahili. One boy, the oldest, watched her intently, walking backward like a guard dog. Leda tried to smile at him.

Inside, she stepped into a battle of smells. To the left, cardamom and clove fought pepper and cumin for control of a stew. Leda sniffed the spicy smoke the same way she inhaled Amadeus's fur after a grooming, but stopped short when she was bitten by Kibera's sharp endnote of sewage.

The boys patted her clothes and skin as they tugged her

toward a woven mat in the courtyard. Leda focused on not tripping over them. She felt woozy after her voyage through Kibera, as if she'd stepped off a merry-go-round. But now, inside the orphanage, if such a thing was possible, it was actually louder, more closed-in, more overwhelming. The kids swirled around her legs like water in a tide pool and Ita followed, the herder.

"We've been waiting for you!" he shouted over the tops of their heads. "They are very excited. We have prepared many things for your arrival."

Leda swam in the most human contact she'd had in years. Maybe ever. Estella had renounced her past and whatever family it may have contained, so Leda hadn't grown up in proximity to anybody other than her mother. She'd sat alone in school, then spent evenings watching children on television, trying to comprehend them in their freeness. Leda always felt as though she'd been born eighty years old.

Now here she was being mobbed by children, her breathing shallowing. Estella's judgments rang in her mind—she was not made for this. Was she crazy to have come here?

And then, just as Leda nearly went down in the mosh pit, Ita saved her. His eyes met hers, a knowing look in them that made Leda feel as if she'd found a wall to lean against. His eyes, dark brown with golden supernovas, stayed locked on Leda as he called out in Swahili to the children. A series of commands, sold with a smile but sure as a sunrise. The children reacted like little soldiers. They took their places on the mat, sitting cross-legged with their hands in their laps.

Leda exhaled and Ita laughed.

"We're happy today. To meet you, Leda."

"Oh, me, too," she rushed out, hoping she hadn't just come across as rude. "Just tired, I think, from—"

"A tsunami of children? Yes. Cannot hear yourself think, is that it?"

Leda nodded, amazed. Yes, that was exactly it. Ita stepped closer. "Lunch is almost ready. Should I show you your new home?"

She looked around the orphanage, at the concrete walls crumbling to the dirt floors, at the open doorways and one wooden door. Shyly, she followed him as he walked briskly to the left of the courtyard. First, he pointed at a closed door, crooked on its hinges. "My office," he said, and walked on. Then he turned, with a wink Leda might have imagined, and said, "And my bedroom." The next room was open and Ita stepped inside, waving her after.

Leda didn't understand what she was seeing. A closet? Shoes lined the edges of the room, in a square around another huge woven mat. She lifted her foot to step forward, but Ita put his hand on her arm. It was warm and soft.

"This is where the children sleep. You may sleep here or—" Ita stepped out of the room "—with Mary."

Mary had been the other name on the website, but hadn't been linked to a picture. Leda's stomach burned with curiosity. "Is Mary here now?"

"Who did you think was creating that delicious smell?" Ita ducked his head under a wooden beam and Leda followed him into the kitchen. A wood fireplace formed the rear of the room, and the rest of it, apart from smoke, was filled with pots and pans and plastic bowls towering off the ground.

Bent over a cauldron that hung above a fire was a sizable woman's backside, wrapped taut in a patterned sarong, brighter than a bouquet of flowers. At Ita's voice, the woman straightened and Leda saw she was old, though to guess her actual age would be tricky.

Leda felt relief gush through her, and she laughed at herself when she realized why. When she'd read the listing online, she had thought perhaps the man and woman mentioned were married or a couple. Now, she knew she'd been hoping that wasn't the case.

Did women shake hands? Leda wasn't sure, so she said, *"Hujambo. Habari ya asubuhi,"* the words piling up in her mouth like cotton balls.

Mary smiled kindly, her face wrinkling like a cozy bathrobe. *"Karibu,"* she said.

Welcome. Leda did feel welcome. She'd never had anyone make such a fuss over her presence, or anything she did, really. Except maybe Amadeus.

Next, Ita showed her where the toilet was—*toilet* being a very loose term. There were two stalls with two hanging sheets. When Ita pulled back the first sheet, Leda's eyes traveled down to the square of concrete. In the middle was a piece of wood with a handle on it, and Leda could only guess that underneath was a hole. The second stall was exactly the same.

"Shower," Ita said of the second stall.

When Leda remembered to breathe again, she met Ita's eyes and saw that they gleamed with pride.

So Leda looked again and tried to see it through different eyes. She remembered how Samuel had said everyone paid to use a latrine and to bathe. This was a luxury. An achievement. He *should* be proud.

"Awesome!" Leda said, and knew immediately she'd overdone it.

But Ita laughed at her effort, not wounded in the least, and led her by the elbow to the other side of the orphanage.

The ease with which Ita touched her—it was unnerving. Even more distracting was how her skin felt under his fingers—

tingly, pliant. Usually, she grew stiff under a stranger's touch. In her fairly limited sexual experience, Leda had always felt clumsy at best, but more often raw and exposed. But as she walked with Ita, she had a lightning-flash vision of Ita's warm hands on her skin. She bet it would be different with him— gentler, yet sexier, urgent.

Leda's head shot up, her eyes darting to Ita as if he'd heard her thoughts. She felt the blood stampede her cheeks. She coughed to try and combat a full-on blush.

Ita paused before the back wall of the orphanage. He looked at her strangely, and she wondered if she was hurtling phero-mones at him so hard he felt it. *Get a grip, Leda.*

"There is a room behind here. It is our medical room, our secret hospital."

He must have known how strange that sounded. But at the same time, she noted the same pride as before that lifted his chin. "Are you a doctor?" she asked.

Ita smiled. But when his eyes moved to the door, his con-fidence faltered. "No. I study." Now he looked embarrassed. "Not like you have studied. Impressive, your education." Leda had sent him her résumé, as if applying for a job. Now she felt stupid about it. "I want to know all about it," he said as he walked past the room.

On the other side of the orphanage, the back half was a three-walled room with a metal roof and another identical mat spread out. "This is for study, and for eating when the rains come."

The next room had a sheet drawn tight across it. "Mary!" Ita called across the courtyard, followed by a question in Swahili that Leda couldn't understand.

Mary's answer boomeranged back and Ita gently tucked

the sheet to one side. "Mary's sleeping space," Ita said, but respectfully, he didn't enter.

Leda hesitated.

"It is okay. You may look," Ita said.

Leda ducked her head inside. This room was much smaller. A mat still covered most of the dirt floor, but this time sported a narrow strip of foam and a folded sheet on one half.

When Leda poked her head back out, Ita watched her expectantly.

"It's…" Leda wasn't sure what he wanted to hear, and her head was starting to spin with the dawning realization that these were her accommodations for the month. "Great."

"So you will stay with Mary," Ita said, satisfied.

Leda looked out to where the children sat, playing quietly, waiting for their lunch. She put a hand out, feeling for the wall, something solid.

Ita's voice was different when he spoke next, with an edge of self-consciousness that was new. "I'm sure where you live is very different." He remained with the sheet in his hand and straightened. "The bed might help you become accustomed."

Leda realized he meant the piece of foam in the little room, but she could no more imagine stretching out next to Mary and having any hopes of sleeping there for an entire month than she could imagine coping with any of it—the toilet, kitchen, the sheets for doors. She would be surrounded at all times. Forget hearing herself think, she wouldn't even be able to feel herself breathe. As if in response, her breathing came quicker.

But then she remembered the morning—traipsing around after Samuel through the maze—all the jagged metal, the haggard faces, the roar and the stench, heaps of garbage, the images leaping out like rabid dogs.

Leda forced herself to breathe from her belly as she looked at her feet. She saw now where she and Ita had walked carefully around the perimeter of the courtyard. The dirt in the interior was swept clean. The children's sandals were lined up like ducks around the mat. The concrete in the bathrooms was new, the sheets clean. She remembered the touch of Ita's hand, felt the lingering calm he exuded. She was safe. Leda felt sure of it. Inside the orphanage, she was safe.

But Ita noted her silence and saw how she looked at her feet. "I have an idea."

He walked back to the room he'd said was a hospital. He slid open the metal that looked like a wall and waved Leda over. She was amazed to see a metal table, and walls covered in posters of anatomy and the periodic table.

"It is our secret, this room," Ita said, looking at the stacks of medical supplies on a table in the corner, and Leda thought she understood. In a place like Kibera, where health services were rare and precious, a room like this would have to be kept secret lest the whole slum descend on it. "You would like your own room. What do you think?"

Did he mean the metal table? Leda could only think of blood and episodes of *Grey's Anatomy,* until she pictured the foam on Mary's floor and found herself saying, "Yes, if it's okay, this is perfect."

Ita nodded and smiled. "Good. I will bring the foam and blanket. Are you ready now to meet the children?" Ita looked past her at the kids when he said it, and the love that radiated toward them landed on Leda, too, like wrapping her hands around a cup of morning tea. She felt glad for the boys, then noted the lump in her throat.

As she gazed after them, Mary appeared out of the kitchen, struggling under the weight of the steaming pot.

"Michael, *msaada*," Ita called, and the word was followed by more Swahili that Leda figured meant the boy should help Mary with lunch.

Michael, not only the tallest boy by a foot but owner of the only serious expression of the bunch, stood and grabbed the pot's handles. He called out and two other boys obediently headed for the kitchen.

As she watched them go, Leda realized Ita wasn't watching the boys, he was looking at her. She felt his curiosity digging into her again, and realized for the first time that she must seem as strange to him as all this was to her.

"Let's eat," Ita said.

The remaining children wiggled with excitement as Leda came closer.

"*Karibu!*" one of the middle-sized boys called out. He put his hand out like a little salesman. "Ntimi," the boy said, indicating himself. He had a smile almost to match Ita's—full of strong white teeth and a joy one can only be born with.

Leda sat next to him. "Leda," she said. "Nice to meet you, Timmy."

It was Ntimi who named the other boys, from Thomas to Christopher, ending with Michael. Then Ntimi scooped up a toddler and plopped him into Leda's arms. "Walter," he said, and everyone laughed as Walter tried to wiggle free.

Michael was the only one not laughing. Leda had a hunch he was a person she would have to win over slowly. "Thank you for having me here, Michael, for letting me into your home."

Michael nodded with a solemn maturity that made Leda want to smile, but she held it back.

Ita, watching closely, doled out a look of approval that warmed her belly.

"Jomo," Ntimi said as he pointed toward a sheeted room by the door, a room that hadn't been on the tour. Leda took it for a guard post of sorts, or a storage space. She squinted. Did Ntimi mean a guard?

"He new," Ntimi said in a quieter voice, just as Leda made out two skinny legs showing from under the hanging sheet.

Another boy. Boy number seven.

"Will he join us for lunch?" Leda asked, though the answer was obvious.

Mary handed Leda a yellow plastic bowl filled with murky water. Leda studied it, unsure what to do. Was it soup? "Wash," Ntimi said, and Leda wanted to hug him.

She wet her hands in the lukewarm water, then passed the bowl around for the children to do the same.

Next, Mary brought her a bowl heaped with rice from the pot. She handed Leda a spoon.

Leda said thank you and waited for everyone else to be served. But Mary didn't go for more bowls. They all seemed to be waiting and Leda wondered if guests ate first.

The first mouthful occupied Leda mind and body, with a collision of flavors she'd never tasted before. Sweet, salty, spicy all at the same time.

Suddenly Leda saw all the eyes on her. She jabbed her spoon back into the rice and felt her cheeks start to burn.

Activity commenced. Mary left and brought back bowls for herself and Ita. Then she set down the big bowl of rice on the mat, the boys huddling around it. Their little hands went to work, rolling little balls of rice and transferring them to their mouths fast as they could carry. Leda looked and saw Ita and Mary dig in with their fingers, too, employing the same technique.

Leda watched, thinking first of hygiene, then suffering a

guilty replay of all the food she'd left on her plate or thrown away in her lifetime.

Leda looked at her spoon, glinting in the sun, and set it down on the ground. Watching Ntimi's nimble fingers, she imitated him, rolling the food into bite-size pieces with her hands. Ntimi smiled at her.

Out of the corner of her eye, Leda saw the sheet flutter. She looked and saw that it was pulled just a crack to the side.

On impulse, Leda stood up and started over. Ntimi stopped and looked up in worry. Michael shook his head ever so slightly. But she went anyway.

Stopping in front of the sheet, she held out her bowl. "You like to eat alone, that's okay," Leda said gently.

No hand reached out for the bowl, but Leda could hear the boy breathing, with a slight wheeze of asthma that made her heart leap. Dangerous out here with no medicine. *Lucky he has Ita,* she thought, just as she heard Ita stride up behind her.

"How much English do they understand?" Leda asked, glossing over the fact that she still held out the bowl of steaming food.

"All Kenyan children learn English in school," Ita said. He glanced at the sheet when he added, "But many of our children have missed much school."

Leda's heart sank. "So they don't understand me." *Of course not.* "Good way to practice my Swahili, I guess."

Ita spoke into the crack in the sheet. When only silence followed, he spoke again in the same even, coaxing voice.

Nothing happened.

"They will understand some, if you speak slowly and use easy words." Ita saw the look on Leda's face. "Don't worry, they already love you. They are so excited you have come all this way for them. It is hard for them to believe."

Suddenly the sheet opened and a small, lanky boy stepped into the sun. He wore a WWF T-shirt, shorts and a scowl like a guerilla rebel.

Ita knelt down and spoke to him, as if he was explaining why the sky is blue or the dirt orange. Leda already loved this manner of his, a solid gentleness much like what she loved about the trees at home—cheerful but sage.

Jomo stood but he didn't meet Ita's gaze. Instead his eyes found something just off to the side and locked on. His face took on a blankness Leda recognized with a shiver. She looked down and saw what Jomo was doing with his hands. He picked and picked at the edges of his thumbs, beside the nail beds. Leda looked down at her own hands, similarly mutilated. It was an embarrassing habit, but one she'd never been able to conquer. Estella thought it was disgusting. *Doesn't it hurt?* her school guidance counselor had asked. But the pain was the point. It grounded her. In public, whenever Leda felt anxious, when she wanted to flee or scream, the picking gave her something to do, something to keep her from losing control, something to control. The only other thing she'd ever found that calmed her, gave her a buffer against the world was—

"Hey, Jomo," she said, reaching into her pocket and startling both Ita and the frowning boy. "Want to see something?"

Leda took the camera from her pocket. It was her favorite— small enough to take out and tuck away quickly, with the manual control to shoot without a flash. It put a lens between her and the loud crazy world, let her compose it, control it, record it from one step away. Cameras gave Leda a way to interact with the world without…interacting.

Jomo's attention snapped toward the camera lying flat in Leda's hand. His yearning was more apparent than he would have liked, she was sure. She set down the food and knelt across from Ita, close to Jomo, and turned the camera on. She didn't press it into his hands; she just started to demonstrate how it worked. *Zoom like this,* she mimed, *frame with the screen, and take the picture.* She pointed the viewfinder toward Ita and snapped.

Jomo grunted, a small slip of amusement.

Ita watched the two of them studying the image of him and he laughed. She bristled and felt Jomo do the same. But it wasn't Ita's fault, she realized. He wouldn't understand. He wasn't daunted by life. He danced happily with the world. He wouldn't understand the comfort of a camera on the sidelines.

But Leda also knew Ita wanted Jomo to be happy, he was ecstatic at the merest glimpse of joy in the glowering boy. She hoped Jomo would know this soon, too. She tucked the camera away, picked up the bowl and settled it into Jomo's hands before he saw it coming. Then she stood up and walked pointedly back to the mat.

When Leda sat down, the children settled back into a ring around her. On Ntimi's cue, they began clapping their hands and rapping on their knees, and while Leda watched, a little taken aback, they began to sing.

It was a song they'd planned, obviously, because everyone from youngest to oldest joined in at once.

Leda let the harmony wash over her and blinked her eyes. When she didn't have her camera out, she would blink to record the memories she wanted to hang on to, to replay later for comfort. She'd had no idea what to make of her first day in Kibera, but just then she wanted to savor the warm feeling wrapped around her like afternoon sunshine on her porch in Topanga. It wasn't the feeling of serenity she felt there with Amadeus, however. This was something new.

A loud banging on the metal door stole Leda's train of thought and took the warm feeling with it.

The children stopped singing but sat obediently, not looking overly perturbed, though Jomo ducked back behind his curtain. Leda tried to calm herself—visitors to the orphanage must be common.

Ita walked over to the door and she heard the voice that filtered through, sounding more like a low growl than a man.

Reluctantly, Leda thought, Ita slid open the door. But he blocked the gap, so Leda couldn't see who was outside.

She turned back to the boys, but the mood had shifted one hundred and eighty degrees. Leda glanced up to see if clouds had moved in. No, the sun was still beating down like a radiator.

The door scraped ajar and a tall, wiry man darted through to jab Ita and cackle. When the man's yellow eyes scurried over Leda's skin, she shuddered and averted her gaze. When he turned to converse with Ita, Leda looked again.

At first glance, Leda might have called him handsome, with his angular face and cat eyes, but beside Ita, she decided, definitely not. The man was a praying mantis, creeping along on folded pincers. Dreads snaked down his back, trembling as he shuffled closer. Dangling, bouncing from his belt, was a battered machete. When he sneered in her direction, Leda recoiled at two rows of stained teeth. Then she saw that his face was covered in scars, several of them burns like hers.

Her hand went to her scar while her mind filled with fifty thoughts at once. The man was clearly a gangster, yet seemed to be Ita's friend. There was a word at Leda's lips, a scary word. *Mungiki*—what the guidebook named Kenya's vicious mafia and more or less warned to *look out for dreadlocks. Mungiki* ran the slums—extortion, female genital circumcision, beheadings.

"So, this is the volunteer?" The man stopped at the edge of the mat, close enough that he cast a shadow over Leda. "You the woman Ita can't stop talking about, two weeks now?"

Ita's face blanched. Wary? Or apologetic?

"Chege!" Ntimi jumped up. The other children greeted him with enthusiasm, too.

Chege turned to Ita and laughed his hyena cackle again. "She speak?" He looked down on Leda meanly, his eyes on her as he continued in a growl before she could answer. "Funny, nah? Here Ita been talking 'bout this educated white woman, smart, rich, talking up a summer storm." Chege smirked, he flickered his eyes over to Ita then back to Leda. "Lot to live up to, this man a big dreamer. He dream big beautiful things. Like an angel come from America, come save everybody."

"I'm not—" Leda said, but Ita interrupted.

"*Kuacha,* Chege," he growled. He held out his hand to Leda and tugged her up to stand beside him. "This is Leda. She is my guest."

"Leda," Chege purred. "Welcome to Kibera, Leda." He put out his hand and she took it reluctantly.

Ntimi interrupted. "You bring gifts, Chege?"

Ita shook his head and steered the boy back to the mat.

When Leda tried to retract her hand, Chege held tight and pulled her closer to him. She squeaked, desperate to escape his calloused grip, but he peered into her eyes and whispered, "Don't tell him you no angel yet. American rich lady come save Africa, and have a little fun." He nodded his head in Ita's direction.

Leda's eyes flickered over to Ita. Were those his words?

"But what if—" Chege's voice rose, pulling Ita from the children into their huddle "—what if us Kikuyu *brathas* don't need your help, Leda? Don't need a *volunteer*—"

"Chege," Ita said. "Stop."

Chege laughed, his smoky breath hitting Leda in the face. "Okay, okay. I play nice." He dropped Leda's hand and slung down his knapsack. "Presents!" he called out.

The second he let her out of his grasp, Leda stumbled back and wiped her hand on her pants. She wrapped her arms around herself then, trying to still the wave of nausea and panic. Chege strode past her, chuckling, and crouched down among the boys.

Leda coerced herself into taking one clean, full breath.

Chege dug in his bag and brandished a coconut, winning "oohs" and "aahs" from the children. He untied the machete from his belt, its edge jagged, its blade sticky with congealed brown stains. Leda watched him swipe it across his jeans, telling herself firmly the stain wasn't blood.

He split the coconut with a single, expert stroke. He sucked down the milk that came spilling out, letting it course over his chin before he dribbled it into the kids' open mouths, like watering a ring of flowers. The children gulped the sweet juice and giggled. With the machete, Chege carved smaller pieces and handed them out.

Leda watched the whole process in a daze, until Chege ran his tongue over the white coconut flesh, one eye leering sideways at her. She looked away, her cheeks burning.

Ita couldn't seem to tell anything was wrong. He looked over at her and smiled, the same pure, easy smile.

As all the children sat content with their treat, Chege stood next to Ita. With a flare obviously for Leda's benefit, he pulled a bulging wad of money from his pocket. "Been a good month, brother."

Ita looked at the cash and the smile was gone, replaced by steel. "No," he barked, followed with daggers of Swahili, fervent hand gestures, and a look searing enough to ignite a forest fire.

For a fleeting moment Chege was surprised, he teetered backward on his spindly limbs. He recovered at the same moment Leda saw Jomo edge into the courtyard.

Chege saw him, too, and waved him over. Jomo hesitated, then jutted out his chin and walked over.

Chege peeled off a leaf of Kenyan shillings. "Ita say he don't want any," Chege said. "He don't like where it come from. Ita always think money cares where it come from. Always. Even when we was you age. Course, then he had no choice."

Chege took Jomo's wrist. He thrust the money into the boy's palm. Jomo's eyes bulged as if he was scared to blink, as if the money might disappear. Now Chege looked up at Leda. "Maybe he think things be different now?"

Leda felt the nausea tip and pour back through her stomach. What had they said about her? What did they think of her here in this place?

"Chege, enough," Ita said, but Chege put out his hand and knelt down next to Jomo.

"But this boy knows. Every hungry boy knows money have to come from somewhere." Chege's coiled stance made Leda think of a feral cat—watching, plotting, waiting. "And somebody always have to give something to get it."

Leda could tell Jomo didn't understand the words, but everything Chege did was a cartoon requiring no caption. Ita's jaw was clenched so tight she wondered how words could possibly escape, but she could see them, piled up behind his teeth, being chosen carefully.

When he opened his mouth, however, Ita's words were swallowed by banging at the door. Deep voices followed, so loud Leda jumped.

Chege laughed. "For me," he said with a wink.

Ita's frown was like a deep etched carving. "Go," he said and strode quickly with Chege to the door. Leda stayed where she was, holding her breath.

When the gate opened, thugs huddled outside, their words like little firecrackers. Leda couldn't understand any of it, but the men looked back and forth behind them as if they were being chased by the devil himself. One man took the machete from his belt and demonstrated a whack. With another glance behind him, he tried to dart inside the orphanage.

Which is when Ita started shouting. He screamed at the men, then at Chege, all the while trying to close the metal door on top of them.

But everybody, and time itself, stood still when Chege hollered into the air. With terse, measured words he spoke to the men, who lowered their heads and nodded. He pointed beyond the door and they left.

Chege turned to Ita. A look passed between them and Ita raised his chin. Chege slipped out though the doorway. But as Ita slid the door shut, Chege's eyes found Leda and sent a chill all the way down into her shoes.

Leda backed away, air locked up in her lungs.

When she sat down on the mat, she found she was shaking.

All the children had scattered off, to their room or to the kitchen. Leda pressed a finger to her scar.

What in the hell had she gotten herself into?

CHAPTER 3

December 30, 2007, Nairobi airport—Leda

THE SEAT BELT SHAKES IN HER FINGERS, AS LEDA buckles in and wishes she could likewise restrain her mind. Above the rushing of the air vents, the rumble of the engines, the chirpy chatter of the stewardesses, Leda hears her own horrible sound track on repeat. The sound of fist on flesh, the crack of machetes, the thud of Ita hitting the dirt. Screaming. Leda hears the awful, high-pitched screams, then realizes they were hers.

She sees Ita silhouetted in the doorway of the shack when he discovered them. Sees him hit Chege so hard the blood is like a hose, instant and coursing. Leda could smell it. She can smell it now.

She buries her face in her hands, presses against the small glass window, like she can make the sounds disappear, like she can snuff out the images.

She can't.

She feels Chege's wet mouth over her ear, stubble slicing her skin, his arms pinning her, sure as shackles, hissing into her ear in a voice that will never leave her again.

Ita found them, but too late. He found Chege sprawled atop her, grinding into her, her body pinned as though beneath a scorpion's tail.

She looks down at her skirt, balling it up in her fists, fighting not to cry, wishing among so many other things that she'd changed clothes at the airport. Thirty hours she will have to look at her skirt and remember. Thirty hours she will be imprisoned in memory.

No, forever. Forever is how long she will have to live and relive this night.

Ita hit Chege and the world exploded. In the grand finale of the fireworks show, Chege's men descended on Ita like bloodthirsty warriors. How many men were there? Leda couldn't count. She'd covered her face and cried, begging them to stop. If the police hadn't arrived—

But the police had arrived and they'd dragged her away. Once they'd learned she was already scheduled to fly out tonight, they asked no more questions. They dragged her away from Ita and left him there. As though her life was more precious than his. *You don't know anything!* she'd wanted to scream at them as she looked down at his bloodied body in the dirt. *Save him, not me! I cannot live with this.*

The child in the seat next to Leda is asking the stewardess for ice cream. The stewardess jokes with the boy, looks hard at Leda, as though she's about to ask her something.

Leda turns farther toward the window in a preemptive response.

How? How is she alive and on a plane? How is the world still spinning? How can the child next to her be deciding between strawberry and chocolate?

Leda thinks of the orphans. What will happen to them? What's happening to them right now?

She burrows into her seat and tries to breathe.

"I liked the zebras best, mummy," the little boy is now saying. "And the hippos. But they looked mean. I think the zebras are nice. Don't you think so?"

"Yes, I think I liked the zebras the best, too."

The mother sees Leda's sullied clothes, sees her mussed hair, the scratches on her neck and arms.

Leda sees the woman's blow-dried hair, her careful makeup, her attempts to hide her scared eyes, the lines of worry. The mother knows what's happening beneath them. She can only guess the horrors responsible for the scratches on Leda's skin and the look on her face, but she knows.

The look she gives Leda is a plea.

Their eyes lock, two women in a world of men gone mad. Leda looks at the boy, who's around Ntimi's age. Then she thinks of the youths who attacked her, their teenaged faces hard as wood.

Leda turns away. She obliges the mother with her child's innocence and her mind returns to the stench of blood cloaking her. She washed her hands in the airport bathroom, but now as her hair falls forward, Leda sees it matted with the stuff. Her stomach clenches when she remembers how, as she cradled Ita's battered head in her lap, her hair caught in the blood on his face. His eyes could barely stay open, as the fire reflected in them raged all around them. The sorrow in Ita's eyes quickened the terror in the gazes of the policemen staring down at them.

I'm sorry, Ita. I'm so, so, so sorry.

CHAPTER 4

December 9, 2007, Kibera—Ita

THAT NIGHT ITA LAY IN HIS BED, WRESTLING with his eyelids as though trying to clamp shut two hippos' mouths. With a grin, he gave in to replaying the day instead. The sudden blooming smile when she said his name, the breathless tinkling sound of her laughter and the way her hair danced to it, dark brown curls swirling. It wasn't like Ita hadn't met white people before, mostly at the clinic. But none like her. Leda was like an American movie star, but from old films he'd seen in black-and-white. Maybe it was the way her skin glowed in the dark, or the curves of her body like flowing cloth. Even when she first arrived, covered in a fine dust, her cheeks looked creamy underneath, like milk. Her green eyes peeked out from her slender face, watching like a bird on a branch, poised and wary at the same time.

She was nothing like Ita had imagined—an aggressive older American woman. Crass, maybe, loud, even wanton, from what he'd seen at the theater in Kibera that showed current movies. Women with plastic breasts and lipstick, who wore little clothing and made dirty jokes.

Leda didn't seem this way in the least. She reminded him of an old-time movie star because she didn't seem real, of this time, or even human. She floated behind him on her first tour of the orphanage, taking everything in like a first visit to Earth. Could she tell that they'd cleaned? Swept? Washed all the dishes? Ita had sensed her discomfort at sharing a room with Mary. He was glad he'd thought of the hidden room.

Goose bumps crept up his skin in the dark. She was nearby, in that room—asleep on the metal table, wrapped in the blanket he'd given her. He imagined her wispy eyelashes, a smile on her face, her slender fingers curled around the cloth.

He sighed. Everything was perfect.

Suddenly his heartbeat sped up like a motorcycle. Nothing was ever perfect, or ever stayed so for more than a fleeting second.

Ita knew why he pictured Leda curled up, smiling in her dreams. He'd known another girl to sleep that way.

He tried to stop the stampeding memory—he put his hands over his eyes, he turned to his side, dug his head into the foam. But he couldn't stop it. The vision of Leda's beatific face was gone, mutated into the image that haunted Ita every day. A different smooth, beautiful face, but darker and twisted beyond recognition by fear, battered and swelling with blood, as she slumped down beside him in exhaustion. Behind her, Chege.

The memory crept away as it had slithered in, leaving only the guilt twisting Ita's stomach like wringing wet clothes.

Chege.

Ita replayed Chege's appearance today, how he pushed his way in to see Leda. How he took her hand, seductively, teasing her, leering at her. Then he'd pulled out that money. *What are you showing off, Chege?* Nothing to be proud of—how his boys made that money.

It was Mungiki creed to despise Westerners, Americans, even as they coveted their clothes and music. Did Chege really not see the hypocrisy? Could he not see what he'd become?

The air in Ita's room seemed to grow hotter as he thought of what Chege had said to Jomo—money in Kibera can only be gotten by giving something up. Filmstrips of memories spiraled in Ita's mind, of how much Chege had given him— so much, everything, saved his life even, countless times. And now Chege wanted to help the orphans the same way, give them money, protect them. It made Ita's blood boil. Maybe it shouldn't. Maybe he should be grateful. But Ita knew what it cost to accept Chege's help. He knew what it meant to repay in regret and nightmares.

In the dark, Ita shook his head, trying to wriggle free of his thoughts. He wished he could be like Leda—clean, new and fresh to the ways of Kibera.

Suddenly, he remembered how she bent down for her suitcase, sending her curls to cover her face. Was it the scar she wanted to hide? A mark like white paint dribbling down her jaw.

Maybe she had memories she wished she could forget, too. Ita felt a tenderness ache through his chest. In his eyes, that only made her more perfect.

In the morning, Ita wasn't surprised to find the children awake early for school, waiting on the mat for breakfast, eyes darting to the secret room.

"She is in there, stop worrying," he said in Swahili. "Do you think she will fly away?"

As he said it, he realized it was his worry, too.

While they stalled a bit, Ita asking them about their studies, Jomo appeared and sat on the mat as if it was the most normal thing in the world. But in the few months since Jomo's arrival, he had yet to willingly come sit with them. Ita's gaping mouth reassembled into a smile.

Mary came outside with the food, and as they debated whether to wait or wake their visitor the door scraped open and there she was, looking exactly like a crumpled angel in the best of ways. He had seen pictures of the men's pajamas American women wore, and she wore a set herself. But it didn't strike him as wanton like the pictures. On Leda, it actually looked quite demure.

But Ita must have been indiscreet with his looking because she seemed suddenly self-conscious and stepped backward.

"Good morning," Ita said, worried she would duck back into her room.

The children echoed him, practicing their English greetings. "Goo-mowning, goo-mowning, Ledaaah."

"Breakfast is ready," Ita said. "Please, join us."

She smiled, but he could see her hesitation, and the flurry of thought scurry across her face. He had noticed this the day before—she was always thinking, dreaming, watching. But he liked this quality, it reminded him of the children, the rapt curiosity with which they regarded the world.

Leda walked across the dirt in her blue pajamas and sandals. She sat down in the empty spot next to Jomo. "Good morning," she said. Jomo didn't look up, but Ita could see the glint in his eye.

The children were at a loss as to what to do with this mysterious species in their midst. It was Ntimi who looked up shyly. He took a moment and then he opened his mouth. "I trust you slept well, Miss Leda," he said.

Ita nearly split open with pride, hearing the phrase they'd practiced.

Leda beamed at Ntimi, too, looking equally impressed. "What a gentleman you are. I slept like the princess in the fairy tale. Well—" Leda leaned in closer "—not the one about the pea."

Ntimi smiled blankly at the foreign words, and Leda noticed. She mimed opening a book. "I will read it to you. I brought lots of books."

That the children understood, and they clapped and chattered in response.

Ita was touched. In her email, she did not say she would bring books. But books were what the children craved, and lacked, the most. A luxury Ita always longed to provide.

Mary set the tray of food on the mat. Leda watched the boys first this time. She washed her hands, then took her loaf of bread and a cup of tea. When she took her first sip, her eyes widened in reaction.

"It's spicy!" she said and licked her lips like a kitten. "And sweet," she said to herself, then poked Ntimi until he giggled.

"Spicy. Sweet," Ntimi echoed and everyone dug in much like Leda, absorbed in the happiness of a shared meal.

Ita watched his little family take in this strange new addition, like they did with each new orphan. A warmth spread through his stomach, like the fullness of a big meal. It must have been the tea, he reasoned.

Once the boys were off to school, Ita and Leda helped Mary with the dishes and straightening. Leda seemed a bit deflated with most of the children gone. Maybe she didn't feel useful enough. She bounced Walter on her hip, which he loved, though he shouldn't get used to it, Ita thought.

Ita pictured the paperwork waiting in his office, but he surprised himself by turning to Leda and saying, "Would you like to go exploring with me?"

She hesitated, these little pauses already becoming familiar, and Ita wondered if it was the image of the slum or the thought of time alone with him that caused that little furrow in her brow.

"I have things to buy," he added, suspecting she would prefer it presented professionally. He was right.

"Oh, okay, sure, let's go. I'll just change my shoes. One second."

She crossed to the secret room. While the boys had gotten dressed, she'd changed into brown pants and a blue T-shirt. Ita wondered if blue was her favorite color. This was something he did with the orphans as they arrived—try to identify their preferences. Jomo always took the blue cup if it was available and had selected blue sandals for school.

Ita didn't have a plan for their tour, and this was very strange for him. He preferred to have a plan for everything, a trait that Chege had teased him about since they were small. For the Kibera laughed at nothing more than plans. But it was what had made the orphanage possible. Ita's business plan had found them sponsors and the space they now inhabited. And planning was what made him a successful safari guide, standing out among the many, Ita believed. He knew how to craft the perfect trip, down to the type of salad and sandwiches he served for lunch and dinner. Everything was meticulously scheduled, so that it looked effortless for his customers.

What about today's schedule, then? His plan had been to let Mary show Leda the housework she would do around the orphanage while the children were at school and Ita worked in his office. Fetching water, washing, cooking—he'd told Mary that American women didn't know how to do these things without machines. They'd joked about the idea of a dishwasher. How funny. Imagine having enough electricity to power a machine to wash the dishes.

But here he was, walking the volunteer out the front gate, watching the mix of emotions dance on her face. How was he to know that the volunteer would be beautiful and shiny and completely captivating? The kind of woman who makes paperwork—something he enjoyed, the figures lined up neatly—suddenly boring.

So Ita led the way around the corner, past the beauty shop and the barbershop next to it. The sun struck them between the maze of rooftops, flickering over their skin through the haze of dust. Ita noticed a spring in his step that he loved to see in the children. Not that he remembered ever being a child like that himself. Chege had always said Ita walked as though he had a rhino on his back.

First stop, he needed to charge his cell phone. Leda had asked him questions about his phone yesterday. She seemed surprised that he had one. But how would he run a business without it? From Leda's descriptions, it sounded as though most businessmen in America had computers. She asked if they had one, making Ita laugh. If anyone knew he had a laptop in the orphanage, he'd have to hire a security guard to live with them. No, Ita explained. He had to pay to use the internet in Nairobi, when he went to check his post office box for the orphanage. When he told her that, he thought of the shillings that had added up in the minutes he'd spent staring at her emails and résumé.

"What's up, brother?" the charging-station man asked. Ita

handed him his phone and saw the man look Leda over, alternately like a skewer of meat and a purple elephant.

Leda noticed. She smiled at the man, at the same time averting her eyes and backing away.

Ita handed over the money and rushed back to his charge.

"So," he said, hoping to soothe her. "What do you plan to teach the children while you are here? Improve their English?"

Leda's face lit up instantly, like the first rays of sun that woke Ita up every morning. "I was thinking about it last night."

He couldn't help but picture her curled up on the table in her blue pajamas, modest enough to hide her body, but thin enough to fuel his fantasy of undergarments.

"I would definitely love to teach them, and read to them, and I've brought several cameras, but—" Leda's voice grew shyer suddenly. "I wanted to see what you thought about the boys' room. What would you think of building them bunk beds?" She made a gesture with her hand like a shelf.

Ita was caught off guard. There were many things the boys needed before wooden beds, but the thought was touching, and the boys would feel like city princes. And did she mean they would build them together? Ita liked the idea of them working side by side.

"Is that silly?" she asked. "I'm sure there are other things they need first—"

He laughed. "They will love bunk beds. You know how to build them?" He hoped he did not sound discouraging. He was just trying to picture her wielding a hammer.

Now it was Leda's turn to laugh. "I have a house in the mountains. I've discovered that I like building things. Flower boxes and a doghouse."

"You have a dog?"

"Amadeus," Leda said, and now Ita knew a way to win a smile from her.

"Mozart. *Eine kleine Nachtmusik,* the boys like. For me, *Requiem*—breaks my heart."

She gasped. But when she smiled, Ita knew she must love the music as much as he did.

"Okay, bunk beds," he said. "We will need wood and nails."

She looked down but her voice was even when she spoke. "I would like to donate all the supplies, please."

A feeling welled up in him that was hard to place—gratitude, excitement, giddiness at the rare taste of money—

"Do the boys like to paint?" she asked.

Surprised again. "Like on paper?"

She smiled. "The walls! We could all paint the orphanage walls together. Would they like to decorate their home? Maybe elephants and birds, rhinos, all the animals from your safari trips."

The boys had never been on safari. But he was sure they would love painting animals on the walls. Ita liked to draw, too, though how long had it been since he had done it? "They would like that." A lump rose in his throat and he turned away. He was moved, imagining Leda lying in bed, dreaming up these plans. "Should we get the supplies today? Wood and nails. And paint. We will have to get someone to help us carry them back."

The day stretched on that happy way, now that they had a united mission. They found the paintbrushes first, but had to go elsewhere for the paint. They laughed as they discussed their plans, designating zebras their place by the kitchen and monkeys in the bathroom.

On their way to get the wood, Ita couldn't help himself from tossing questions at her like chicken feed. He wanted to know everything at once. But she didn't answer. Before his eyes, she caught herself, breathed in and said coyly, "You first," with a little smile. But Ita would bet it was a practiced defense, that smile no man would deny.

"I grew up here," he said, watching passersby stare as they walked. "I tried to leave, I wanted to become a doctor. I was on my way, starting school, helping out at a clinic here, but then the orphanage came to be and—" Ita put out his hand to help Leda over a creek of dribbling brown water. The touch of her skin sent shivers through his arm.

Leda caught his eye and looked quickly away. Did she feel it, too, the electricity? "And?" she asked, her voice high in pitch and a little shaky.

"And what?" he said, his hand still closed over hers.

Leda slipped out of his touch and bounded a step ahead, leaving him feeling embarrassed. He was acting like a schoolboy in love. The realization brought him back to Earth and he remembered what he'd been talking about. Broken hopes. How time steals them away. "And days became years," he said. Could she know what that meant? Dreams dashed, time squandered on poverty, years that raced by as he dealt with one pressing problem at a time? It hurt Ita to speak of his dream, getting further and further away now, of being a doctor.

"I know what you mean," she said softly.

Ita believed that she did, somehow. He felt the questions returning, piling up—

"But how does an orphanage just *come to be?*" she asked, and he laughed in spite of himself.

"With a Michael." He looked to see if she'd learned the children's names yet. "The tallest boy, the oldest."

"The protector," she said simply.

Ita missed a step to look at her. "Yes. That's Michael." He pointed out a shadowed walk-through, but stopped before entering so they could catch their breath. "A friend brought him to me. She was sick, and she was out of time. Back then, my dream was dying, too, slipping through my fingers—" Leda was watching him with her wide green eyes. She had this way of making him feel as though they were alone in a quiet room, not in the midst of Kibera traffic. "It seemed like a sign from above. How could I say no?"

Ita looked to the sky, remembering so clearly the four-year-old boy with the serious eyes, hiding behind his mother's spindly legs. "I thought I would take him to an orphanage, but no one would take him."

"Why not?"

Ita sighed, feeling the old anger bubble in his blood. "His mother died of AIDS and people thought her child must have it, too. They didn't want a sick child. One who would die or infect others."

Leda chewed on her bottom lip. "So you took him in."

"Yes," Ita said and smiled, remembering. "I took him everywhere, delighting in everything he did. People saw that I loved him, clothed him, fed him, and—" Ita meant to laugh, but it came out like a sigh, remembering the rainy season after Michael arrived, after Ita had to quit school "—then people started leaving children at my door like flowers."

A man knocked Ita's shoulder, snapping him back to the present. It wasn't safe to stand still like this in the back paths of the slum. Better to keep moving. "You never know, right?" He started toward the shadowy corridor.

"Know what's coming next?" She stepped into a ray of sunshine.

Ita slipped into the alley. "Never know when you'll meet the person that will change the path of your life."

The corridor was only wide enough for one person at a time. A man squeezed past Ita, then jumped when he saw Leda entering the passage.

"*Hujambo. Habari ya asubuhi,*" she said and wriggled past him, so formal and adorable it made Ita want to kiss her.

He turned around, and as though fate meant to grant his wish, she was watching her feet and ran right into him. It threw him off balance, and they ended up pressed against the mud wall. Ita had just a moment to feel her slender frame, the down on her arms brush against his skin.

She looked up at him, her breath retreating across her pink lips.

"You're right," she whispered.

Ita looked at her, a feeling of wonder washing through him.

"You never know," they both said in unison, then laughed shyly and slipped apart.

CHAPTER 5

December 30, 2007, Kibera—Ita

GOD'S BEEN RAINING KEROSENE.

Ita watches the flames clawing the night sky. When he tries to force air into his iron lungs, ash coats his tongue, clogs his throat. He doubles over, hands on his knees, and feels his body heave with vomit. But when he opens his mouth, it's blood that drools onto his foot. He coughs, and blood splatters the dirt. Ita wonders if his wounds will prove fatal after all.

He must make it back to the orphanage. He must find a hold on the present. All is lost for him, but the boys deserve a chance.

He nearly faints from the pain of standing, but grits his teeth and thrusts one foot in front of the other. He'll keep to the alleys—he can hear the rioters out on the main paths. He creeps unsteadily between the homes, his back scraping along the mud shacks. From inside them, he hears the chorus of whispers—plotting, pleading, praying.

One more corner and he'll be there. The fire is behind him; it hasn't reached their neighborhood. He realizes, with a pang of shame, that he dreads seeing the children. He dreads their questions, their tears, their bulging eyes. Ita doesn't have any comfort to give. He's afraid if he opens his mouth, he might tell them the truth.

The life we have been building, the one I wanted to give you, planned so carefully—it's over.

When Ita knocks quietly on the door, there is an instant rustle.

A tiny whisper asks who's out there. Michael.

As soon as Ita answers, the door slides open.

Michael's eyes go wide as cashew nuts, and Ita realizes he must look as monstrous as he feels.

"Jomo?" Ita asks.

Michael nods.

Ita sighs. He is safe. Jomo is inside and safe. Ita drags his swollen body inside.

Michael watches with his ancient eyes. "All the children are in bed. Mary, too. I told them they must stay there until you returned." Pride peeks through Michael's scared voice. Ita sees that the boy is clutching Ita's rifle. He floods with tenderness for this boy whom he has promised so much.

"You did very well, Michael. I knew I could count on you. You must sleep now. I will need your help in the morning."

"But—" Michael darts another look at Ita's wounds.

Ita puts out his hand, takes the rifle. "I'll be okay. I can fix it." He nods toward the secret room. But he has no idea if he can fulfill that promise, if he can fix anything this night has destroyed. "Go on," he says in a voice he knows Michael will obey.

Michael sighs, the same old man's sigh he had when he was five years old. *"Lala salama, mpwenda baba."* He says it so softly as he turns to leave that it takes Ita a moment to realize what he's heard.

Goodnight, dear father.

Ita watches him enter the bedroom, then begins the painful trudge toward the room with the medical supplies. *Leda's room.*

There are footsteps again in the courtyard at his back, scurrying, urgent.

"Ita—" Mary's whisper hisses into the night.

Ita turns. Mary's face is crinkled paper, soggy in the creases.

Her family, he realizes with a pang. The orphans are not her family, not like they are for Ita. Mary's kin is out there, in the chaos, in the fire. Her daughter, Grace, lives by the railroad tracks with her husband, with Mary's grandchildren. But Mary is here. She stayed. "Thank you, Mary. Thank you for staying with the boys. What can I do? Do you need me to go check on your family?"

A tear winds crookedly through the wrinkles of Mary's face. Ita realizes he has never seen Mary cry, not even close. She's looking at his battered body. "You cannot. Look at you. What did they do to you? Where is Leda?"

"She is gone." But Ita has no words for what happened to him, because it is linked to what happened to Leda, to what Chege did. He wonders when he will be able to say it aloud, if ever. Dizziness rolls over Ita like fog. He pitches forward, his stomach heaving into his throat.

Mary scuttles toward him, grips his shoulder.

Ita recoils from the pain. He must stand. He must reassure her, if he wants to be alone. "It's okay. In the morning—"

"No, I must go now. My daughter—"

He shakes his head firmly. "No. You cannot go out tonight. It is not safe for women."

More tears seep into Mary's scrunched face.

But Ita must be firm on this. He cannot go back out there now and hope to protect an old woman. "Does Paul have a phone?" Ita asks of Mary's son-in-law, taking out his cell phone.

Mary shakes her head.

Ita nods. "I'll go with you tomorrow. We will walk in the sun, in the light that has to follow this darkness. Grace will be all right. She's strong and brave. Like her mother."

Mary understands. Ita has decided. She stops her lip from trembling. Then she reaches up and puts her hand gingerly to the side of Ita's face. He closes his eyes and the scratchy parchment of her hand on his cheek brings the flicker of a memory, decades old. A mother's touch. If he doesn't open his eyes, he will disappear into the sensation, spiral into the void, searching for solace in memories lost and drained away.

His eyes fling open when Mary's hand slips away. Without another word, she turns and shuffles off to her room to spend a sleepless night.

The moment of comfort evaporates, and Ita knows he might collapse any minute. He hastens across the courtyard to the hidden room.

Inside, he lights an oil lamp. He sees the pile on the floor, but wrests his mind away from thoughts of Leda, of the memories in this room. Instead, he looks at himself in the small mirror.

At the first glimpse of his face, Ita sees a statue glued back together all wrong. His eyes, nose, jaw—everything's in the wrong place and wrong proportions. The swelling—that explains why his vision is so distorted, why his head pounds like a pump about to blow.

The only other time he has ever seen his face like this, a mangled toy to be thrown away...

The only other time was the day he met Chege. The day one life ended and another began.

Ita soaks a rag in a bowl of water. He presses it to his forehead, covering his eyes, covering the vision, and tries not to remember.

But everything—the blood coating his teeth, the pain in his limbs as though they're clenched in a lion's jaw, the hopelessness flooding his veins—it's all so much the same that Ita can't help but remember...

September 22, 1989, Kibera—Ita

Ita hears them, the boys, he hears them coming, but he doesn't care.

After two weeks on the streets, he is already tired. He's tired of running, tired of begging, tired of trying to hold on to a life that's bent on wriggling out of his fingers like a worm. *So, let it. Let it all go. Mother. Home. School. Hope.* He hears the boys tearing down the alley, their footsteps the sound of his plans being trampled.

When the boys turn the corner, Ita sees they are older than he'd expected. Teenagers.

There is a moment where they stop and Ita looks up and they look at him and there is still a thread of time in the fabric of fate when they might just move on.

But then one of them spots Ita's backpack. And when he nudges the boy next to him, that boy looks at Ita's shoes. And then the third boy, the tallest, with a tattoo freshly done, he rallies them all with a certain look. Seconds later, as though choreographed, they all jump Ita.

The tall boy is the fists. He likes it, Ita can tell. He likes beating him, likes beating anyone, probably, maybe because he's holding in the same bellyful of seesaw emotions as Ita. This way, when his knuckles crack on Ita's cheekbones and his knees make Ita's ribs pop, some of the feelings can get out and away, and leave space for him to breathe again.

That's what Ita hears the loudest—the boy's breathing, heavy in his ear. But that doesn't mean he can't hear the other boys unzip his backpack. He can hear them celebrating the spoils, tossing out the books as they find the food and clothes, the medicine. Ita can hear, just barely he can hear them tell the tall boy to stop, that it looks like he's dead, stop, he isn't moving, he's—

The next thing Ita hears—it must be a dream. There is a new voice. It is a madman shouting. A madman shouting in a kid voice like a whistle.

"Get away from him!" the voice is screaming. "Get away or I kill you. I kill you all."

Ita bargains with his eyelids. They weigh more than two rhinoceroses, but they must open. *Open and I will let you close for good. Before I go, before I die, I want to see the madman.*

Ita's eyes open to glimpse a dreamy sliver of absurdity. The teens, they're frozen, frozen in place by the owner of the whistling voice.

He's the skinniest kid Ita's ever seen. His hair looks like he cut it with a broken bottle. His eyes shine like he swallowed a flare. He's standing atop an overturned jerrican, and he's still barely taller than the shortest of Ita's attackers.

Doesn't look like he has got a lot going for him, Ita thinks.

But he does have a machete.

The attackers don't seem to notice; they've begun to thaw. They giggle, Ita doesn't see which one starts, but now they're all hyenas, cackling in the dust. The tallest boy, he zips up Ita's backpack and slings it over his shoulders. He laughs as he walks toward where Ita lies. Ita's eyes are about to close, having upheld their end of the bargain.

But he fights himself to watch the tall boy come slip the shoes off his feet, and to see the incredible thing that happens next.

The miniature madman makes a sound. It cannot be called a scream—it hardly fits the description of any human sound Ita's ever heard. He waves his machete in the air. When he brings it down, it whacks into his own forearm until blood squirts out in the shape of a rainbow, splattering Ita's attackers. With the bubbling blood, the madman smears his cheeks, like war paint.

The last thing Ita sees is the blood-smeared kid spring from the jerrican and charge, roaring like a hound let loose from hell.

The last thing Ita hears is the backpack drop in the dirt beside his head. But then his senses are extinguished, replaced by the sound and color of nothingness.

When Ita comes to, it's nighttime, the most dangerous time in Kibera. He struggles to cobble together his thoughts, rocks tumbling into a river.

"Good. You not dead."

Ita looks, and the machete-wielding psychopath is sitting just beside him in the dark.

"Chege," the psycho says.

It will hurt to speak, Ita imagines. "Ita." He was right.

"Go back to sleep, Ita. See you tomorrow."

In the morning, Ita wishes he was dead. *Still might happen,* he consoles himself. Everything hurts. Everything.

"Morning," the psycho says brightly.

Ita wonders if maybe he is a spirit, a spirit guide into the other side. Should he talk to him? Can he ask questions?

Like…where is my mother? Is she here? She's dead, too. She just died two weeks ago—

"Hey, you okay? You eyes rolling back into your bones again. How much longer you expect me to sit here?"

Ita's ears normalize for a moment. They're near the tracks, he can hear the trains. So they're in the landfill. Now Ita can smell it and his stomach turns.

"I'm just kidding. You can sleep. Just don't die."

Sun's going down again when Ita next wakes up. His mind is clearer. He understands he can die now, if he wants to. Or not. Because he saw what the psycho named Chege was sitting on—the backpack.

"Inside." Ita isn't sure if the words came out or not. "Medicine."

"I saw. Which one?"

"Pill. Orange."

Ita's mouth feels orange, stuffed with Kibera dust.

"Got it. Here. What's it for?"

"Infection."

"How do you know?"

"My mother. Sick. A long time. I learned—"

"You Kikuyu, yeah?"

"Yeah."

"Me, too."

Ita doesn't answer.

"It your mother's fault, then, that Kikuyus not take you in. She go with men? Get money? She got *that* sickness—"

"Shut up." Ita rolls up to his elbow, ignores the lightning strikes of pain, blood frothing in his mouth. "You shut up, you—"

"Shhh. Hey. I no judge. Your mother love you so much, she do it for you. That makes it okay."

Ita sees his mother's face, a skull painted brown, her trembling bone fingers giving him her necklace, the gold sparrow sparkling in the setting sunlight, her voice, scratched raw, saying, *I'm sorry, I'm sorry, forgive me—*

"No, it doesn't," Ita says and blacks out, back into the in-between.

Two more days, and Ita doesn't take any more of the pills. Best to save them. When he finally sits up, Chege nods in approval, and they sit on the field of trash where no ground is visible.

"You live here?"

Chege hears the judgment. "Now you do, too."

"Why?" Ita asks. He is genuinely curious—why choose to live in a trash heap?

"Because here you won't run into those guys again. Because here you can sleep, even if you stink like a cockroach."

The backpack is zipped, sitting between them. Ita opens it up. It's all there. The books, even the food. He looks at Chege in surprise.

Chege twists away. When he swivels back, he holds out a crooked carrot and a mushy tomato. "Eat these."

Ita knows he must have been saving them. "How'd you get them?"

Chege shrugs. "I stole them from an old woman." He pats the machete resting across his knees.

Ita looks at the food in his hands. If he eats it, he will break the promise he made his mother, and himself. The promise that he would try to be good, die if he must, but not die shamed, like her.

"What did you do to the guys that attacked me?"

"They not coming back, don't worry."

"I'm not worried. I want to know."

Chege's face is blank, placid, cracked dried blood still visible on its skin. "Just eat."

Ita looks at the tomato. The pang in his stomach tells him he's starving, his body desperate. He pops the tomato in his mouth. The skin splits and the mush bursts in his throat like rotten flesh. He almost chokes, but gulps it down.

"Why are you helping me?" he asks Chege, and chomps the carrot, so dry and old it's furry on his tongue.

"I'm not!" Chege huffs. "I'm leaving. I just didn't think you should die yet."

Ita looks at Chege's face, staring straight ahead.

"You smart," Chege says quietly then. "You read books. There just some things you didn't know yet." He picks up a bottle cap and chucks it. "Now you know."

But Chege doesn't get up. He doesn't leave. He sits, huddled over, feet dug in. Anchor to the ship thrashing in a storm.

December 30, 2007, Kibera—Ita

Ita wrings the rag out over the bowl of water and studies his face in the cloudy mirror.

He knew the terrible things Chege was capable of, but to betray him like he did tonight, to do that to Leda…

How could you, Chege?

Hatred pumps to the rhythm of Ita's blood. His reflection, staring back—the monster in the mirror—a mis-sewn Frankenstein's creature, everything about him grotesque and misshapen, distorted by the electrifying visions that won't stop coming. He sees Chege on top of Leda. Sees her white legs in the red dirt, rows of scratches like lions tried to devour her. He sees the look in Chege's eyes. Guilt. Pure and clear. Guilt and regret bubbling out as Ita lunged at him with his fists. *Good.* Ita remembers the blood spouting from Chege's nose. *If you don't die from guilt as you should, I should kill you. You are poison. You take everything that is beautiful—*

Now it's a different memory vying for Ita's mind. A memory more than a decade in the past, but somehow sharper with time. That look, sick and shamed, twisting across Chege's face—Ita's seen it before. That was Chege's face the day he loomed above Ita as he wrapped his arms tight around a different, trembling, sobbing girl, the smell of fear mixed with the scent of her blood and sweat. *I'm sorry,* Ita whispered into her hair. *I'm so sorry.*

Ita covers his face with his hands, trying to blot out the images, but it makes them grow stronger and louder.

He opens his eyes, stares at the monster in the mirror. *You see? You knew. You knew Chege would betray you again. What he did to Leda is your fault. You let him get close. Close enough to covet her, to hate her.*

Ita remembers how Leda scrambled away in the dirt, her face stained in tears. He remembers her screams. She screamed while the men beat him. Screamed at the world, at fate, sobbing and screaming until she collapsed and pulled Ita's head into her lap, rocking him until the police dragged her away.

Now she's gone. And she's never coming back.

Ita hears a noise outside. His engorged body turns to iron. The sound swells like the roar of a charging animal. It's a pack of men—tearing through the alley. They stop at the house behind the orphanage. Without the thin metal wall, Ita could touch them. The men rip a door from its hinges. Women scream—

Ita grabs the rifle. He must get to the front door.

Then he hears a noise behind him. Inside. In the court-yard, at the door.

He grips the rifle with both hands and spins around.

As the shouting outside turns violent, fists thudding against skin and bone, the door to the hidden room scrapes open.

Ita aims the rifle, holds his finger on the trigger.

But what appears in the crack of moonlight is Ita's night-mare memory come to life. Ita's childhood self, misshapen, a child-sized Frankenstein's creature come back to haunt him.

The little monster blinks, eyes wide and watery.

Ita lowers the rifle, gasping.

"Jomo."

The boy's face is swollen, bruised and taut, as if it will split open. Blood is crusted in his eyelashes, still wet under his nose.

"My God, Jomo, come here."

Jomo looks like he will take a step, but the roar outside changes again. The women screech, outrage at its highest pitch, until a new sound follows the fists—the whack of ma-chete on bone. The screams become the wail of hopelessness.

As Ita looks upon Jomo's broken face, he hears the women's tears rain down on crimes they will never forgive.

"I'm sorry," Ita whispers.

They stand perfectly still, Ita and Jomo, facing each other, listening to the attackers running off, receding into the mer-ciless night.

CHAPTER 6

December 11, 2007, Kibera—Leda

HER THIRD DAY IN KIBERA, LEDA WOKE WITH A smile curved like a fortune cookie. The blanket Ita had given to her was clutched in her fingers; she wriggled her toes into it. She could already hear them, the children, outside in the orphanage clanking pots and chattering. On the other side of the wall of her little room, she could hear people shuffling past in the alley, a rise and fall of greetings and "good mornings" Leda was surprised to find comforting rather than scary in their proximity.

The buoyancy she felt in her heart didn't hold for her body, however. Even with the foam beneath her, Leda's body felt as rigid as her metal bed. For a moment, as she stretched her aching limbs, Leda imagined what she normally awoke to—gentle light through the curtains in Topanga, Amadeus licking her fingers, the first glimpse of her things lined up neatly, then the expanse of the scruffy mountains, the quiet ritual of her morning tea.

But not this morning. Leda opened her eyes. She surveyed the sheet-metal door, its dented ripples and patchwork surface of dirt and paint and rust. She flipped over and looked at the ceiling, which was much the same. A two-foot space surrounded the metal table, her bed, on all sides like a moat. The far wall was the one that connected with the outside world, an effect more like a folding screen than a real barrier. Nothing at all like her house in Topanga, blanketed by trees, or her childhood home facing the sea. She tried to think of the word that would best describe those houses. Not isolated as much as—

Insulated. That was the word.

That was her comfort zone—being alone. But now, as she pictured the Topanga house she loved, the house that had seemed wild and warm compared to mother's ice-cold mansion, now it too seemed sterile.

Leda turned onto her side again, facing the interior of the orphanage. She replayed scenes from the day before. First, cringing at how she popped out in her blue pajamas when everyone was ready for the day. Then her abashed realization that they probably didn't own pajamas. Did she look ridiculous or pretentious? Ita had laughed, though not meanly. His eyes never looked meanly at anyone. Stern, maybe, with the children, and with that nasty gangbanger Chege. But even with him, Ita showed a generosity of spirit that surprised her. After growing up with Estella, who emanated distaste, an annoyance, at her presence, Leda found Ita's kindness unsettling. But warming.

When they'd ventured out into Kibera together, she'd studied him from behind, marveling at how he moved with ease, with purpose, winding through the slum. He was a better guide than Samuel, telling her little flecks of gossip about the neighbors, connecting different locations to stories about the boys. *Ntimi wanted to get his haircut here. I had to explain it was only for women. He still wanted to go. Ntimi likes to be around ladies.*

She was saddened by Michael's story, of how the orphanage came to be. *All the boys have stories like that,* she reminded herself.

Ita's eyes as he told the story—they filled with a love so pure and rich, Leda had almost felt jealous.

Then she remembered the dark alley. The part of the day she'd been thinking about ever since. Leda closed her eyes to picture it better—how she squeezed past the old man into the darkness, how she lost her footing, bumping into Ita, and them squeezing up against the wall together.

How his eyes filled with desire, with wonder, with appreciation. Leda couldn't believe how he left his emotions free to jump off his face like that, but she loved it. She'd heard his breath quicken, felt his body stiffen, sensed that he was breathing her in like a sudden perfume, memorizing her for later. And then they'd said it, at the same time, in harmony like an impromptu song...

You never know.

They'd come so close to kissing, Leda could still taste it. She'd felt the hotness of his breath, his hands rising to her sides, seen the tuck of his chin, the flutter of his eyelids.

She got up off the table. No pajamas today. She put on the brown pants from the day before—she'd noticed everyone repeated clothing—but dug a bit for the teal blouse with the ruffled collar, the one that brought out her eyes.

After she swiped her face clean and brushed her hair into a ponytail, Leda went back into the bag for some lip gloss and perfume. *Just a light spritz,* she thought. Not too much.

With a smile and a near twirl, she stepped from her slippers into sandals. It wasn't until she put her hand out to the door latch, catching a glimpse of herself in the small mirror, that she remembered something else. Something that Chege said. *American rich lady, out to have a little fun.*

Leda's hand recoiled. And hadn't he looked at Ita when he said it, like it had been Ita who had advertised her that way?

Leda wiped the gloss off her lips.

I'm here for the children, she thought as she swapped the sandals for sneakers. She debated the blouse, hovering over the suitcase, until she caught herself with a *this is ridiculous,* and stepped outside.

And there they were, waiting.

"Good morning, Leda," Ita said with a gentlemanly nod of his head.

She started forward, drawn to him, already feeling more relaxed.

"Sleepyhead!" Ntimi shouted with his Cheshire cat grin, his big square teeth ready to chomp on life. He pointed at his head and giggled, thinking the wordplay hilarious.

Leda faltered in her path, self-conscious. *Lazy rich lady sleeps through breakfast.*

But Ita chuckled and swatted Ntimi on the head, and his laugh was kind. It rolled across the distance to Leda and snagged when he caught her eye.

Ntimi waved Leda closer, impatiently. He had little Walter in his lap, pinning him down—the toddler with the potbelly and enchanting giggle.

Michael's smile had already faded, the gentle stare resumed. The other two, Thomas and Peter, started in on the bread and Michael, catching it in his peripheral vision, smacked their hands.

Leda smiled. She snuggled in next to Ntimi and rinsed her hands in the bowl of water.

"Where's Jomo?" she asked, but nobody answered.

Leda ran her eyes over the perimeter of the orphanage. The wood for the bunk beds was there, waiting. The cans of paint were stacked along the walls, too. Leda smiled, remembering how excited the boys were to hear of the plans.

There. Leda spotted Jomo—well, his feet, anyway—peeking out under the sheet in the same little spot he'd hid in before. As if he could feel her watching, the sheet moved aside a tiny crack, and the sunlight found a crescent of Jomo's face. Leda smiled. Jomo's glance dove straight down. But Leda kept her eyes on him, let him feel the smile linger. Sure enough, he looked back up and saw her still looking. He tried hard as he could to stop it, but the corners of his lips curled ever so slightly. Then the sheet swung closed.

Like a ghost, Leda thought, his presence wispy and fleeting. A ghost of what? Of the child he could have been?

She chewed on her bread and tried to follow the chatter of the boys. She didn't get a chance to slurp down much of her tea before the boys were up and scurrying off, Ita on their heels, doling out hurry-ups.

Leda scolded herself for sleeping in. She'd have to get up earlier to maximize her time with them before school.

Mary came out to round up the dishes. "Good morning," she said quietly. Mary didn't speak English, so her efforts were all the more touching.

"Good morning, Mary. Thank you for breakfast."

"So," Ita said, returning, and Leda's stomach fluttered. "Today I thought Mary could show you the housework."

Leda's stomach sank. But she scolded herself again. About time she made herself useful. Ita probably thought she didn't know how to clean.

"Of course—" she said, but Ita interrupted with a smile.

"So I can finish the paperwork piling up, and later I can take you to the clinic. Would you like to go with me?"

"Can't wait," Leda said. Was it her imagination or did Mary chuckle?

Ita shut himself in his office and left Leda to star with Mary in a comedy skit. The older woman rambled off explanations to which Leda smiled and nodded and said, "I'm sorry I don't understand a word," to which Mary smiled and nodded and in Swahili said, Leda imagined, "I'm sorry I don't understand a word." Mainly Mary pointed at pots and rags and Leda had no idea if she wanted them cleaned, carried or filled with something.

But by the end of three hours, Leda knew many things. For one, she knew the cooking never stopped. Ever. The breakfast pot got washed and put back on the stove to boil water for washing, then for the lunch stew. After that would come dinner, plus more boiled water for tea. Leda wondered where the water came from. It would be an awful lot of water to carry.

Now, Leda knew that the house had four very important jugs that must always have water in them. Two waist-high jugs in the bathroom area contained water for bucket baths and flushing. In the kitchen, the one on the left was for general cooking and washing. The one on the right was smaller, and Mary made a big fuss over this one. "You, you, you," she kept saying and pointing at Leda. After a rousing game of charades and bubbling noises, Leda figured out that one was boiled water for the tourist. One peek inside at the swirling sediment and Leda made a mental note to buy more bottled water when she went out with Ita.

Pantomime can't help but make for laughter, and it wasn't long before Leda and Mary were fast friends. Mary got into it and it became a game. Leda even mimed her life back in

America, drawing air pictures of the mountains and the ocean and the way Amadeus greeted her at the door. Mary watched Leda with amusement and Leda loved to watch her, too, so strong and capable, so sure. This was Leda's favorite trait to discover in people, ease and calm, and was delighted to study it up close in Mary. Estella was a bundle of nervous tension, anxiety and impatience. Being around her mother was like tiptoeing through a cactus field.

Mary's fingers wrapped around ladles or cups or piled up the logs for the fire with force and grace. If Leda's fingers were too slow or the logs were crossed wrong, Mary rearranged them with a "tsk" and preciseness that Leda adored. *This is how we wash the boys' clothes, make them look smart and clean,* her strong hands said. *This is how we keep the men fed and happy,* her smile said. "Ita," Mary said, and she straightened up her back, pretended to sit up straight in a chair. She spread out imaginary items—a cup of tea to the right, four stacks of paper lined up, just so. She jabbed at an imaginary calculator with a serious look carved into her face. She tapped a pretend pencil against her forehead.

Their combined laughter continued until Ita stuck his head out the door and called, "What's so funny?" making them laugh all the harder.

A moment later, Ita stepped out of the office entirely. He looked at the two of them with a fresh smile and a warmth Leda was starting to crave like kids crave summer. "Ready?"

The slum outside burst at Leda with clashing colors and sounds and smells. Ita took off at a brisk pace, and Leda scurried to keep up. The paths between houses were so narrow they barely fit two people, especially being divided down the middle by a ditch of wastewater. At times, Leda could stretch out her arms and touch both sides. In other spots, the path was soaked in slime and turned to slippery, splattering mud.

Everywhere, beneath the houses and the stalls and the latrines, was the same red dirt mixed and packed together with every kind of trash: broken glass, plastic bags, rags of clothing, empty lighters, soiled cardboard, food wrappers and bits of wood and metal.

Leda discreetly peeked into some of the homes that were open. Most of them looked to be one room, no more than eight feet by eight feet, filled to the brim with teakettles and buckets and clothes, plus people who jumped when they caught Leda looking. A dozen people slept in one house, it appeared.

Intermittently, the narrow pathways opened up and a tiny store—a *duka,* Leda reminded herself—would appear. Soft drinks, candy, cigarettes, cooking oil—all were displayed on a stand like a desk.

When they made it out onto a main road, wooden vendor booths lined the street as far as Leda could see, often two deep. Before them, on the ground, other vendors laid out their wares. Vegetables, clothing, electronics, phone cards, hair products, lotion, fried sweets—the assortment was mind-boggling. After a bit, the booths gave way to giant garbage piles that industrious children, goats and chickens hunted through.

Past the landfill came more mud houses. "We have to stop," Ita said suddenly, waiting for Leda to come up beside him.

"*Hodi!*" Ita called out before a door.

There was a pause, and then a woman's voice called back, "*Karibu.*"

When the woman came to the door, she had a weary smile for Ita, but then she saw Leda next to him.

Ita spoke soothingly in Swahili, gesturing to Leda, his smile on overdrive. Finally the woman looked at Leda and smiled obligingly as she welcomed them inside, but Leda could tell that she was weighed down with troubles.

Inside, at the corners of the small room, Leda could see the stick frame for the mud structure, but most of the walls were covered with newspaper pages, photos and a poster for Raila Odinga. On one side was a low wooden bed frame, with rags balled up for cushioning. There was a mat on the dirt floor with a small stove atop it and a few cooking utensils. The woman removed her sandals and stepped onto the mat to pick up an ancient teakettle.

Leda looked down and saw her filthy tennis shoes standing on what was effectively the woman's kitchen table.

"Pole," Leda apologized quickly and jumped off the mat. She started to sweat as she stood nervously, unsure what to do with herself taking up all that space in the tiny room. The woman poured tea for Leda, and Leda was touched by her kindness. Even though the tea was hot, the scent of cardamom and cinnamon helped combat the smell of raw sewage in the air.

Ita and the woman continued to speak, seemingly oblivious to both the stifling heat and Leda's awkward hovering. Leda tried not to stare, but she saw the pain on Ita's face as the woman spoke in low rushed words. She didn't have to understand the woman to feel her anguish.

Ita listened far more than he spoke, and by the end he took the woman's hands in his. They stayed like this for a quiet moment that made Leda's heart ache, and then it was over.

The woman retracted her hands and stood. She smiled weakly at Leda. *"Karibu,"* she said.

Leda nodded, wishing she could do something for this woman, but not knowing what.

As the woman took the teacups from them, Ita removed some money from his pocket. He pressed it into her hands even as she shook her head.

Should she offer the same? Leda wondered. Would this woman rather accept money from someone she thought could afford it? Leda fumbled with her money belt, tucked inside her waistband, but Ita was already leaving through the door and the woman looked at Leda's hands strangely. Leda felt her cheeks burn. She wanted to explain, but knew it would come out garbled and wrong.

Instead she hung her head, thanked the woman for the tea, and followed Ita outside where he waited in the path.

"Is she okay?" she asked, when obviously the woman wasn't okay. "Can I help her?"

Ita looked into Leda's face, his expression reminding her of a character in a silent movie. She thought she saw approval and judgment, sadness and hope, travel across his face in overlapping succession. Finally he sighed.

"She will be okay. She is a good, strong woman."

He turned but when he saw that Leda wasn't going to follow, he added, "Her husband has gone."

"What do you mean gone?"

"She doesn't know. Drinking, maybe. Another woman. Maybe dead. We shall see."

Ita turned and continued down the wide road, people filling in the space behind him.

Leda watched for a moment, considering each person streaming past her. All different heights, all slender. And all of them concentrating, their faces set in lines, lost in their thoughts. She saw the same tiredness she'd seen in the woman's eyes. Not anger, Leda thought, not bitterness. Just exhaustion.

She remembered how Ita had grasped the woman's hands as she spoke. Why weren't they angry? Why weren't they bitter? How could they have been through so much, every day, and still smile? Looking around, she saw tired people, yes, but also much happiness amidst the flurry of activity.

Both sides of the path ahead were lined with people selling their wares—cinnamon-sugar *mandazi* frying in a dented bowl over a wood fire, a tray lined with wilted greens and dusty fruit. A Mariah Carey song belted from an unseen boom box, presumably nearby the skinny old man sitting next to a tray of CDs. All around her, people greeted and joked loudly with one another. As she caught up with Ita, two young kids bounded up to him with their mother and right away everyone was laughing heartily, Ita the loudest. He introduced her and the mother gave her a wide smile.

Leda thought of her brief night and morning in Nairobi at the hotel. There, the staff had smiled too grandly, too big, at the tourists. In Kibera, it was different. Here they didn't have to pretend.

Leda appreciated that. She smiled back, bent down to greet the children before they were off again on their way.

The more she tried to keep track of where they were going, the more the winding structures blurred before her. Leda stopped short before a concrete wall plastered with political posters. She leaned in to study them.

In the one on the right, Kibaki, the current president, stood in a suit and tie against a vibrant blue background. *Kibaki Tena,* the slogan read. Leda took out her pocket translator book. Kibaki again.

The one next to it was a man against a white background,

pointing off to the right and above. *Pamoja tusonge.* Together. *Mbele.* Leda flipped to *M,* as Ita came up beside her. *Mbele.* Forward.

"Raila Odinga," Ita said, "The savior of Kibera."

Leda looked at Ita's face, for the voice was a tone she hadn't heard from him yet. Half sarcasm, half hope.

"The same age-old battle between old and new?" Leda said, thinking of the upcoming elections in the U.S., Barack Obama the new cool kid on the block.

"The new man promises, while the old man sweeps broken promises under the rug." Ita's smile was nowhere to be seen.

"Which one will you vote for?"

He looked around. "I am Kikuyu," he said softly, and tugged at her elbow as if they should go.

Leda struggled to remember what Samuel and the guidebooks had said about Kikuyus, the leading tribe. They'd been persecuted and now ruled.

"Kibaki is Kikuyu."

"Let's go, Leda," he said and moved on without her.

But that's not all, Leda thought. *Mungiki,* the gangsters, they were Kikuyu, their secret rituals based on Kikuyu rites.

Leda envisioned Chege outside the orphanage door with his crew, his long dreadlocks falling down his back, his skin and teeth marred from drug use, and the men who followed his command, their dreads spikier and shorter, but with shifty yellowed eyes to match. What had Chege said? *What if us Kikuyu brothers don't need your help?*

The elections would happen while she was there, just before Christmas. Up until this point, Leda had thought of that as a bonus. Exciting—to be a part of history. She'd been waiting to ask Ita about politics.

But his reaction made her remember something else—

something a favorite professor had once said. *Nothing is more dangerous than promises. And elections are full of big promises.*

Ita didn't turn back to speak to her again until they reached the clinic. But as soon as they got close, Leda saw him slip into a new skin. His shoulders lifted, his step stiffened. They walked past a sluggish line waiting out front, four people wide and maybe twenty deep. As they passed, many of them called out to Ita. He smiled, but far more seriously than usual. His professional smile, Leda decided. The front of the line was a check-in table where a young Kenyan man and woman sat, performing quick checkups with stethoscopes and tongue depressors. The woman smiled widely when she spotted Ita, and the young man nodded respectfully.

While they exchanged pleasantries, an older couple appeared. These two were European, Dutch maybe, Leda guessed, looking over the man with frizzy blond hair and sunburned skin—the type just simply not engineered for hot weather. His eyes were piercing blue but emanated warmth. When he greeted Ita, the radiating warmth increased tenfold. He waved at Leda, then suddenly became frazzled, looking down frantically for his stethoscope and finding it around his neck. Leda couldn't help but laugh. She liked him immediately. The woman greeted her stiffly and scolded Ita for not coming around often enough. But Leda could tell from the glint in her eye she was very fond of Ita, too.

"Mariska," Ita cooed and gave the woman a hug.

"Where you been, old friend?" the man asked Ita with a grin. He looked at Leda. "Is *this* the volunteer?"

Ita smiled proudly. "This is Leda." He turned to Leda and said, "This is Martin. He helped place the advertisement. His idea."

"Though I must say you improved on it. Did you screen photos, you dog?" The man punched Ita's shoulder playfully and grinned at Leda. "What a beauty you are, my dear. American, is that right?"

"From California," she said.

"Welcome." Martin took Ita eagerly by the shoulder. "Come. We've made some upgrades this season I think you'll appreciate." To Leda he added, "Brain works of this brilliant young man here." He patted Ita's shoulder and the affection bathed Leda, too, as she followed them into the clinic.

"The feeding room," Ita said with a grin.

Martin laughed. "Turns out you were right."

Leda looked at the room to which they gestured and saw a table where young volunteers were handing out juice and small meals.

Martin continued, "Ita spotted a problem with our system. Raising all those boys, he knew a meal solves as many aches as antibiotics. We used to have fights here, after people walked all day only to wait in a long line. Now people know if they wait quietly, they will get their turn. Plus some chapati and lemonade."

"Of course," Mariska said, pointing at the swollen line, "word is getting out."

They continued and Leda's tour showed an ingenious use of the small space. There was an IV station, a mini operating room for sutures and a curtained space for female issues.

"And is this an NGO?" Leda asked Martin. "Is it—"

"Free? Yes, all free. Donations from a variety of sources, but Mariska and I, we pretty much run our own ship here. I'm a doctor in Amsterdam, but twice a year we set up out here and try to help how we can." Martin turned to Ita. "And when we're lucky, we have Ita to help us. Brilliant doctor this man will be one day."

Ita looked away. Leda tried to discern if it was shyness or something more like frustration.

As they continued, Ita asked detailed questions about patients' diagnoses, new medications. Other things, procedures, he asked about, Leda couldn't follow but was impressed by the lingo.

When they reached a small room in the back, Martin waved Ita inside. "I brought them for you, hoping you'd stop by."

There wasn't room enough for more than the two men, but from the doorway, Leda saw Martin produce a stack of magazines. She craned her neck, trying to see what they were.

"Medical journals," Mariska said at her side. "Ita has a mind like a computer. I dare say he could pass his exams today, if such a thing was possible."

Leda relished the excitement she saw on Ita's face. And she loved the mentor role Martin took with him.

"Ita found us, but Martin recognized the skill in him immediately. I protested, but it wasn't long before Ita was helping with sutures, minor surgeries, diagnoses. Martin is right. It is what he was born to do." Leda got chills at the statement, watching the man in question pour hungrily over the journals. "Makes you think about the world, doesn't it?" Mariska said softly.

Leda was forced to look at her, with the underlined question mark hanging between them. "What do you mean?" Leda said, gazing into the woman's wide face, pink in the heat.

"Makes you think what a person like Ita could have done with money and privilege."

Leda flinched.

Ita looked up and saw the two women in the doorway.

He flipped shut the journal and hugged the heavy stack to his chest. He smiled at Leda, making her stomach flutter. "Ready to go home?"

On the walk back to the orphanage, Leda's mind went into hyperdrive. She watched Ita, the journals clutched under both arms, a swagger in his brisk step.

What a person like Ita could have done with money and privilege.

Probably Mariska had no idea just how privileged Leda was, but the comment stuck in her heart like a fishing lure. What had Leda done with the money she was so lucky to have? She'd squandered it, really, desperately seeking a calling. But here was Ita, born to save people, to save lives, thousands maybe, over a lifetime. Leda started to roll an idea around in her mind. When she asked Ita how much university in Nairobi cost, the answer was shocking. All four years cost less than one year in the U.S.

A scholarship fund. Who was to say making a sound investment wasn't as good as finding a calling?

CHAPTER 7

December 11, 2007, Kibera—Leda

THAT NIGHT, AFTER THE BOYS FINISHED THEIR homework, Ita presided over bedtime. Leda used the opportunity to slip off to her room alone. She shut the door behind her, forgetting the lack of electricity, and had to fumble in the dark for the oil lamp.

When she finally got it lit, she sat down heavily on her makeshift bed and found herself breathing a deep sigh of relief. In her earnest effort to fit into this new world, she hadn't realized how exhausted she was at the constant companionship.

Now Leda realized the enormity of her coming here. It wasn't just Kibera's relentless poverty or danger that troubled her. It was the closeness, the suffocating proximity to so many human beings and the emotional vulnerability she felt as a result. Leda knew how to do one thing perfectly—be alone. If there was an award for solitude, she could win it.

Now nine pairs of eyes watched her like a reality television marathon.

And Ita's eyes—

Ita's eyes were devoted. They were certain. They were patient.

All the things Leda doubted in herself.

Just as she wondered whether she should put on her pajamas and pretend she'd gone to bed for the night, there was a soft knock at the door.

She straightened up. She smoothed down her blouse and took a deep breath.

The knock came again.

"Coming," she said, and the word boomeranged around the metal room.

When she slid open the door, she was surprised to find herself face-to-face with not Ita, but Mary.

As usual, Mary spoke a river of words Leda couldn't fish out a meaning from, but her lilting voice soothed Leda immediately. *What would it have been like to have a mother like Mary?* she found herself wondering for the second time that day.

When Mary spoke again, this time she waved Leda forward and nodded her head toward the courtyard. That's when Leda saw that someone else stood out there. A woman in a flowered dress, talking quietly with Ita.

Leda followed Mary into the warm, buzzing night. Apart from the wafting smell of waste, Leda welcomed the air that breezed across her cheeks. When they passed the wash area, she heard giggles and saw the dancing shadows of stragglers still cleaning up for bed.

"Leda," Ita said, and she noted the easy pleasure with which he said her name.

The woman turned. She was about the same height as Leda, but much curvier.

"This is Grace, Mary's daughter," Ita said.

The woman nodded her head. "Good evening, Leda. I'm

happy to meet you." Grace had the same bright voice as her mother.

"So nice to meet you, too," Leda said, which was true—she was relieved to meet another person who spoke English.

But Mary interjected before she could say anything further. She nudged Grace's elbow, chattering excitedly and eyeing Leda.

Grace answered with a laugh rich as roux, then turned to Leda. "I've come to do my mother's henna for a wedding. She wants to know if you'd like me to do your skin, too. For fun."

Leda paused, and Grace noticed. "It's a Muslim wedding, a tradition," she explained. "We are Christian. But there are many Muslim friends in Kibera and I have made a little business for myself by learning to do the henna painting."

"Grace is being very humble," Ita said. "She is a well-known artist, and Kibera women line up to be her canvas." Then he added something, probably a translation, to Mary, who beamed.

Why not? Leda thought. "In that case, I would be honored, Grace. Paint me!"

December 11, 2007, Kibera—Ita

Ita watched Leda reclined under Grace's flurried strokes. *If I were an artist,* he thought, *this is the image that would haunt my dreams.*

It was late. Mary had been painted first and had since gone off to bed. Ita held a medical journal in his lap, of which he hadn't read a single word.

His gaze was like the light of the oil lamp, flickering and lingering over Leda's face, from her smooth forehead down the narrow slope of her nose, catching at her flower-bud lips, over her delicate chin…

Ita was surprised that when he blinked he'd already memorized her face, the hue of her marble skin, the curve of her cheek. Even her scar he knew, the smudge like a painting left out in the rain. He let his eyes travel to the outstretched arms Grace was adorning. He'd seen Leda pick at her fingernails, but now he saw that she'd scraped off swaths of skin near her thumbnails. The rough, mutilated skin was in such contrast to her sleek beauty, it stung Ita to see it, but made the tenderness he felt for her all the more searing.

Leda's eyes stayed closed, not peacefully, but squeezed shut. She had shared few details about her mother and childhood, but from them and her other behaviors Ita could glean she was not a person used to people. It was as if she lived in a world all her own and was shocked when someone got close enough that she had to see them, not as decoration, but an entity as real as she.

With a start, Ita realized how Kibera must feel for her, like drowning. She needed space and quiet, this woman, rare commodities, but Ita made himself a promise that he would find ways to give her these things. The boys had taught him much about navigating broken people. Leda reminded him very much of the orphans when they first arrived, little minefields to map out, one careful step at a time.

Grace murmured something. She was finished with Leda's hands and arms.

Leda opened her eyes and nodded. Grace slipped down Leda's blouse enough to bare the space above her breasts to the glow of the lamp.

Leda caught Ita watching and smiled shyly. It was too late to look away, so he smiled back. Grace looked over her shoulder and caught him, too. She looked back and forth between the two of them, suppressed a knowing smile, and returned to her work. She painted flowering vines sweeping across Leda's collarbone, leaves fluttering, blooms dancing in the lamp's orange glow. Her palm concealed the small cone of dye, so that the black edges of the petals seemed to flow from her fingertips. She was a magic painter.

But Leda was the muse.

Ita couldn't believe his luck, couldn't believe she was here, this beautiful woman with her angelic skin, so delicate, like a museum vase, so precious and vulnerable it had to be protected, guarded—

Ita flinched.

Watching Leda in the flickering light, he couldn't keep out the creeping feeling in his stomach, the queasy sloshing of regret, acid flooding his gut. The last time he'd had thoughts like these, held steadfast intentions to protect fragile beauty, to save a woman he loved, her skin as smooth and inviting as morning tea—

He'd failed. He'd failed himself and failed her.

I haven't forgotten, Kioni. I haven't forgiven myself. I never will.

CHAPTER 8

December 12, 2007, Kibera—Leda

IN HER DREAM, RATS GNAWED AT HER NECK and Leda couldn't fight them off because her wrists were pinned at her sides in red-hot handcuffs. The rat bites began to itch, itch and burn until she was yoked by a collar of fire.

She woke up panting, whimpering in the late-night—or early morning—darkness. Her hands flew to her neck but stopped short of touching her skin. Something was wrong, very wrong.

In the pitch black, she remembered the henna, Grace's beautiful handiwork. On her arms and neck. That was the burn she felt—flowers on fire.

The itch was like nothing she'd ever experienced, but she was too scared to touch it. She swung her feet around to the edge of the table and fumbled her way to the lamp, the enflamed flowers strangling her breath away.

When the lamp wrapped its orange sphere around her, Leda looked at her hands. Blisters.

Oh, no.

She had to wash it off. Immediately.

Her mind started to race. How would she get to a hospital in the middle of the night? How would she survive the itching long enough not to scratch off all her skin? Would she be scarred? Flower scars to match her face. She felt tears gather in her eyes.

Ita. When they'd been at the clinic, the doctors had had every confidence in him.

Ita can save me.

In moments, Leda was up and sliding open the metal door, shuffling through the dust in her sandals.

She rapped on Ita's door, restraining herself from banging.

There was an immediate response. He was up, standing on the other side.

"Who is it? What's wrong?"

"It's Leda, I—"

The door opened and Ita's face appeared, lines of worry highlighted by the moonlight.

Leda didn't say anything more, because she felt sure she would cry. She brandished her arms like a zombie and threw back her head so he could see.

"Does it burn?" he asked. "Itch?"

She nodded her head and tears again welled in her eyes.

"It's okay, Leda. Shhh, shhh, it's okay. I promise."

Ita put his hand on her waist to steer her back through the courtyard, but she jerked away. She nodded her head that she would follow him toward the bathing area.

He led her into the bathing stall. He left for a moment and returned with a rag and a stool.

So blinding was the pain and the itching that it took all Leda's effort not to scream into the night. With her eyes squeezed shut, she heard Ita dunk the rag in the tub of water. She felt him approach.

"Give me your hands," he whispered.

She held out her flaming arms, imagining the Wicked Witch of the West hissing and bubbling, dissolving into a puddle.

Ita wrung the wet cloth over her wrists and a blessed gush of water rained down on her skin. The fire sprang back almost immediately, and she yearned for more seconds of bliss.

"Again," she said. "What's happening?"

"You're allergic. We'll wash you for comfort and then I have medicine."

The next time he wet the towel, he blotted it gently over her skin, the coolness of the water and the pressure of his touch bringing precious seconds of release from the trauma. He moved to her neck, pressing the towel firmly against her hot skin.

"Will it scar?" Leda whispered.

She opened her eyes to see Ita's face, gauge the truth. What she found was tenderness. She had the clear thought that he would never lie to her.

"What a beautiful scar to have," he said. "Eternal flowers."

"Frankenstein flowers."

"Scars are not monstrous, they are very human. A testament to the design of the body and the strength of the soul. The boys have many scars—stamps of survival, of the audacity to survive in a place where no one wants you." Ita looked suddenly far away. Then he came back. "I tell them since they earned so many badges so young, life will be very happy for them later."

Leda's face felt hot. "I would not tell them that."

He touched her cheek to lift her chin, his thumb near her scarred jaw. She lifted her face out of his reach. His eyes flooded once again with tenderness. "Scars are a reminder that you are not your body, or the bad things that happen to it. You are your soul and your soul is always free to be happy and beautiful. You, Leda, are very beautiful, body and soul."

Leda let herself linger in his gaze, cradled like a hot towel after a winter bath. The plush feeling was so foreign, she found herself savoring it like a new favorite food, until doubt wormed its way back in. She must have frowned, because Ita's gaze changed to concern and he set about soaking the rag again.

After he had finished washing her skin and the painful itch had subsided, he led her out into the courtyard and back to her bedroom, where he moved to the far wall and rustled through a box. Leda didn't know if she should close the door. She left it open. But as she watched his shoulders through his shirt, saw how the material stretched to contain them, she found herself imagining what he would look like without it, wondering where his scars were hidden.

"Found it." He turned and caught Leda looking flustered. "Are you feverish? Please. Come sit. How do you feel? Dizzy?"

Yes, she wanted to say. *But not from the henna.* "I'm okay. I feel much better after—" *your touch,* she thought "—the water."

She sat on the table. *My bed,* she thought.

"Where are your pajamas?" he asked, grinning. He motioned for her to hold out her arms again.

She had gone to bed in her clothes, not wanting to disturb the henna. "You think they're funny?"

"I think they are enchanting," he said, and laughed his rolling thunder laugh, though more quietly this time so as not to disturb the sleeping household.

The intimacy of his laugh gave Leda goose bumps. He noticed. "You sure you don't feel a fever?"

"I feel—" she could think of a hundred words to insert next "—better."

But it wasn't long before the maddening itch of the blisters started to come back, with a fire of desire in her stomach to match her searing skin. She winced.

"The water's relief is temporary, but this will help." Ita unscrewed a tube of cream. As she watched in anticipation, he squeezed it onto his fingers. Her body stiffened and she averted her eyes.

Ita came close, so close that if she looked up, her nose would rest beneath his chin. He could kiss her forehead—

Leda let out a shuddery sigh and tilted her head back, letting the light spill over her. She shut her eyes. She felt him hover and the silence swelled between them. Her heartbeat grew so loud, surely Ita could hear it.

He stepped in closer still, and she could sense his desire like a dragon breathing in the corner. Leda was amazed that with blisters over her body and her scar spotlighted, he could want her.

To get his footing, he pressed against her legs.

Leda wanted it, she wanted nothing more than for him to touch her. But when he did, his fingers spreading the cream at the base of her throat, her body acted on its own, wilting under his touch.

He paused.

She opened her eyes, humiliated. But Ita's gaze wasn't offended or daunted. It was patient. Kind.

The coolness of the cream faded and the itching returned with a vengeance. The urge to scratch was a desperate hunger, matched in intensity only by another sudden desire. The desire to throw herself into his arms and press him to her, tight as her burning fingers would allow.

He saw it. Saw the hunger in her eyes, her soul's desire winning over her body's resistance. He reached behind him, took up the tube of cream. He spread the slippery white salve over each collarbone, down over her breastbone, delicately across the space above her breasts.

This time, Leda leaned into his touch.

He finished with her neck and chest, then moved on to her hands, lifting them gently from her sides and encircling both at once. He worked the cream over the backs of her hands and the tops of her fingers, until they were left holding hands. Warm, wet, slippery hands.

"There," Ita said, his voice low in his throat. "Better?" he asked, as if to say *May I?*

Leda met his eyes, slow as the air was thick. She felt strong and sultry under his gaze, but it unsettled her too, on some primal level.

"I feel like—" Ita whispered.

She held her breath. She wanted to know how he felt, more than anything in the world.

"Like I won't want you to leave."

As soon as he said it, something happened. She tried to name it, to understand the change she saw on his face, felt in the air. But she couldn't. Simply that something had shut off, like a faucet in another room. Leda knew the moment was passing, the words she could reply with shrinking. Shrinking to none.

Ita cleared his throat. He smiled, but it was ten degrees cooler than before. "Will you be able to sleep?"

She thought about it. She felt the warmth in her belly, the undulating heat between her thighs. No way would she be able to sleep. "Yes, of course. Thank you, doctor."

Ease found its way back to his face. "I will give you a pill to help with the itching. But it will make you sleep heavy. You may miss breakfast," he said with a wink.

She laughed. "You noticed I'm not much for mornings, huh?"

He laughed with her, then stepped away and walked back to the box of supplies. As he rustled through it for the medicine, he took his phone from his pocket. Leda heard it vibrate, saw its lit-up screen.

Ita's head shot up toward the courtyard at the same moment Leda heard the knock at the front door.

"I'll be right back," he said and slipped out of the room, sliding the door shut after him.

She sat on the table and tried to think what to do with herself, with what had just happened, with the image of Ita's hands sweeping over her skin.

She didn't have long to sort it out before she heard voices outside. Ita's voice was low, careful of the sleeping children. But the chuckle, the oily, snarling voice—that belonged to Chege. And it was coming closer.

Leda's muscles tensed, her limbs curled into her body.

Ita and Chege stopped just outside the door, speaking in rapid, sloppy Swahili Leda couldn't decipher one bit. It continued for several minutes, the back-and-forth, before she heard a pause and Chege say the word *mzungu.* That word she knew plain enough. White person. Her.

Ita hesitated, then answered quietly. Leda looked at the door. *No lock,* she thought as she heard Chege's retort and Ita's voice rise with his next words, an explanation, a shuffle, a protest—

Chege burst into the room, his thin face puffy, his eyes red and hazy. He was drunk, Leda could see it immediately—the look was the same on an affluent mother in a Malibu mansion or a gangster in Kibera.

And there was Leda, her blouse still pulled down to just above her breasts.

"Burned by the African paint, huh, *mzungu?*" Chege said with a sneer. He poked a crooked finger at Ita. "You pay the doctor?"

The burning returned in full force, like it was Chege spitting the fire onto her skin. "What?" Leda squeaked.

"Three days—you use the water, eat the food. Now Ita fix you." At this he twisted his lips into a dirty smile. "You think it all free?"

Ita barked something at Chege, something Leda hoped meant *Leave her the hell alone.*

Chege shot back slimy words as though taunting Ita. The way Chege's eyes traveled over her skin, Leda was glad she didn't understand, but as he went on, his voice grew firmer, insisting.

She looked to Ita. He had a sickened, sheepish slope to his face.

He agrees, she realized.

Chege smirked at her.

She didn't know what to say. On one hand, of course it made sense to reimburse Ita for medical supplies. Doctors don't work for free. No one does. Especially here, where everything was so valuable and her money could mean so much. But logic couldn't overcome the feelings coursing through her veins. Shame, yes, but also indignation. Leda straightened, tugging her blouse up onto her shoulders, the pain making her breath catch.

"Of course I'll pay," she hissed. She stepped down from the table and reached for her money belt. With her back to the men and her hands shaking like a pond in an earthquake, she took out way too much money. She spun back around and thrust the money into the air.

"Take it, Chege. You seem to be the bill collector." She pursed her lips until Chege snatched the cash roughly from her fingers. "Now please get out of here, both of you."

"Leda—"

She heard the regret in Ita's voice, but she didn't care. It was too late.

"Just go," she said.

And as they left, Chege's parting snicker echoed in the small room.

A long time later, once Leda had turned out the light, wrapped herself in a cloak of soured thoughts, and tossed and turned like a cement mixer, there came a knock at her door.

"Leda, are you okay?"

If I don't answer, he will go away.

"Leda, may I come in? Just to check on your skin. Give you the medicine."

"I'm asleep," she answered, more awake than an owl at midnight.

"Please," Ita said so clearly outside the door his lips must be pressed nearly into the frame.

Before she could think better of it, she said, "Come in."

Ita slid open the door and moonlight slithered into the room at her feet.

He crossed the room with his head down and lifted a foil package of pills from the box of supplies. He pushed one through and held it out to Leda. "I apologize for my friend. You didn't have to give any money."

She took the pill, staring at him evenly. "Is he really your friend?"

Ita inhaled. It was a heavy sound, like a vacuum in a sandbox. In its rush, Leda noticed other sounds of the night, the distant clatter of the slum.

Finally he said, "Chege, I know like I know the sun and the rain—good, bad, always coming back. Does that make someone your friend?"

Yes...but... "No. You two are different."

"Are we? We grew up together, without families. Chege taught me to survive." Ita's eyes darted away in the darkness. "I owe him more than you can imagine."

When he said *you,* Leda knew he meant *someone like you,* and her skin bristled.

But he was right, she realized. She couldn't imagine. She reviled the idea of depending on anyone, but wasn't that because she'd had the luxury of never having to? Even if her heart suffered, her basic needs—shelter, food—were always secured.

She checked Ita's face. His eyes were focused a million miles away. She looked around the tiny, dusty room. With Chege, maybe, money was about power, like in the U.S. But Ita wasn't being greedy or mean. He was surviving, trying to give the boys a better life, a chance.

"Me and Chege," Ita said suddenly, "we share the same story. The struggle to be good."

"But you *are* good," Leda said, eager to point out the success of the orphanage.

"Maybe. Or maybe I'm atoning." He crossed to the door. "Good night, Leda."

CHAPTER 9

December 31, 2007, Kibera—Ita

MORNING'S COME, WHETHER ITA CAN BELIEVE
it or not.

Lying on his foam mattress, he feels like he's been strapped
to train tracks all night, pounded by steel wheels. His skin is
hot and itchy, a wool suit he wishes he could peel off.

First thing he sees when he opens his eyes—his bloody
clothes on the chair.

So then it is real. Everything really happened. The devil
has taken the reins.

After another moment, he gets up, stacking himself like
broken dishes. He looks at his phone. Leda is still in transit.
He can't call her. But she's safe, returning to her world where
things are white, clean and quiet.

And Ita is here, the metal wall the only thing separating
him from hell. He listens. There's none of the normal din of
morning. He hears a roar like military trucks in the distance.
He hears whistles and shouting, popping noises like gunfire.
He can make out chanting. The protesters are out there.

Protesters. Ita thinks about the word. *We have plenty to pro-*

test. But what he saw last night was murder. Rape. Betrayal. Mayhem. Men peeling off their humanity to let loose their darkest demons.

Before he is forced to picture Chege again, Ita thinks instead of all the children out there, in the front lines to violence. The rioters—they were innocents once. But after a lifetime of Kibera's picture show of injustice, they have all the emotional fuel they need now to set the world on fire.

He recognizes the scent in his nostrils. Not the cooking of breakfast, but billowing towers of smoke.

People are fleeing. Ita heard them in the night, the frenzied commotion of flight. People are running back to the country, to their homelands.

But we have nowhere to go.

An orphan watching over seven little orphans.

The boys.

He rolls his broken body out of bed and drags himself to their room. Eyeing the smoke in the sky, he scans the sounds of violence. But inside the orphanage—only silence.

Ita pulls aside the sheet to their room and looks in. They're awake, he can tell, but glued to their bunk beds, pretending to sleep out of fear.

"Morning is here. I'm here."

Ita watches them weather the same process of waking up, swallowing the new reality. But when they turn, one by one, and peer at his broken face, they lose the words on their lips.

"Michael," he says and leaves the room.

Moments later, Michael stands before Ita in the courtyard, squinty, but alert enough to be wary.

"You must keep them quiet. You must keep them calm. Understand?"

The boy nods in his solemn way, a priest at confessions. "How long will you be gone?"

Ita doesn't know the answer to that. "As short a time as possible. I must go with Mary to see her family. And if I can find it, we'll need food, supplies—" Ita stops. Why worry him more than necessary? "I'll hurry."

"Be careful, too."

Ita smiles at him and puts a hand on his shoulder. How long have they been a family now? Seven years? Seems impossible. But long enough for Michael to know what family means, finally. For both of them to know the meaning, Ita realizes. "I promise."

Ita crosses to Mary's room. Before he can open his mouth, Mary's voice comes from behind the sheet. "I'm ready."

He waits and Mary opens the sheet and passes him. She turns back. "The tea is on the fire and the bread is on the plates, covered. Do you think they can manage? Are you sure we should leave them?"

His heart swells with her worry for the children, sees the warring emotions on her face for her two families. Finally, he nods. "They are safe. Enough. Michael has my gun."

Their eyes lock. There's only one gun. *Safe enough,* Ita thinks. *What does that mean?* No one is safe in Kibera anymore.

"Let's go," he says. "I will bring some medical supplies."

Mary's face loses some of its bravery as she turns toward the courtyard and the entrance to the orphanage.

Ita walks in the sun beside Mary, his bruised limbs protesting every step. The streets are quiet, a strangled silence like a hand clamped over a mouth. But he hears the roar of a mob not far off, the crackle of fire. The smell of smoke is strong, burning his nose and throat.

They wind their way through the back alleys, expecting the worst to arrive at any minute.

The phone-charging man is nowhere to be seen, his kiosk barren. As Ita expected. His cell will die this morning, his bridge to the outside world burned up like everything else.

The beauty shop on the corner is gone, reduced to sizzling rubble, the ashes of sacrifice. Ita's gut twists into knots. Fire can spread ten blocks in two minutes in Kibera. He looks at the smoking hole where the beauty shop stood and hears Mary take the same breath as he. Death stood right here, looking over their shoulders while they slept.

They move on.

As Ita scours the burning structures for any food kiosk intact, images of Chege and Leda flash before him, making his feet stumble over the rocks and debris. His body shudders uncontrollably, both at the images of destruction before him, and the images aflame in his mind.

Once they turn a corner, the next block comprises only rubble and hastily restacked shacks—sheets of metal or wood strapped to rickety sticks. Bedsheets drawn tight over any open spaces, windows or doors.

Ita thinks back to Friday, two days and an eternity ago, when the sheets flapped open, people milled in and out—a barbershop, a butcher, a CD store inside. He curses himself for not stockpiling supplies when the election drama began to build. For not anticipating that this would happen. For allowing happiness to let him forget the first lesson in Kibera— bad times are coming.

The eerie calm makes his skin prickle. Just as he becomes aware of it, two young men duck around a nearby corner. One carries a bow and arrow, the other a machete. Mary's gaze drops to the ground. Ita sees her muscles grow sinewy across her old bones. But the men never look at them. They're laughing. Ita's stomach churns at the sound.

A burning pile of tires and metal blocks the next turn. Ita stops. He leans uneasily against a mud house. The flames are high, menacing. And they're new—men must be close.

Ita strains his ears, listening with his whole body. Inside the house, he hears a woman shushing her children, a rushing mix of *mtoto, mpendwa, pole pole sana. Dear child, so sorry.* Ita grits his teeth. This is the morning all parents feel that they have failed their children.

An old man looks out from the house across the alley. He stares at Ita, a brave face atop shivering knees, then relaxes when Mary reaches Ita's side.

Off to their left, unseen, there comes a shout, *No Raila, no peace!* A rally cry. *No peace!* Voices echo back.

Instead of turning, the old man and Ita look into each other's eyes. Ita recognizes the same, tired look he feels in his heart. He has no stomach for war cries. Kibaki's arrogant speech accepting his rigged reelection—what did he think would happen? Did he know that men would gore each other in the streets?

The old man ducks back inside his home and Ita and Mary move on.

Ita should never have agreed, should never have *invited* someone like Leda to this place. He remembers the mob last night. Men in the street, barking and howling, thrusting their machetes into the smoking air. Human flesh cut like wood for fire, thwacks on the legs of women and children as they ran screaming.

And Chege. Sprawled atop Leda like a clawing predator, a monster, a depraved, starved demon in the night—

Ita tries to shake the image from his head. He can't think

of it now. Mary is too vulnerable out here. They still have blocks to go. He twists his torso and feels blood he missed, dried now, cracking on his back. He must focus. They must get to the house.

They slink down an alley to the right. The houses on both sides are quiet, too quiet. How many people are hiding? Prisoners in their own homes.

But around the corner, they hear it. A wail. A second voice surrounds the first, trying to comfort and contain, trying to quell the woman's cry. But the wail comes from a deep spring in the human soul, one that can't be stopped, Ita knows.

Mary gasps and takes off past him. A mother knows her daughter's cries.

He rushes after Mary, as she calls out her daughter's name. He catches up to her at the door and they tumble inside.

Ita takes in the frantic scene—children piled up in a corner, tears on their faces that erupt anew the second they spot their grandmother. Grace is on the other side of the room, bent over a form on the ground. The smell of blood saturates the air with foreboding.

Grace looks up, her eyes glassy with grief. She sees her mother, but when her gaze shifts to Ita, she looks to the sky. "Sweet Jesus, we are saved!"

Ita steps closer, surveys the man's crumpled body on the floor. Her husband, Paul Omolio. He'd just seen him at Christmas. Now he's a mass of blood and bruises, beaten nearly unrecognizable. Ita stoops down just as Paul's eyes flutter open.

The man's foggy eyes register who's crouching over him, and widen like a bush monkey's. "Out! Out, devil!" The words drool from the man's lips, blood frothing at the corners.

It takes Ita by surprise. Does he have a fever? He puts a hand to Paul's forehead.

But his touch is a trigger—Paul convulses like he's having a seizure. His words grow stronger, clearer. "Monster! Kikuyu!"

Grace and Mary flutter to his shoulders like angels.

"He was attacked just this morning," Grace whispers, her words scurrying into Ita's ear. "At a protest rally for Odinga. Men dragged him away and beat him."

"Monsters!" Paul points a finger at Ita. "You—"

"Shhh, my love," Grace coos and takes her husband's hand. "Ita's a doctor. Let him help you. Please."

In a lower voice, she tells Ita, "Mungiki retaliation. Against us, Luos, for the protests."

Protests, Ita thinks of the word and how vile it has become. *What did they expect? You murder Kikuyus in* protest, *and think the Mungiki won't strike back?*

"They cut him, Ita," Grace says, but it is Mary's sudden shudder of breath that lets on just what Grace means. Ita looks to Paul's groin, sees the epicenter of blood. The fly to his pants is unzipped.

Paul's eyes roll back, his body goes slack.

Echoes of preelection chatter boom in Ita's mind. *We cannot have a boy as president,* the other tribes said of Odinga. Ita's stomach somersaults. Uncircumsized Luo men teased about forgoing manhood rituals.

Ita grits his teeth. Paul is right. Monsters do these things to men.

Taking items from his pockets—sutures, antiseptic wipes—Ita scans the room. "Rags," he says. "Or clean clothes."

Grace moves quickly, brings him a folded pile.

Ita positions his hands over Paul's groin.

"Look away," he says to the women, and gets to work.

After struggling to gingerly remove his pants, Ita gets one quick, stomach-churning eyeful of the damage before Paul comes to life like a man set on fire. As Paul screams at him, his fingers jabbing him in the chest, Ita tries to focus, to assess his other wounds. He counts the machete wounds on his arms and torso, his neck, above his left ear.

But now Paul's raving pierces his concentration. "Mungiki monsters. Chege—"

Ita's heart halts in its cage, then hammers the bars. "Paul... did Chege do this?" Careening back on his heels, Ita feels like he's falling into a black hole in space. Could Chege have done this? How can Ita doubt it, after what he did to Leda, after all that Ita knows he's done? Chege's bloody machete, his tall tales of revenge, conquests, always being hunted by the police. On some level, hasn't he always known what Chege was capable of?

Ita's going to throw up. He's certain of it. The regret inside, the horror, it's bubbling and stewing and it has to come out. It's too much. He can't keep it inside.

Paul continues to scream, spittle landing on Ita's face and neck. Ita struggles to his feet, backs away toward the door, tripping over children, trying to get a grip on time, on his mind. He sees Mary's twisted face, Grace's eyes desperate and scared.

But Ita needs air. He needs a second or he is going to lose his mind.

He whips the sheet to the side and stumbles back out into the street, red dust flying around his ankles.

He hears Grace collapse into sobs as he staggers blindly away from the house. Over the wailing of the children, he can't make out her words. Ita slumps to the ground, his back scraping the sticks. His head drops into his hands, a welcome pocket of darkness to blot out Paul's accusations. But Ita can't stop his stomach from roiling, or his head from pounding.

How did everything fall apart? Was there ever a time that things could have been different, for he and Chege both, for everyone? Since the day Chege saved his life—was there ever a day that this wasn't their fate?

Ita opens his eyes, and like an answer from the heavens, he sees suddenly where he is. Everything is different—the houses, the stores, the streets—but when Ita looks up the hill surrounding Kibera he sees the train tracks, the depot.

This is where they found Kioni. This is where Ita did something right, where he saved her. The place and time where Chege still had the chance to become something different.

With the dusty air filling his throat and the prick of déjà vu running up his spine, Ita lets the shivery trigger of remembrance take hold of him.

April 19, 1990, Kibera—Ita

Eleven-year-old Ita crouches in a dark alley, watching Chege delight in dumping out the day's prize—a woman's purse. Ita feels the familiar thud in his stomach, imagining the woman screaming, weeping in the street. At the same time, he worries for Chege. "The Mungiki will kill you, you know." In Kibera, the Mungiki played both perpetrator and police. It was how they maintained their power over the people.

But Chege is quiet, which makes Ita peer harder into the dark for his friend's face.

"What is it? Did they see you?"

"I talked to one of them. He said...said I good enough to work for them."

Ita hears the veiled pride in his voice. *Bad enough to work for them,* he thinks. "Chege, no—"

"Not you. You won't ever be with them. You go to school, get out of here. It would be easier, with help. But me—what else can I do?"

They hear men shouting in the distance, coming closer. The streets are empty at night, unsafe. Anyone who is out has nowhere to go, like them, or they're up to no good.

But as they both crane their ears to decide where they should run, Ita hears another noise, closer this time. A sound like a scurrying insect or animal that wakes you in the night. But it carries another sound—a whimper over quick, panting breaths. A girl. Running away from something, and Ita would bet it was from the men they heard.

The patter of footsteps stops and the whimper tucks itself away somewhere.

"Ita, let's go." Chege heads away from the men whose words are coming into focus. They're drunk, angry. "Now."

But Ita heads toward the quiet noise. He knows where it is hiding. He has used that spot before, too, tucked behind the crates, trying to find a place to read. He ignores Chege's second call to flee. "I will leave you," he says. But Ita knows he won't.

When he's close to the stack of crates, the little breath stops short.

Flattening himself, he peers behind the wall and there she is. A girl as pretty as any Ita's ever seen, her hair in tiny braids tipped with colored beads. The tattered pink dress she's wearing trembles as her eyes go wide at Ita's appearance. Her face puffy and streaked with tears, they stare at each other without blinking.

"Come on," he says. "Come with me."

The little girl shakes her head. Her eyes are so big they scare him, like they might crack open, spill out a river of tears to drown him.

"It's okay. Hurry. They're coming."

"Come here!" The men are close, too close, one, maybe two alleys over. "Where'd-she-go-that-little-bitch-slut?" one slurs, and it's not hard for Ita to picture a big slobbering giant.

"Ita," Chege hisses. "What are you doing? Leave her."

"I'm not leaving her," Ita says, his eyes never leaving the girl.

Her head darts in the direction of the men, back at Ita, down at her feet. She's beginning to see what he knows about her hiding place. It's a trap.

Ita puts out his hand.

The little girl takes it.

"What's your name?"

"Kioni," she says.

Her voice is a bird in a thunderstorm, the roar of men a dark cloud rounding the corner.

The slapping of Chege's footsteps is the rain.

"Kioni," Ita says and squeezes her hand tighter. "Run."

December 31, 2007, Kibera—Ita

"Ita!"

Ita jumps at the sound of Grace's voice.

"I thought you left!" Her face is puffed out like a blowfish.

Still reeling from the memory, he shakes his head.

Grace looks like she is about to say something but stops herself. Looking closely at him, she asks, "You okay?"

He looks up into her eyes. He wouldn't know how to begin to answer that question.

She nods. "I apologize for my husband. It's the fever. And the shame."

But Ita has to know. "Was it Chege?"

Grace looks at him. "No," she says, eyes soft. Then they ice over. "But it was men like him. They dragged him from the rally, beat him, stabbed him. They used a broken bottle to cut his member. They said they would rape me, rape the children. And Paul—" Grace looks away. "He's seen you with Chege. With Mungiki. And you are—"

"Kikuyu," Ita finishes for her. Grace's last name by marriage is Omolio. Omolio, Odinga. Names that start with an *O* betray Luos at checkpoints. But what is a name? Ita's name comes from a man he's never seen with eyes old enough to remember.

"Ita."

The tears on Grace's face swell like a river in the rain.

He looks at her. Women will bear the brunt of this storm, for it is they that are the most vulnerable to both man's cruelty and their suffering.

Ita pulls himself to his feet. "Let's go save your husband."

CHAPTER 10

December 31, 2007, Topanga, CA—Leda

AFTER THE NOISE AND THE SMELL AND THE clash of people on the flight, in the airport, in the cab line, after picking up Amadeus from doggie care, and enduring the ever-present cloud of strangers' *"Happy New Years"* everywhere, Leda is finally home.

She pauses before the front door, Amadeus's carrier under her arm, and digs out her keys. She turns the metal over in her palm—the key to her old life.

But when Leda enters the house, breathes in the stillness and the space spread before her, what rises in her throat isn't calm, but panic.

Like swimming in open sea, the impression of smallness floods her, and she can only think one thing—*What a waste.* All that space, the ardent cleanliness, the expensive flourishes—all for one person. The silence screams it loudest of all—the guilt Leda rightfully feels. She's always felt the guilt vaguely. From now on, images of the people she met in Kibera, the orphans, they will give her specific faces to feel guilty about.

Amadeus eyes her strangely, frozen in place by the door. Leda looks down on him, her storm of emotions knit together into a blanket of depression that wraps itself around her shoulders and leads the way to the bedroom.

She passes the bathroom and considers taking a shower. The shudder moves so fast through her shoulders that her hands flop like fish at her sides, and she realizes she doesn't want to see her naked body. She'd rather pretend it didn't exist.

She makes it to the bed and crashes down upon it. Rolling over, she takes her phone from her pocket. She'd turned it back on at the airport, found three messages. Two were a chipper girl with status reports on Amadeus at the doggie hotel. The other was a wrong number.

One month, she was gone. Including Christmas.

All this space and fuss for one person no one cares about. That no one should care about. And the one person who did, a million miles away, hasn't called either.

But maybe he couldn't call. Her heart crumbles at the thought of what's keeping him from doing so. At the thought of him in the inferno.

Leda looks at the phone, her heart beginning to beat again. There is the number, ready. Waiting.

She dials, but already she is afraid. Afraid for him to answer. Afraid for him not to.

It goes straight to voice mail. His phone is off.

Dead.

But then it is beeping and Leda knows she has to speak into the voice mail system.

"Ita." Saying his name makes her dizzy. Leda slumps against the wall, her left hand on the smooth paint. *Tell him what you would want to know.* "I'm okay." *No, I'm not. I'm alive and not much else.* "That's not true. I'm not okay, but I'm home.

And…I'm…I'm sorry." She hangs up the phone and throws it at the rug.

Leda thrusts her head under a pillow, feeling the world spinning away from her. She will be the first woman to drown in air, she thinks, gasping beneath the pillow, her heartbeat like a war drum.

After a minute, she peeks out and stares at the phone on the rug.

She snatches it up and hugs it to her chest. Then, the silence a monsoon on a tin roof, she buries herself under the pillow and miraculously falls asleep.

CHAPTER 11

December 12, 2007, Kibera—Leda

LEDA WOKE IN THE MORNING TO HER NOISY
new home.

She heard scampering feet and giggles outside the door,
trailed by Ita's rich laugh. Pots and cups. Brooms and flapping
wet clothes and splashing water. The clinking, clattering routine of a new day. It was a palpable difference from her home
in Topanga, where the birds and the wind competed to be
the noisiest, and neither was louder than the classical music
on Leda's laptop. And Estella's house, where she'd grown up,
was glass and sky and sea, and anytime one of them spoke
they made the other jump.

Leda lifted herself to an elbow on the metal bed. The skin
on her neck and arms screamed in protest, and the memory
of the previous night, with Ita and Chege, came back to her
in the little room. The tube of cream still sat on the table.

She looked at the half-empty tube and thought of Ita's
strong, smooth hands on her skin, moving across her chest
above her breasts, sliding down her arms, encircling her wrists

with the cool, slippery cream. Remembering, she felt her nipples harden under her shirt.

"*Hodi!*" a little voice squeaked, making Leda jump.

The stampede of little footsteps had halted outside the door.

A whisper came next, Ita's, something Leda couldn't make out.

"May—" the little voice started.

Ita's whisper again.

"May…we…come in?"

Leda smiled. "*Karibu!* Come in!"

The door slid aside and light flooded in, sparkling, but not as bright as Ntimi's smile. "*Habari ya asubuhi. Hujambo, bibi.*"

Bibi was a term of respect, for a lady. "*Hujambo,* Ntimi."

"Good morning," Michael said. But more instructional, for the boys, than as a greeting for Leda.

"Good morning, Michael," she said and smiled as widely as she could manage.

Michael held a tray with both hands. He stepped around Ntimi and toward Leda until she saw what it held. A cup of tea and a chunk of bread on an orange plastic plate.

Leda scooted over and Michael set the breakfast down on the blanket.

Ntimi beamed. He motioned with his hand, a grand invitation that Leda was happy to oblige. She picked up the cup carefully and sipped the tea under the many little eyes, making a loud slurping noise on purpose. "Deee-licious!" she proclaimed and the boys laughed. And it was. The tea was milky and spicy sweet. It would be difficult to ever go back to Earl Grey.

When she looked up, Ita was watching her with a look sweeter than the tea. The haunted look from last night was gone, as if it had never happened. "So," he said. "You lived."

"Not funny," she said.

"No, it isn't funny." His lips settled into seriousness. "I will have to apply the cream many times, at night, so you heal properly."

Leda almost spit out the tea. Was that as naughty a glimmer in his eyes as she thought? She got turned on again, seeing it. "Yes, doctor," she said, finally.

Ntimi figured out what they were talking about—though hopefully not the subtext—and he came over to inspect her burns. *"Pole, pole,"* he said as studied the blisters.

Ita cleared his throat with a cough. "Well, we will let you get dressed," he said, followed by, *"Kwenda, kwenda"*—*go, go*—as he herded the boys out the door.

Leda watched them go, leaving nothing but a cloud of dust as they went.

Then Ita reappeared. "Can I get you anything? Anything you need?"

She looked at his face, full of kindess and a wriggle of worry that Leda suspected was about whether she was comfortable there, if she was happy with the room and the food. She looked longer at his soft, full lips. She thought about it—if there was anything missing, anything she needed. She knew the answer in her bones.

"Not at all," she said. "I am…complete."

And as his smile bathed her, before he turned and gently slid shut the door, Leda felt how true it was, what she'd said. The lingering shadows of the night—Chege's nasty comments, the awful handing over of the money—Leda knew she shouldn't ignore them, but she didn't want to chase away the new feeling settling inside her.

Happiness.

★ ★ ★

The feeling carried Leda through the day, as if she'd boarded a hot air balloon to float high above the usual malaise of mental chatter.

After the boys left for school, Mary took Walter with her to run errands, so Ita and Leda were left to build bunk beds alone.

As they stacked piles of wood and counted out the nails, a giddy anticipation hung between them, as if they were waiting in line at an ice cream truck. The sweat and labor of it became harmonious, the passing of nails and wood a duet like slow dancing.

When Leda stepped outside to get more wood, she realized what was different today. Her mind, usually racing off on a desperate hunt for answers, certainty, seemed to have found whatever it was searching for or happily given up. Even the anticipation with Ita felt warm and buttery, not something to fret over, but to relish. Leda paused before going back into the boys' room. She put a hand on her chest. No tightness, no vise to unscrew. She stepped back inside and Ita's eyes were waiting for her, calm as the feeling above her heart.

"Is this enough?" she asked, holding out the wood in her arms.

"Definitely," he said, and waved her over.

"So, how do we fit four bunk beds, that is the question, right?"

"Four?" he asked. "I thought two. Don't you think the boys will like to sleep side by side, two or three together?"

Leda smiled. All her American notions were challenged here. "Back home, people are so concerned about privacy."

Ita looked at her softly. "Because they are raising children to be alone." He paused and the hum of the slum outside made his point. "What would be the point of that here?"

She stood in the doorway and thought about it, about having been raised to be alone. That was the right way to put it, she realized. She'd just never thought about it like that. She stared off, thinking of America's individualistic society, designed to raise individuals.

"Leda," Ita said with a grin. "Where do you go when you do that?"

She blushed, caught. It was funny, most people never noticed her daydreaming, let alone whether or not she wasn't in the room anymore. "I'm back," she said. She set down the wood slats on the ground and knelt next to Ita.

For the next two hours, they attacked the project of the bunk beds, all the while chatting like chess players in the park—easily, for the joy of it. Ita asked her about her studies, her house, her neighborhood, neighbors, Amadeus.

Leda answered everything, politely and happily, but she felt like bread in a toaster, burning with questions of her own.

"How did you meet Chege? What was he like?" she asked, taking the hammer from Ita. "It's hard to imagine him as a child." If Chege was his friend, there had to be a reason. Something had brought them together.

After Leda banged in both nails, though, Ita remained silent.

She looked up. He met her eyes, and his thoughts were clear. He'd heard the judgment in her voice. "I-I'm sorry." Leda stammered. "I didn't mean—"

"Is it easy to imagine me as a child?"

She smiled. "Yes."

He didn't return the smile. A storm of emotion clouded his face. "Kibera is a difficult place to be a child. In the way that you mean it. A difficult place to be innocent. Good."

She quashed the urge to change the subject. "What did you do?"

Ita looked as if she'd pinched him. Then he set his jaw and looked at her evenly. "Begged. Stole. Robbed. Hurt people." He stared, testing her. Daring her to condemn him.

Her palm around the hammer grew sweaty. "I'm sure everything you did, you had to. It's different when you do something bad to survive."

"That is what Chege would say."

Ita straightened, took the hammer from her hands and lifted a frame into place, leaving Leda huddled on the ground, her empty hands trembling. She'd failed the test, disappointed him, she knew. Watching him—his purposeful hands, his regal posture, his skin smoothed over his beautiful face, she had the strangest thought. *I know how Chege must have felt. Why he wanted to help Ita, protect him.*

"Well, it was for a reason," she said. "Look what you've accomplished. The orphanage. The safari business. School. Tell me about school."

Ita's shoulders had dipped, relaxed as she mentioned the orphanage and safaris. At the word *school,* his muscles tensed again. "Finishing grade school was a miracle. Then I got sponsored by a family in Nairobi. Who wanted to help a slum kid with..."

"Promise," Leda finished.

He shook his head with a smile, remembering. "It was like a dream, starting at the University of Nairobi."

"I'm sure you were the perfect student." She pictured him on the campus grounds, suddenly ensconced in marble and grass.

"It was perfect. So perfect I should have known it couldn't last." He hammered a nail into the wood.

Leda's smile faltered and fell. "What happened?"

He didn't answer, hammered four nails, one after another, hard.

Not easy things to talk about, she realized, mad at herself again. She fumbled for a way to change the subject but before she could think of anything he started speaking again.

"Everything fell apart, like Kibera homes when the rains come. My sponsor family lost their fortune, but no one told me until it was too late. I asked the doctors at the clinic, foreigners I knew, for help, but…talk of money makes people curl up like bugs in a fire."

Ita struck a nail as forcibly as squashing a beetle. Leda looked at the blisters on her wrists, remembered last night's argument with Chege, how she thrust the money at him and kicked them both out of the room.

"The university sent me a letter. It was over. That's when Michael arrived."

Leda couldn't take her eyes off the blisters on her hands. So ugly, marred. Her calves shook from squatting. She was furious at herself for upsetting Ita, upsetting their lovely afternoon. It was hard for him to talk about it. *But he wants to.* Each time, she realized, he'd hesitated, then told her the truth. Her legs stopped shaking. She moved closer to him, helped position the wood he'd picked up.

Ita noticed her hesitating, staring at him. "What?" he asked.

"That female doctor at the clinic, something she said about you. I keep remembering it." She paused and lost a little nerve, having him so close she could smell him, feel the heat coming off his body. Ita looked at her, waiting. "She said imagine what someone like you could have done with money and privilege."

"Someone like me?"

She lowered her eyes, so she would say it. "Someone driven, brilliant. Someone deserving."

He sighed. "And does the world care what people deserve and what they get?"

Leda swallowed hard. *No,* she thought. *The world has a shitty accountant.* People like her get too much and fall short and people like him—

She could feel the ease slipping away for good. She couldn't be the one that drove it away. Her mind came up with Americans' favorite daydream game. "What would you do with a million dollars?"

He was surprised, but he took the bait. With no mulling, he said, "I would build a bigger orphanage and a big school. I would hire good people to run it and then I would go back to school, myself."

"No cars or houses?"

He laughed. "How much is a million? I'm sure it is enough for cars and clothes and a house." He looked off into the distance. "And I would go places. I would see the sea. I would go the places you have gone."

His lack of bitterness made her feel queasy with guilt. "You see? You deserve it. You would do good things."

"So would you, since you are here," he said. "Your turn. What would you do with a million dollars?"

Leda looked away, startled. But of course that's the question he'd ask next. She'd been careful so far, when she spoke of Estella, of her life in California, not to say anything too specific. Why? Why was she hiding her wealth from him? For safety, she probably would have said. But no, it was that same feeling causing her stomach to churn. Guilt.

Ita was still smiling, but he wasn't stupid. He saw he'd

struck a nerve. His next question was softer. "Would you have a family?"

She felt a golf ball roll to a stop in her throat. "I'm not so good with them."

"With families?" She knew he wanted to understand, but that he wouldn't press too far. He would wait a million years until she was ready.

"With relationships," she said. "Not like you are, I'm sure."

"I'm not good with relationships," he said, surprising her with his change in tone.

She looked at him, reconsidering. Ita was around her age and single. That wasn't so strange in California, but it must be here. There had to be a reason. There had to be hurt there. *Maybe relationships just haven't been good to you.*

Ita snapped back from wherever he'd gone off to. "But I'm good with kids." He was trying to make light. "Before it's too late, before they become too—"

"Damaged," she said. "Haunted?"

He shook his head. "They are those things," he said heavily, and Leda could hear his unspoken qualifier—*in Kibera.*

Suddenly there was a rattle of metal and a thump, and they were both on their feet. They were headed for the door when they heard the footsteps running toward them.

Ita yanked aside the sheet. "Jomo! What are you doing?"

Jomo stood where he was, his chest heaving like a bird fallen from its nest. He didn't answer, just looked at them both, blocking the entrance to the bedroom, first in confusion, then in suspicion. *What are you up to?* his narrowed eyes asked.

"Bunk beds," Leda said.

She watched the boy's face grow curious.

But Ita's face was tinged with anger. "Jomo. Answer me. *Kwa nini si wewe katika shule?*"

Why aren't you in school? Leda translated slowly. But Jomo's eyes traveled to the dirt at his feet, his mouth showing no plans to answer. Her heart went out to him, remembering being yelled at as a child for sneaking off, for being quiet and wanting to be alone. It was like looking in a mirror. She would have the same body language as Jomo now—drawing pictures in the dirt with his sandal, mind off on a mission elsewhere.

"Come in, Jomo." She waved him inside. "You just wanted first pick, didn't you? Pretty smart," she said and tapped at her temple. But she stepped aside so Jomo could enter the bedroom with plenty of space.

Jomo's eyes went wide as he surveyed the beds, almost finished. He walked to one of the bunk beds. The top bunk was just above his head. He put out a hand to touch the wood.

"Ladders," Ita said. "*Ngazi.* To climb up." He pointed at the mat, where they had almost finished the first ladder. "Want to help?"

Ita knelt down and picked up a slat of wood that would be a rung. He used the measuring tape and pencil to mark off the right spot. Then he turned the ladder up sideways, lined up the slat of wood and struck a nail to hold it firm. After, he put the ladder flat and held out the hammer to Jomo. Leda held her breath.

The boy took the hammer. He knelt down on the other side, across from Ita. He picked up a nail with his slender fingers. Jomo chewed his lip as he held the nail in place and then whacked it repeatedly, stopping when the nail was all the way in. With a tiny nod, he reached out for the measuring tape. He'd been paying close attention. Jomo took the pencil and marked off the spot for the next rung.

Leda watched Ita as he watched Jomo with gentle, approving eyes. She could tell that he was holding himself still, not wanting to break the moment. She felt such a tenderness for them both that she had to put her hand to the door frame to steady herself. The love Ita showed these boys who came to him broken and bruised touched a deep part of her she'd almost forgotten about, the part of her that had once believed she could trust, love, without shielding her heart.

"Very good, Jomo," Ita whispered and Jomo froze. "I bet you will be an engineer. *Mhandisi*."

Jomo understood. He didn't smile, but his lips lost the grimace he carried around all the time. The boy flipped the ladder over with a thunk onto the mat, buoyed with new confidence.

When he finished the rung, he didn't look up. He looked at the mat and seemed to be waiting.

"Jomo," Ita whispered. "What would *you* do with a million dollars?"

Leda inhaled.

Jomo looked up, uncomprehending.

"What would you do with five dollars?" Leda asked slowly, compromising with his frame of reference.

Jomo looked at her. His expression was shy, but he was no dummy. His eyes searched her face.

"Movie," he said, serious as can be. The first word he'd spoken to her.

Leda couldn't help it, she laughed aloud. Then she asked earnestly, "Is there a movie theater in Kibera?"

Ita snorted. "Of course."

"Friday," she said, slowly, *"Ijumaa,"* looking at Ita to see if her translation was correct. He nodded, smiling. "It's a date."

CHAPTER 12

December 14, 2007, Kibera—Leda

FRIDAY AFTERNOON, LEDA FINISHED HELPING Mary in the kitchen, one ear open, waiting for the kids to come home from school.

Even still, the banging on the front door made her jump.

She rushed out to see the boys tumble in on Ita as excited as she'd ever seen them—a tangle of smiles and exclamations, predominantly the phrase *movie night*. They'd taken to the expression Wednesday and had said it at least a thousand times since, a rallying cry.

"Movie night!" Ntimi shouted in lieu of hello. "Movie night, Leda!"

"Movie night, Ntimi, and how was school?"

"Good. Good," he said, tugging at her arm. "Go!"

"Okay, okay," Leda laughed. "Food first."

Mary appeared as if on cue, wiping sweat from her brow, Walter at her heels. She carried a bundle—cloth wrapped around the chapati they'd made. Leda was already obsessed with chapati, a buttery cross between a pancake and a tortilla.

Much better movie food than popcorn. Mary handed the bundle
over to Leda.

"You sure you don't want to come?" Leda tried one more
time.

Mary shook her head and smiled. She waved her hand at
the boys and said something in Swahili that made them laugh.

Then all the boys looked up at Leda at once, as if to say
Let's get a move on, lady.

"Okay, boys, let's go!"

The first steps into Kibera were as jolting as ever, but Leda
found she was starting to get used to a few things, like how
to walk without looking down the whole time, ergo not running into anybody, and how to breathe through her mouth
so she didn't feel locked in a Porta Potty.

In the dwindling afternoon sun, Leda watched the vege-
table stands glow on the side of the road. She listened to the
rise and fall of gossip, the belting music or radio behind every
door, and the chickens competing in squawkiness.

But most of all, Leda relished the chatter of the boys. They
told her about their day, in halting English that was already
improving. Ntimi showed her a coin he'd found, kept a long
time, that he wanted to use for movie snacks. Leda tried to
picture what that would be. She told Ntimi about popcorn
and he laughed, like it was a punch line. Even funnier than
snowfalls, which she'd told him about the day before.

And then, not too far at all, they arrived. Not that Leda
understood that right away. They'd stopped in front of a mud-
stick little house just like every other. It had a metal roof, a
bent metal door, and no windows. It was marginally bigger
than the house next to it, maybe twelve feet by twelve feet.

"Here!" Ita said.

People were filing in. A couple. Three male friends, laughing. Everyone that spotted Leda stopped mid-sentence to stare.

Inside was so dark, Leda's heart revved as her feet skidded to a stop. Ntimi and Michael piled up at her back. Synchronized, they each took one of her hands, wove around her, and led the way.

She sat where they instructed, in the middle of a long wooden bench. While the boys divided themselves evenly on either side of her, she checked to see where Ita would sit. She caught him looking at her and blushed. Both their eyes flittered away, but her heart leapt when he shimmied past the boys and squeezed in next to her.

The room was packed, and Ita pressed up against her. The temperature soared from all the chattering, wiggly bodies bumping together. It made Leda think of a video she'd seen of jiggling atoms in a molecule. But as the hot flesh of Ita's forearm came to rest conspicuously against hers, she found herself thinking of very different videos she'd come across online.

Leda had the urge to pinch herself, both to distract herself from the warmth spreading through her lap, and also from the overwhelming novelty of the moment. As her eyes adjusted, she could see ten long benches, like pews in a church, scrunched together so closely she had to slide her knees under the bench in front of her to fit. By peering left and right through the jostling people, Leda could make out a TV on a stand at the front of the room, not more than 30 inches, and a rickety DVD player.

The movie tonight was *Enchanted*. A new movie in the States, it had to be pirated. Leda thought it hilarious—Patrick Dempsey bringing his fairy-tale good hair to Kibera.

Ntimi beside her couldn't sit still any more than a jumping bean. He jabbered endlessly to Michael, who was listening, but looking around like a Secret Service agent at the same time. Leda smiled, seeing their personalities shine even in the dark.

Ita was unusually quiet. Was he self-conscious to be out with her? Apprehensive? Or simply as hyperaware of the intimacy between their forearms as she was?

Leda turned and pretended to look at the walls, keeping her arm squished insistently, sweatily against his. Soon she really did become fascinated by the construction. The crisscrossed frame was made of squiggly tree branches, holding the mud-stone mixture sandwiched between. The back wall was a T-frame of branches, but with burlap sacks strung taut across them. Leda guessed that was why you'd want your roof to overhang so much, because otherwise the rain might just wash this straight down the street into the gutter.

Just then a man came around to collect the fees. Leda had tucked away the money for all of them in the little pocket of her pants, so she could hand over the approximately four dollars fairly inconspicuously.

Still, the man took a second to understand it was for all of them, and Leda saw that Ita dipped his head.

No previews, just a jerky start and then, sure enough, *Enchanted,* with Patrick Dempsey's wavy mane, played on the meager TV speakers. Everyone was immediately rapt, huddled together and craning for a better view. Leda yearned to know what they thought of the posh New York apartment on-screen, or the fancy clothes and city luxuries. What would they think if they knew she lived with similar privileges, half a world away? Would they rob her? Or just hate her for it?

Leda couldn't see the movie, even if she kept weaving like a boxer for a keyhole peek, so she gave up. She snuggled in safely between her new favorite boys, and took in the experience. The smell was strong, but not so bad. It smelled like people, like people who cooked tomato stew and played soccer in the dusty street with their children and told stories by the light of palm-oil lamps.

The closest and best scent was Ita's, his singular smell Leda could already pick out.

As the movie played on, people laughed and whispered and said who knew what about Patrick's perfect hair and Amy Adams's musical numbers. Leda didn't understand any of the Swahili whispered around her, but she felt the buzz of the room make her arm hairs rise—the communal happiness of moviegoers everywhere.

When Ita moved his arm to the back of the bench behind her, almost an embrace, it sent butterflies fluttering down her spine.

She leaned back, snuggling into his arm, and smiled in the darkness.

When they returned home, Mary had just put Walter to bed. She tried to usher the boys off, too, laughing at their imitations of the actors. Ntimi held out his hand to Leda and then twirled her around in demonstration, more gallant than Gene Kelly. Leda laughed and laughed, spinning at the end of his little hand.

Off they went, finally, to be tucked in and off to dreamland, leaving Leda and Ita alone in the courtyard under the stars and the clouds in the sky.

"Thank you," he said.

"My pleasure," she answered, and realized how husky her voice sounded, especially saying that particular word.

Ita was a sight in the moonlight. His skin was smooth and flawless from his straight brow over his mountainous cheekbones. He must have scars somewhere for his face to be so perfect, Leda found herself thinking. Maybe she just wanted to do a body check.

But he took her silence for propriety, she realized too late. "Good night, Leda. *Lala salama.*"

Safe sleeping was the exact translation, she knew. What if she didn't want to sleep safe that night? What if she wanted to be daring, dangerous?

Mary walked out into the courtyard, stopped when she saw the two of them, inches apart.

"Good night, Ita," Leda said softly. "Sweet dreams." Another thing she didn't want to do that night—her dreams would be anything but sweet, she suspected. "Good night, Mary."

Leda and Mary walked together the length of the courtyard, before Leda let herself into her little room. She didn't need the lamp tonight; she'd learned her route to the bed, led by the moonlight that trickled in near the roof.

It felt as if it took her a million years to fall asleep, watching the metal roof as though it could rain down slumber and calm. Her body was on fire, and not just the itchy burns from the henna. She felt literally kindled from within. Alive. She kept searching for the right word, and while she did, she pictured Ita's face. He was so firm, sure in everything he did. But ever kind about it, and patient.

With the children, he seemed to really want to understand each boy for who they were, not mold them to his wishes or change them from their essential natures. Only someone sure of who they were could be that way—secure enough to let others be themselves and love them for it. The way he'd been with Jomo the other day, the way he treated Mary, Leda— everything Ita did was sure-footed. And constant. Leda knew those boys could count on him for life, that his love would never flicker.

While cleaning his office the day before with Mary, stacked in between the medical journals from the clinic, Leda had found Ita's notes—meticulously hand copied in block lettering. From library books or the internet, Leda didn't know. But those notes showed a dogged dedication, a drive that was as magnetic as it was admirable.

What if she'd grown up with Ita in her life? she wondered. Wouldn't everything have been different? She felt safe with him. Safe from harm, yes, but more than that. Safe to be herself. Ita read her like a classic novel, willing to start at the beginning and work his way through. It made her feel like never before—special. And capable, like she could do big things, different things. Good things.

Leda smiled, snuggled into the scratchy blanket, and fell fast asleep.

December 14, 2007, Kibera—Ita

Ita lay in bed, his body buzzing as though plugged in at a charging station.

The buzzing seemed to chant Leda's name. She was a sudden new star in the sky, everyone excited at its discovery. Anything she looked at—the children, Mary, the neighbors, the food—lit up like a sunrise. Like a rainbow after the storm. Hope. Leda was a second chance.

The things she knew about the world, the places she'd been. He'd never met anyone like her. She reminded Ita of what he'd dreamed of becoming as a child—educated, worldly, elegant.

When was the last time he'd felt these childlike stirrings of the heart? Ita had stored them away long ago, accepted the dogged responsibilities of manhood. But Leda was fascinating—she showed there was a different way to be, a way to be an adult and still leave room for wonder.

There was hurt there, buried deep, but joy, too—a combination that made her seem like a child Buddha.

But she was no child. She was very much a woman, Ita thought, and squirmed in his bed. He thought of the way they'd sat together in the movie theater. He'd felt the warm curves of her body when she'd leaned against his arm. He could still smell her perfume in the night air. He pictured her skin glowing in the flickering light.

Suddenly, his phone vibrated on his desk, making him jump. He snatched it up quickly to still the noise.

Chege.

Ita jabbed at the ignore button. No way was he coming down from his high. Whatever it was Chege wanted, it wouldn't be good.

But after the phone buzzed three more times, the spell was already broken and Ita answered.

"Outside," Chege said and hung up.

Ita crept across the courtyard to the door. He took a deep breath, stood where he could block the entrance, and slid open the metal as quietly as he could.

"Let me in," Chege said, his fingers curling into the crack.

"Why?" Ita looked around—Chege was alone, the street empty.

"Ita," Chege said, his voice like a roll of his eyes, as though he knew Ita would open the door and was simply making things difficult.

"No," Ita said.

"Why?" Chege hissed. "Because of her?"

"Because I said no."

Chege laughed. The tone of it flooded Ita with anger. He started to slide the door shut in Chege's face.

"Okay, okay, just—" Chege bent over, peeling off his outer shirt. He took a gun from his waistband, wrapped it in the shirt. "I need you to hide this for me."

"What did you do?"

Chege looked him hard in the face. "Nothing you haven't seen me do before, brother." He shoved the bundle through the gap and it fell to the ground.

"Things are different now," Ita said.

"What's different?" Chege sneered. "Me? You?"

"Everything. We are not children anymore. There are ways to survive and respect life at the same time."

Chege kicked the bundle farther inside the orphanage. "Someone wins. Someone loses." He looked at Ita's hands by his sides, not picking up the gun. "Ita. We can argue philosophy later. The police coming for me." When Ita didn't budge, he added, "I have money. For your trouble."

"You killed someone with this gun today?"

Chege was getting impatient. "Someone who deserved it."

"Ah. For a good cause, then?"

"What your problem, eh? What I always tell you? This is life."

"It doesn't have to be."

Chege peered over Ita's shoulder, smugness dawning on his face. "Ah. Now I see. This for her. You a holy man now, a good Christian, 'cause that white woman sleeping in your house. Or is it your bed she sleeping in? How white pussy feel?"

"Shut up." Ita wedged himself in the doorway, intercepting Chege's leer. "It's not like that. She's not like that."

Chege shook his head. "Look at you. You think you in love with this woman."

Warmth swirled in Ita's stomach, wound tingling through his limbs. He couldn't help himself, he felt the smile curl his lips like a happy snake in the sun. "Maybe."

Chege was stunned, the teasing look wiped clean away. "No. You not loved a woman since—"

"Since a very long time ago. We were kids. Leda is different. She's the kind of woman I always hoped existed. Smart, cultured, wise—"

"And you think you can a have a woman like that? For real?"

Ita met Chege's mean gaze. "Maybe I can."

"She'll leave."

"You leave, Chege." Ita kicked the gun back through the crack. "Now."

"I need your help."

"I said no."

Chege didn't respond for what seemed like an eternity, a look smeared across his face Ita didn't recognize. Chege wouldn't try to change Ita's mind anymore, but there was something else, something gripping his mind and tongue.

Chege didn't say it, whatever it was. He stuffed the gun back into his pants, put on the crinkled, baggy shirt and disappeared into the night.

Ita slid the door shut, and saw that his hands were shaking.

The next morning, Ita awoke feeling itchy and anxious. It was early; he didn't hear anyone else awake. He got up, dressed quickly, shedding dark dreams and Chege's words from the night before like snakeskin. Outside, he peeked at

Leda's door, but knew she'd still be fast asleep. The thought made him smile, imagining her in her pajamas.

In the kitchen, he startled Mary making tea.

"Good morning," Ita said.

"Looks like you're having a good morning," Mary said and grinned into her pot of tea.

"Good morning!"

Ita and Mary both jumped a foot at Leda's voice. They turned to see her freshly scrubbed and smiling, dressed in a pink T-shirt high-collared enough to cover the henna scabs.

How many clothes does she have? Ita wondered, but the truth was he couldn't wait to see them all. Each item brought out a new light in her. Today she had a perfect flush on her cheeks—the color of lychees ripening at the market.

"Today we paint?" she asked excitedly.

He chuckled. "How about we eat breakfast first?"

"So practical." She made an adorable *tsk-tsk* sound. "Okay, I'll go wake the boys."

"What?" Ita asked Mary once Leda had gone and Mary caught him watching her go. He tried his best to stop smiling like a neighborhood fool, but his lips had no intention of cooperating.

Mary shook her head and stirred the tea.

"We need to plan," Ita insisted, but Leda wanted to just start painting. Ntimi, of course, was on her side.

"An elephant!" he shouted and pointed at a swath of wall.

"Yes!" Leda agreed. "Gray or purple?"

Ntimi laughed. "No purple elephant!"

"Are you sure?" She looked through the paint cans and took out green. "I think I saw a green one once. Maybe he was sick?" She pretended to vomit out of a pretend elephant trunk, making Ntimi laugh again.

She opened each can, and laid out brushes across each one.

"Wait," Ita said, already imagining the chaos and the mess that was seconds from ensuing. "Are you sure—"

"Birds!" Leda picked up a brush and dipped it into the black paint. On the wall closest to her, she painted three lowercase *M*s in quick succession.

The children collectively sucked in a breath and turned their wide eyes on Ita, waiting for him to erupt. He saw their big eyes like a row of vervet monkeys and laughed. This made their eyes grow even bigger.

"Paint!" Ita said. "Monkeys! Lions! Rainbows! The sun!" He looked at Leda and then he reached over to pluck up the brush from the orange can of paint. He walked beside her and painted an enormous orange circle between Leda's birds. She clapped.

The boys sprang into motion at once, grabbing up the brushes and dashing off for their own piece of wall. Ita filled in his sun while Leda watched.

"Are you going to do the green elephant next?" she whispered close to his ear.

He felt the tingle go down his neck. "Anything you wish," he said.

He heard her take a deep breath, sucking the warm air away from his neck. She stayed there, crouched behind him, watching him fill in the sun, one slow, even stroke at a time.

When the sun was finished, neither one of them moved. It was a pause Ita wanted to live in forever. When Ntimi shouted for Leda to come see his painting, Ita was sad to see the moment end. "Now I shall fix your birds," he said.

"Hey!"

He took the paintbrush from her fingers, the black paint already drying in the sun.

"What kind of birds should they be, then, huh?"

"Sparrows," he said.

"Leda!" Ntimi shouted. "Look!"

But Leda didn't leave just yet. She nodded at Ita, seriousness smoothing out the scar along her chin. "In the States, sparrow tattoos signify freedom, but also coming home. Did you know sparrows mate for life? And in Egypt, sparrows signify dead souls living as stars."

Ita watched the hairs on his arm stand up. How did she know these things that spoke to his soul?

"Hope," Ita said. "For us, sparrows mean hope and dignity. And love—the love we all deserve, no matter who we are or where we are from."

CHAPTER 13

December 31, 2007, Kibera—Ita

WHEN ITA RETURNS TO THE ORPHANAGE, the boys rush forward like miniature infantry, only to fall back at the gunfire realization that Mary isn't with him.

Michael says what everyone is thinking. "It's just us now?"

"Yes," Ita says.

"Mary will stay with her family?"

"Yes," Ita says again, desperate to lie down. He has no idea how they will survive without Mary, even though it was he who insisted she stay with Grace, with her real family at a time like this.

Ntimi has the next question. "And Leda will stay with her family, too? She isn't coming back?"

Ita feels sorry for them, but they deserve the truth. "No, she isn't coming back. It's just us now."

Nobody knows quite what to do after Ita says that. He steps farther into the courtyard, closer to them, and then past them. "Michael, come, let's cook lunch."

With food in his stomach, Ita's head clears enough for him to see the days stretched out before him. No school to send them off to. No business to attend to. And no Mary to help. They will be here, like this, staring at each other, each with an ear peeled to the outside, waiting for the fire to come for them.

First, and fast, Ita knows, they will run out of food and water.

When he closes his eyes, he can picture the week before— Christmas. Leda with her hair that shook when she laughed, the children gathered around her, tugging on her as if she were an angel about to take flight any second.

When he opens his eyes, the boys are staring at him, their eyes bulging in their sockets. Fear.

Without a word, Ita spreads open his arms. Jomo takes a step back, but the rest of the boys hurry in, arranging themselves around and on top of Ita's legs. Walter, miraculously without a sound, curls up in Ita's lap. Michael sits down shoulder to shoulder with him.

Even though it presses on all his bruises, Ita keeps his arms wrapped tight around the youngsters, their jutting bones reminding him of little birds.

"Jomo," Ita says as the boy turns and walks away.

"Let him go," Michael says.

Ita looks at Michael, then again at Jomo walking off on his own to the bedroom.

"Let it go," Michael says and Ita can't help but think he means all of it. Leda, Mary, the life and future they'd been building the last seven years.

Let it all go.

That night, Ita stretches out on the mat beneath the boys' bunk beds, staying until they fall asleep.

Listening to their breathing, he looks up at the structures

he and Leda built together. The flowing wood grain reminds him of her long tapered fingers. Of how she pursed her lips when she hammered the nails, how she laughed when he teased her. He lets his eyes count the nails. Even while it makes his chest ache, it soothes him to remember the hours they spent in this room, to remember Leda here.

That is how he drifts off finally—playing back his reel of memories, from the day she arrived with her suitcase and her smile, her watchful eyes surveying Ita from head to toe, the first time she came to breakfast in her blue pajamas, the first day they went out to explore Kibera, movie night, and the afternoon a few days later, the first time they—

Ita's eyes fly open in the dark. How long has he been asleep?

He's sitting like someone jabbed an iron rod down his back. A noise. Coming from the courtyard. From the front gate. Ita rises from the floor, scanning the boys' faces, praying they won't wake.

He tiptoes out of the room. What was it? A knocking, he thinks. But there's a hissing in the night, too, that sounds like his name being called.

He reaches the door, the rifle slung over his shoulder. When he holds his breath to listen, he hears the breathing on the other side. A man. Chege?

Ita's stomach flash floods with acid.

But then his name comes again in the night, leeching through the padlocked gate, and it isn't Chege. "Ita, it's Samuel. Let me in."

Samuel. The man who brought him Leda. "Samuel. What happened?"

"Please." The younger man's voice seeps through the metal like a bleating goat. "Help me."

Ita tenses his protesting muscles into a ready stance. But he doesn't open the door. He doesn't know if he has any more comfort to give, strength to help other men battle the darkness. He has the boys to protect—

"It's my girl," Samuel's voice sobs, shuddering though the door. "Please. You have to help her."

Ita doesn't hear a girlfriend, only Samuel's labored breathing. But the desperation of his plea rings in Ita's ears. He's been crying hard.

"What can I do?"

"You are a doctor, people say."

Ita's heart races. If the violence staggers on, how many more will come for help?

When he opens the gate, he looks out into empty air. Then he looks down. Samuel's crouched on the ground, slumped over something dark and lumpy.

The man looks up, the whites of his eyes shining from a grotesquely swollen face, and Ita sees what he's cradling in his arms.

Slung over his knees is a woman, unconscious.

They're both bathed in blood.

Ita can't see her face in the shadows, only her form. In the darkness, her broken body becomes Leda's, pinned beneath Chege. It becomes Kioni, unconscious in his arms as he listens for her breath, begging God not to take her, not to stain Ita's hands red with her blood.

He failed them both. Maybe this woman he can save.

Ita bends down.

Samuel's eyes glisten with gratitude. Together, they lift the woman through the doorway. Ita locks the door behind them. Surveying the dark courtyard, Samuel clutches his girl tighter, rocks her gently. Ita can't tell if she's alive. There is a frozen sea between the two men, fate being decided, like dice rolling in slow motion.

"This way," Ita says. He points toward the hidden room.

Inside, Samuel lays the girl on the table while Ita closes the door. He crosses the room and lights the lamp. In the bouncing glow, he readies his equipment, dons plastic gloves. The scent of blood blooms in Ita's nostrils.

Now he turns to inspect the woman, his heart cracking, one fissure at a time. Her clothes are torn, her hair matted with blood. She's been struck in the face, and all along her body, methodically, it seems. Blood oozes from wounds on her scalp, her neck, and her clavicle…but it's not enough to explain the quantity of blood that has them both glistening and sticky. "Are you hurt?" Ita asks Samuel.

Samuel doesn't look up, his eyes are locked on the woman. "Don't worry about me. Save her. I'll give you anything. Hurry. Please."

Ita opens the woman's tattered blouse, undoing the buttons one at a time instead of tearing them.

His fingers freeze when he finds the source of all the blood.

A loop of intestine protrudes from the bottom of a jagged gash—she's been stabbed in the stomach. There's so much tissue damage, Ita suspects a machete. When he lifts her skirt to check her legs, he decides, yes, machetes did this. A gang attack, most likely.

Then Ita sees the girl's underwear, soaked through with red. He looks up, catches Samuel's eyes across the table as they well with tears, his face cracking like an egg, jagged pieces falling in on themselves. Thick tears drip onto the woman's broken body, the woman Samuel loves, the woman he would give anything to save.

What Ita needs is time to stand still, so that he can think.

The violence outside, Samuel's weeping, the blood pumping through the woman's body, the memories of Leda stampeding through his mind—everything needs to stop, give him two seconds to think, to plan how to save her.

If he was in the clinic, the plan would be clear. He would do a laparotomy to assess the damage. He needs to open the gastrocolic ligament, decide the type of procedure she needs. The wound is close enough to have nicked the liver. Her lungs could be compromised. The colon or bladder could be injured, spilling their contents, causing peritonitis. Large blood vessels could cause a bleed-out.

Gently, Ita tips back the woman's head and leans in to check her airway. When he shuts his eyes to listen for her breath, he can smell her skin beneath the blood, so close to his. Almost, he reaches out to stroke her cheek. Instead, he sets his fingers to the tip of her nose—it's cool to the touch. Her breath is there, but shallow. When he touches her jugular, her distant pulse is a rabbit skidding through the brush, quick and terrified. Time is turning its back on this woman. Fury swells Ita's chest. She doesn't deserve to die like this. She can't.

"How long has she been unconscious?" Ita asks.

"Not too long," Samuel says, as though what he says can change what happens next.

"She's in shock."

He moves to her hand, checks her capillary refill time by pinching a chipped red fingernail clogged with dirt.

He sees the panic fill Samuel's eyes as the seconds tick off in the room—rising at the same rate as the dread in Ita's stomach. No. *No!*

Ita turns back to his supplies. Buried deep is an IV of saline solution. It is more precious than Samuel can possibly know. Ita squeezes shut his eyes, feeling dizzy. He spins back around and starts the woman on an IV, twisting the clamp to allow a steady flow, not a drip, of crystalloids for shock.

He puts out his hand. "Give me your student card."

Samuel starts. "What? Why?"

"I need it. Or any card, of any kind. ID. Student. Doesn't matter."

Samuel fishes in the woman's pockets. He hands her student ID card to Ita. "Her name is Mercy," he says, seemingly more to himself than to Ita.

Ita looks at the card while he douses it in hydrogen peroxide. The woman in the picture, Mercy, is beautiful, with regal cheekbones and big smiling brown eyes. Her eyes are like Kioni's—brave and kind. At least, what Kioni's eyes used to look like.

Ita blinks. He has to keep a grip on reality. He presses the card over the gash, forcing the intestines to slip back inside the wound. He packs fresh gauze over the card and then a towel. "Press. Hard." As Samuel does as he's told, Ita tapes around her body, top and bottom of the towel. "Keep pressing."

But as Ita winds the tape, he sees the skin under Samuel's hands changing.

With trembling fingers, he reaches out and touches the lower half of Mercy's abdomen, his heart skipping a beat. Her skin is rigid and distended, darkening in the glow of the lantern. She's bleeding internally.

Ita's teeth clench so hard they feel as if they will shatter. He throws his head back to the metal roof, glares at the god that made this forsaken world.

She needs surgery. She needs help Ita cannot give her, not here, not with the supplies he has.

With tears racing to his eyes, Ita struggles to breathe. Ita will fail a third woman tonight. A woman named Mercy. *Oh Lord, where is your mercy now?*

Gently, while Samuel continues to press desperately on the gauze, Ita slips a towel under Mercy's feet to raise them. Respectfully, he lowers her skirt. He covers her legs with a blanket.

Samuel notices his movements slowing down. He watches, his eyes jumping about, weighing Ita's every act.

"Samuel," Ita says softly.

The man's eyes stop flittering and double in size, his anguish filling the room like smoke. "Come on, Ita. Please."

Ita's own wounds throb as he shakes his head, like punishment. Judgment for his failure.

"Please," Samuel says again, louder. "I brought her here because I heard you can help—"

Ita grits his teeth. "She needs a hospital."

"You're the hospital. Look!" He gestures around the room, at the posters, at the supplies. "What does she need?" Samuel holds out his arm, making a fist. He looks down at the veins bulging to the surface, in the crook of his arm. "Take my blood. Take my organs. Anything you need from me. Please. I don't have any money. I brought her here. I brought her here." More tears pool at the corners of his eyes. "It can't be my fault. Please. You have to save her."

"I can't save her," Ita says, and the words stab his heart. "She needs surgery."

Ita looks down on Mercy's still body. The human heart pumps several liters of blood a minute. A human female has no more than four liters of blood. He has to tell Samuel the truth. He can't send him into the night, with no money, lugging her heavy body to a faraway hospital, where it will only be too late. It already is too late. "Samuel," he says and waits for the poor man to look at him, so he will see Ita's eyes and hear the truth. "She's going to die. Very soon."

"No!" Samuel stands up so fast he tips over a metal pan with Ita's tools, sends them flying. The noise of metal on metal shatters the night.

Ita looks sharply at the closed door. He imagines with dread Michael's head suddenly peeping through the door.

"I can make you." Samuel's eyes look to the ground behind Ita. Without having to turn, Ita knows what is there.

The rifle. He carried it into the room with them, set it against the wall.

Ita shakes his head. A tear finally frees itself from his eyelashes. "I'm sorry, Samuel. I wish I could save her, truly. I wish so many things could be different than they are." He takes one ragged step and picks up the rifle, slings it silently over his shoulder. "I will leave you to say goodbye."

Samuel's iron face melts at the words. He spins away from Ita as if he no longer exists. He sees only Mercy, on the table. The dice have stopped rolling. No more shouting or pleading will stay fate's cast.

Ita watches, sadness tearing his limbs apart, as Samuel sinks onto the stool beside his beloved's body. He kisses her bloody face till his lips sheen. He smoothes back her hair, plucking tiny rocks from the strands above her forehead. He cups her face with both hands. "Mercy." The name comes slow and soft as honey, like the sweetness of her spirit filling the room.

Samuel whimpers, begging her forgiveness, as Ita edges out of the room, the whispers of *my love, my life* hissing like a branding iron, marking Samuel the eternal possessor of the worst moment of his life.

Ita pulls open the thin door and reenters the long, cruel night.

The sheet to the boys' room is drawn. Miraculously they haven't woken. He carries a plastic stool a small distance away from the hidden room to sit and wait. To wait for what else this night may bring.

New Year's Eve.

It's the first time the thought registers in his mind and sticks.

He flashes on how he and Leda talked about it, dreaming what the New Year would bring them.

She told him about celebrations in America, men and women drinking bubbly liquor and kissing each other at midnight. The memory is a sharp pang in Ita's side. Leda isn't celebrating tonight. She is suffering.

Ita looks into the courtyard where Leda sang with the boys, where they played, where she painted elephants and giggled with them. He sees her face turning around to smile at him, the laugh that sprang from her like fresh clean water.

At least she's alive. She didn't meet Mercy's final fate. She is somewhere safe.

December 31, 2007, Topanga, CA—Leda

The hot water scalds her and Leda endures it resignedly, watching her skin turn the color of shame, the color of regret and blood and pain. She lifts her face to the showerhead and opens her mouth, thinking it could burn her or drown her or both and that would be okay. The water fills her mouth and pours over her chin; it rains and rains, drawing her blood to the surface like a sunburn.

But now the water feels heavy, pounding the bruises on her body, raking the scratches, pooling in the pockmarks where the rocks ground into her shoulders.

Suddenly Leda isn't in her shower anymore, with Amadeus whining just outside. She's back in Kibera, the scene of her last night replaying in amplified slow motion. Every drop is the men's fingers clawing at her arms, Chege's dreads falling across her face, the necklace snapping from her neck, his long fingers wrapping around her throat, dragging her toward the door—

Leda drops into the white tub, choking and gasping, and watches her battered legs splay out in front of her. A stranger's legs. There it is again—the feeling that she's inside a stranger's life.

She went. I came back.

Leda doesn't know how to stop the panic ripping through her veins, shredding her thoughts into shards. The water becomes broken glass.

Somewhere, far, far away, she hears the phone ringing.

Ita.

Leda's heart pounds at the thought. Her toes curl, gripping the slippery white of the tub. She scrambles to get her legs underneath her, turns her eyes away from the bruises. She covers them with the hanging white towel.

Halfway down the hall, the ringing stops and Leda stops in her tracks, her heart hammering away under the wet cloth.

She waits. No beep for voice mail. But if it was Ita, then he's okay. She moves again, one foot in front of the other. And as she does, the phone rings again.

This time she dashes. "Ita—" she says into the phone when she reaches it, her fingers gripping hard enough to make the plastic creak.

"What?" comes the crackle in reply. "Leda?"

Leda slumps into a chair. "Mother." She wraps the towel tighter around herself, putting up a shield. But maybe Estella's calling to welcome her back. Maybe Leda can tell her what happened, and her mother will comfort her for once. Her heart sinks. Does she even deserve it? After what she does to those who show her kindness?

"You're back," Estella's voice comes tersely. "I have news."

"Yes," Leda says. "I'm back." She should have known—Estella is only capable of thinking of herself. Only capable of thinking of her daughter as it impedes or facilitates her life. She has news—probably new curtains for the house. Leda contemplates just hanging up.

"Are you sitting down?" Estella says.

Leda pulls her knees into her chest. "Yes."

"Okay. Listen. There's no good way to do these things. Let's just get it over with." Estella's voice speeds up like a metronome gone haywire. "The cancer is back. I've got one kidney and the MRIs show it's got spots. We're waiting on more tests." Estella pauses to take a quick breath, like she will race on. But she doesn't. The metronome broke. No more words brave the silence between them.

Leda feels the guilt as her uncharitable thoughts inflate her stomach like a balloon. "Oh, Mother—" She sighs, the balloon bursting and air rushing out all at once.

"Take some time to let it settle, Leda. I have."

Leda's heart jumps. Wait. "When did you find out?"

"Just before you left." When Leda can't find any words to eke out over the dropping feeling in her stomach, Estella adds, "But I needed time, like I said."

She was calling to tell me before I left. That's what that call was. Leda clenches her eyes shut. "Do you want me to come over?"

"No, no," Estella says. "You've just returned. Enjoy a little peace and quiet. Tomorrow you can meet the team."

Her considerateness catches Leda off guard, but then she registers what she's said. "The team?"

"I'd like to call them the Death Squad, but apparently they have rules of decorum."

"What?" Leda's mouth is so dry, the word putters out like a dying leaf blower.

"A team. I've got three nurses, an assistant for shopping, plus an on-call doctor. There's a lawyer, too, for the eventual… arrangements. You won't have to worry about a thing. Oh, wait! Tomorrow is New Year's Day. They're not coming tomorrow."

"Mother—" Leda squeaks.

But Estella rushes on. "You can come still, if you want. Or another day. Whatever you want, I understand."

"Estella—"

"I have to go. Happy New Year." Estella hangs up but Leda is sure, on her last words, she heard a distinct break in her mother's voice.

CHAPTER 14

December 17, 2007, Kibera—Leda

SUNDAY HAD BEEN A LAZY DAY OF FINISHING UP the murals and lounging on the mat, teaching the children how to play hangman and tic-tac-toe.

Come Monday, as they waved goodbye to the boys on their way off to school, Leda said to Ita, "Let's go into Nairobi today." Ita turned to her quizzically. She knew he must have work he'd been putting off. She sped up her case. "I want to get a suitcase I left checked at the hotel. And I have things I'd like to get for the boys. And—" Leda knew she was about to blush, and she still couldn't believe Ita brought out such schoolgirl reactions just by looking at her with those big eyes. "I thought I... I'd like to... Figured the least I could do...was take you to lunch."

He smiled instantly. "Lunch?"

Leda begged her cheeks to stop boiling. She knew it was a useless endeavor.

He nodded. "I have to check my mailbox in Nairobi. And I would love to have lunch with you."

She smiled, way too big. "Okay. Great. I'll just—" She spun

around before finishing her sentence, her cheeks competing to head up Santa's sleigh.

As she walked back to her room, Leda felt her heart flapping like hummingbird wings. She couldn't stop the singsong thought in her head. *I've got a date.*

In her room, feeling light-headed and clumsy, she swapped her sandals for tennis shoes and brushed her hair into a ponytail. She smeared on her sunscreen with trembling fingers.

She applied mascara and lip gloss, then rifled through her suitcase for more products, contemplating that blue eyeshadow that had to be somewhere, and blush. *Yeah, right.* First of all, she certainly didn't need any more help blushing. Secondly, any more makeup would melt right off in the day's heat.

In any case, Ita had spent a whole week with her sans makeup and he still seemed pretty smiley about their date. She allowed herself a little shimmy of her hips before opening the door calmly to find him waiting right outside.

His smile stretched from ear to ear. "Ready?"

"Ready."

Off they went, Ita leading the way as usual, and Leda trying not to go down in the muck.

But today, she finally felt as if she was getting the hang of it. A week ago, she couldn't figure out why people didn't just move in two directions—on the right and left side of the ditch. Now she knew it was because you couldn't. The ground was so uneven, it was impossible to stay balanced in a straight line—you'd slip straight into the ditch of sewage. So you had to hop back and forth from one side to the other, jumping in and out of the way of passersby like a dance. It was actually quite fun.

The other amazing thing was that in the dizzying expanse of identical mud shacks, Leda recognized their route to the main road. She knew the charging station, the beauty salon, the stall where Mary bought the charcoal and another where she bought soap and canned foods. Leda looked around for the path to the place they bought their water, but that one escaped her. On that walk, she'd staggered along under the weight of two massive jugs of water, her teeth gritted the whole way.

Leda kept up with Ita easily at first, her footing sure and fast, but after a few more twists and turns, she was as lost as ever.

"Are we going a different way?"

"Yes," Ita said. "Almost there."

The path took a hard right and she saw where it ended—in a giant parking lot. Now she understood the roar of noise she'd heard in the distance. Squared-off minivans called *matatus* lined up and jerked around each other like bumper cars, their drivers shouting and smiling in equal measure. Children were everywhere. As usual, when they spotted Leda, they swarmed around her, calling hi-how-are-you-how-are-you-how-are-you. Now Leda knew it wasn't a question. It was synonymous with, *Hey look, a white lady. Look at you, white lady!*

Ita left her mobbed by kids and approached several *matatu* drivers. At the third one, he waved her over.

Leda untangled herself from the children and wove through the throng of people. No lines. It was a free-for-all.

Most of the *matatus* were white or tan, one sliding door and three square windows in back, a minibus. The majority had seen better days, were purely functional.

But there were others. Ones as shiny as any Ferrari, in red and yellow or black and purple, with racing stripes, graffiti, graphics and paint jobs like an illegal East L.A. drag race. They brandished spray-painted names like Brutal, Pyscho and

Black Betty. The one Ita waited at was tattooed with a voluptuous woman and the name So Sick. Leda froze and gaped.

Ita laughed. "Come on!"

She stepped forward and he steered her inside the vehicle, into the first row of three seats. She scooted over to the window seat and he jammed in beside her. A couple squished in next, the girl sitting on the boy's lap. Five men of various ages piled in, then another trail of young boys squeezed past into the last row. It all happened so fast, Leda's head spun like a washing machine.

Another man tried to squeeze in on their row, but Ita barked at him and reached across the woman's lap to shut the door.

People started passing forward their fare money. Once the door shut, it was almost dark. All windows but the windshield were tinted black, and the inside of the van was all black, too. Black lights rimmed the top, making the graffiti inside fluoresce.

The young driver revved the engine and veered off into the fray, shifting gears like a race-car driver. Music banged from the speakers at decibels Leda knew with painful certainty would result in tinnitus somewhere down the line. When she opened her eyes from wincing, she saw the mounted screen played rap videos to accompany the music.

Only when Leda saw Ita laughing at her did she realize her mouth was still open as if she had a broken jaw. Not that she could *hear* him laughing over the music, but seeing him made her laugh, too, because the whole scene was pretty funny.

As the *matatu* climbed the hill, she watched the expanse of Kibera from above—the checkerboard of rusted metal roofs bulging out from either side of the railway. Leda saw the towering wall topped with barbed wire that separated the wealthy suburbs and shielded them from having to contemplate Kibera over their morning coffee. But they were headed in the other direction, past the blocky beige apartment buildings, presumably public housing with their uniform drab hue and flapping laundry strung above dirt yards full of weary mothers and scampering children.

Driving away was different than driving in. It wasn't that Leda was used to Kibera, exactly, but that now she saw it with different eyes. Instead of reading about the water problem in a guidebook, she could see it clearly—water pipes running through and under Kibera into Nairobi to feed the golf courses and the government lawns rushing green past her window. This meant water had to be brought back into Kibera, bought at exorbitant prices, five to a hundred times what people paid in those government apartments one mile away.

Was that what Ita was thinking about? Did he have new eyes, too, now that she'd been staying at the orphanage? Did sitting beside her make him think of the injustice? Did she represent everything that was wrong with the world— entitlement, disparity of wealth, racism, elitism, a hundred other *isms* that made a place—no, a phenomenon—like Kibera somehow possible?

Outside her window, Leda watched the billboards—incumbent President Kibaki and challenger Raila Odinga vying for drivers' eyes, minds and hearts. Could Odinga really change things? Would he make Kibera a priority, as he claimed? How much would it cost to build large-scale water projects and public housing? Sanitation facilities? Leda was beginning to understand what this election could mean. Where in the U.S. she was excited about Obama for his lofty ideals—bipartisanism, responsibility, youth empowerment—here, an election win could mean water, food, life and death.

Leda sneaked glances at the other passengers, all of them presumably residents of Kibera. The men mostly stared straight ahead, bopping their heads to the music and looking cool, like young men everywhere acted in the presence of gangsta rap. The couple shouted into each other's ears, as if they were in a nightclub, then nuzzled one another, oblivious to the world as they bumped and rubbed along. The election was in a little over a week. Leda felt excited for them. She imagined the celebration in Kibera if Raila Odinga won.

January 1, 2008, Kibera—Ita

It's another two hours before Ita hears any movement in the hidden room from his post on the stool. Though his body aches, he gives Samuel as much time and privacy as he needs.

When the door scrapes open, Samuel fills the frame, Mercy's body cradled in his arms.

Ita nods. He rises slowly and leads the way to the front gate. Samuel doesn't say a word as they pass through the courtyard. Respecting the sleeping children or lost in grief, Ita doesn't know.

At the gate, the two men's eyes meet across the threshold. There are no more words to be spoken. No gratitude. No apologies. Just the look between strangers that says *kwaheri* and *kila la kheri*.

Goodbye and *better luck to you* in this mad world.

After Samuel's gone, Ita trudges back to the little room. With bleach and water, he scrubs the blood from the metal table and gathers up the bloody blankets. He cleans himself, too, with the last of the hydrogen peroxide.

An hour passes before Ita reappears in the moonlight and carries his stool to the front gate.

He leans his head against the metal, and before he knows it, he's fitfully asleep and dreaming of Leda.

He sees her face, her alabaster skin glowing in the light of the stars. But then suddenly there's blood everywhere—dripping into Leda's green eyes, down the ends of her dark hair, bubbling over her lips, spilling down her neck. She's trying to speak, but can only gurgle. Now she's on the metal table in the hidden room. She's wearing Mercy's clothes, her soaked underwear, her body is bludgeoned by machetes. *Save me,* that's what she's trying to say. *Save me. Ita—*

As he gasps awake, one hand on his throat and the other reaching out to keep the rifle from falling to the ground, Ita sees the night has finally passed. He can't see the sun yet over the orphanage walls, but it's out there, rising, relentless, throwing spears of light into the smoke.

A noise outside makes him jump to his feet and realize that perhaps it wasn't the dream that woke him but rather whatever is out there.

The answer comes as a soft knock at the gate. His heart leaps into his throat as he stares down the metal door.

We are not safe here. They should flee like everybody else was fleeing to their villages, their homelands. Kikuyu is a death sentence now. Ironic, since Ita has no Kikuyu family. Never had Kikuyu neighbors or relatives come forward to help them. As far as Ita is concerned, he has no tribe, no ancestral village. But that also means they have nowhere to go.

He tries to think. It's the first light of dawn. Early. Who could it be? A neighbor wanting food? Mary returning?

"Ita."

His mind stops dashing over possibilities and plunges into a vortex of time. His ears ring in the silence as he strains to hear the voice again, to see if it could be true. Ita would recognize that voice in a monsoon, the voice that haunts him in the darkest hours of the night.

"Ita," the woman's voice comes again. Not pleading. Not begging. Just there, existing, waiting.

And then he is staggering forward, tripping, fumbling with the gate.

Even when he sees her, he doesn't believe it.

But there she is.

Kioni.

CHAPTER 15

December 17, 2007, Nairobi—Leda

BY THE TIME THE MATATU SCREECHED TO A halt, and Ita gallantly took her hand to help her out, Leda's mood floated like a bobber on a sunny lake. Yes, she'd just torn through a big strange city in a vehicle like a *Pimp My Ride* episode on steroids. But with Ita at her side, she felt both protected and free to be a little wild. It was as if with him, in his world, she could be a different person, a stronger, better one.

On the street, Leda looked up. Across from the hotel was another block-shaped, beige-colored structure, but this one had a pointed copper archway atop two altars bearing hieroglyphic-like carvings.

"The Kenyan National Assembly," Ita said. "Parliament."

Leda gazed in awe at the imposing building and its regal neighbors. Nairobi was an impressive city, teeming with bright hotels, green parks and regal architecture.

Ita stood beside her and looked, too. She could tell his gaze was more conflicted, but when he turned to her, his smile was there, just for her.

Their first semiofficial date had begun.

She smiled back. "Shall we?"

They strode toward the Intercontinental, a towering white structure with green awnings. Nine days after her arrival, Leda's first night's stay in the hotel seemed like a far-off dream. She drifted through the glass front doors, smiling at the doorman, Ita a step behind her. At the front desk, the receptionist confirmed Leda's bag was there and asked if she would like a porter. When she saw Leda hesitate, she asked brightly, "Would you like to have lunch first?"

Leda turned to Ita, but he was busy ogling the surroundings. "We can have lunch here, if you'd like. There's a beautiful Italian restaurant." She remembered what she'd seen—formal dining with Renaissance paintings, heavy draperies and white linen. The look on his face told her it might be a bit much. The truth was she always felt uncomfortable at those types of places, too. Estella didn't dine out, and Leda had more practice playing the part of the ramen-expert college student than the fancy heiress. "But I'd rather dine by the pool."

"The Terrace Restaurant," the woman at the front desk said. "They have a lovely buffet."

Leda waited for Ita's response. It took him another moment to figure out both the women were waiting on him.

"Yes," he said.

Leda eyed Ita, getting a little nervous. He was suddenly edgier than usual. She turned to the woman. "Thank you. I'll return after lunch for the bag."

Leda led the way to the patio restaurant. It was warm outside, but not the stuffy, beat-down heat of Kibera. The Terrace was casual but elegant, with linen napkins and tablecloths and wooden chairs beneath cloth umbrellas. The turquoise pool provided a bright backdrop and misty coolness.

A host escorted them to a table made private by carefully

manicured hedges. The young man pulled out Leda's chair and, after she sat, took the crisp linen napkin and spread it in her lap. She took a sip of lemon water before she noticed Ita still standing, watching her in a daze. She suddenly felt silly seated and started to stand.

Ita laughed. He shook his head at himself and sat down. "Sorry," he said. "It's just so—" he turned his eyes squarely to Leda "—beautiful."

Leda blushed and ducked her head, but inside she was delighted and hungry with anticipation.

When their waiter appeared, they ordered beers and headed for the buffet. She noted Ita's gasp. The buffet was an explosion of excess—a parade of fruit and flowers, twenty-plus lined-up platters, piles of sandwiches and pasta salads, flanked by stations of prime rib and rotisserie chicken. Leda chose her favorite things, added an extra spoonful of potato salad, and laughed when Ita overloaded his plate before he got halfway down the line.

When they took their seats, she stared at her plate like a Jenny Craig patron about to go AWOL. "I had no idea I was so starving," she said, muffled by a mouthful of lemon-caper potato salad.

"I know what you mean." Ita fit a huge slice of roast beef in his mouth and Leda wanted to kick herself for using the word *starving* so casually with him. She wished he could eat like a king every day for the rest of his life.

The beers arrived and from the first clink, Leda allowed herself to settle into the scene like a well-rehearsed play. Their conversation never clashed, never collided. Rather, it rose and fell like ripples on a pond. They hit every cue for wit and camaraderie.

They talked about their lives, about the boys, expressed

their concerns and theories on Jomo's silence. They agreed how much they wished all the children could be there with them. They made each other laugh, taking turns imitating what each of the boys' reactions would be to the buffet.

Leda gushed how thankful she was for Ita's kindness in hosting her. She admired with all her heart what he had accomplished at the orphanage, the haven he'd created.

Embarrassed, Ita mumbled something that she could only guess at by the look on his face and his body language.

"Did you say guilty?" she asked. That she couldn't believe—not from him. "You've achieved impossible feats. The only thing that's ever held you back is funding." She felt her conviction about him solidify even as her own guilt bubbled. "*You* have nothing to be guilty about."

His silence told her he'd heard the change in her voice, saw the look scurry across her face. In the blink of an eye, the tone of their afternoon changed.

"I'm the one who should feel guilty," she whispered. "I should have done so much more with my blessings. With my life."

He gazed at her, considering her words thoughtfully. "How did you get the scar?" he asked softly and only then did she realize she was stroking it. "A burn," he guessed correctly. "From liquid, I would guess."

Leda saw no disgust, no pity, nothing but concern on Ita's face. Where every other time in her life, she would have changed the subject, instead she confessed, "Boiling water. It tipped over on me from the stove."

Ita reached out, slowly but surely, and his fingers caressed her face, halfway between a lover's touch and a doctor's assessment. "It wasn't treated properly."

Leda didn't feel shame at his words. She felt *his* anger, and it only emboldened her. "I was eight. And I'd been left alone. For days." She stopped. It was more than she'd meant to say.

He nodded. "You have spent much time alone." His hand was still cupping her cheek.

For a moment, Leda melted into the warmth of his palm and the world disappeared. *Yes,* she thought, and his touch only made it that much more true. She could feel it—his compassion like a cocoon designed just for her, designed to help her grow and change and turn into something better, beautiful.

But as the moment lingered, the gushy feeling faded and her body tensed. Suddenly, she felt awkward and ridiculous hunched over in his palm. She glimpsed a patron staring, registered the clinking silverware around them and kids splashing in the pool. Her heart began to race. She had the budding desire to run. Ita's skin was hot, too hot on hers. Like the cozy warmth of a radiator turning dangerous, and she jerked out of his touch.

She saw the tiny wince on his face and her heart sank into her lap. God, she was terrible at these things.

When she dared to look again, however, Ita's distress had vanished, replaced with empathy. Gently, he asked, "Have you ever married, Leda? Do you have a boyfriend?"

Leda picked at the skin on her fingers. "Neither. Like I said, I'm not good at relationships."

"Maybe they weren't good with you."

His face held a divine understanding. For a moment, she considered his words. "No, trust me, I'm a wrecking ball."

"Not you," he said. "Your little monsters."

"Did you just call me a monster?" She smirked. But, come to think of it, that was a pretty accurate description of her behavior with men.

Ita didn't smile. "No. The little monsters buried inside us. They're not you. They swallow your regrets and bad memories so you can sleep at night. But sometimes they get out, take over and do terrible things."

Leda's skin prickled, feeling as if he could see right through her, see the memories she'd never told anyone about, ever, the nights she carved lines into her skin to prove she existed, prove she was alive. But it made her wonder, for someone to glimpse such ugliness—

"Then you, too, have been unlucky in love?"

He didn't answer, but he didn't have to—his eyes filled with flickering remembrances of his own ghosts. The longer he looked at her, the further away he swept, and Leda almost thought she understood, could glimpse a life of being let down, abandoned, ignored. *That* she understood all too well. "Kioni," Ita said into the sky.

Leda watched his face contort as he uttered the name. Like the path of a tornado, guilt twisted his features, rained regret into his eyes. Before her, Ita's face hardened into a mask she hardly recognized. A mask of darkness, chilling even in the heat.

Just then the waiter appeared above them. "Two more beers?"

"*Yes,*" they said in unison.

The laughter brought the bliss of levity rushing back. Ita peeled off his mask and tossed it aside. His smile toasted Leda along with the clink of a frosty glass.

Minutes later, they were back to funny stories and smiles, but the darkness had brought a fuzzy intimacy that still wrapped around Leda's shoulders. She felt far closer to him now, closer maybe than she'd ever let herself get to anyone. She tentatively accepted it, but deep in her bones, she had to fight the flutter of panic, fight the feeling that the closeness would crush her.

"Excuse me," she said suddenly, rising clumsily. "I have to use the ladies' room."

She teetered over hot coals all the way to the bathroom, past the diners and the food and the waiters. When she pushed open the door, she landed smack in front of a harshly lit mirror.

Her hair was a tangled mess, her face without makeup flushed and shiny. Her dusty clothes were rumpled beyond precedent.

But the overall impression of the vision Leda saw in the mirror amounted to something surprising.

She didn't look like herself at all, not one bit. Tanned and tousled, she realized she looked instead like a contented, happy version of herself she'd never known.

How long until I ruin it? she asked the radiant woman in the mirror.

Scared of the answer, she pictured Ita's face, calm and confident. She remembered him walking tall at the clinic, guiding the children through their homework at the orphanage. Everything he did was imbued with strength, goodness and purity of spirit.

Please, give me a little longer.

December 17, 2007, Nairobi—Ita

Watching Leda walk away, Ita was locked in an afterglow, the world like a masterpiece painting left to dry. Every cell in his body felt alive, bursting. He recalled accounts from drug users in the medical journals—the high that made them feel like the best version of themselves—smarter, funnier, the most dazzling person in the room.

With Leda, he felt that kind of euphoria, as if everything could be different, better. With her, as with the doctors at the clinic or his peers at the university, he felt infused with inspiration. But more than in the doctors or students, in Leda he'd found a kindred spirit. Unlike them, she looked at him as a true equal, as a friend. *And,* he thought, *maybe as more.* The electricity between them was intoxicating. This angel, sitting across from him in a beautiful sliver of a perfect day, wanted to know everything about him, understood so much, so many secret things, pieces he'd tucked away so long ago. Ita felt free to be alive, to be happy, to hope.

But as the minutes passed, as her absence sank in, the glow receded and Ita peeked through the clearing fog at his surroundings. He saw the waiters clustered in a corner, whispering as though about him.

The luxuriousness of the restaurant, the marble and glass, the crisp white linen, the impossible blue of the pool—it imparted Ita with the prickly suspicion of a dreamer about to wake.

What could he possibly offer a woman like Leda? With her array of clothes and the house she'd described, the gilded life she'd rejoin in just two short weeks. What could he gain from this liaison but a broken heart? Ita glowered at his dirty fingernails. This lunch cost more than he'd spent on the children's clothes for the year.

Inspecting the other diners, he felt ill at the injustice of the world. It was better if he didn't see this, didn't have to think about it. Didn't have to imagine what he could do with one tenth of the money these tourists spent here on holiday. What he could give the orphans with that kind of money. What he could have given Chege—the chance at a better life, a better soul. And Kioni—

Kioni. With these rich people's pocket money, he could have spared Kioni her suffering.

At the thought, Ita's stomach lurched into his throat, threatening to reject the lunch he'd gulped down so happily, so greedily. How could he even think he deserved someone like Leda? Deserved to be happy?

He closed his eyes against the wave of self-loathing, but when he opened them, he noticed something—the dirt under his fingernails wasn't dirt. It was paint. Black paint and some yellow and blue, from painting the murals.

Ita smiled in spite of himself, remembering Leda helping Ntimi with his elephant, coaxing Jomo into painting zebra stripes. It was easy to imagine how life would wilt when she left, lose luster and shine.

He took a sip of water and gave himself a talking-to. She was here for now, and he could enjoy it or not. He could let the little monsters play him for a shadow puppet, or he could savor these two weeks like the sun returning after a long, lonely storm.

And, besides, there was one thing he could offer Leda.

December 17, 2007, Nairobi—Leda

Leda returned to their table, feeling like a deflated balloon drifting across concrete.

But Ita looked more like a circus clown hopped-up on Red Bull. "You're back. I have a surprise," he said in a rush.

As she took her seat, she felt the tingle start back up in her stomach.

"Ready for it?" he asked.

"Ready," she said.

"Come with me on safari."

Birds took flight in her stomach. *Really?* When? How?"

"I had hired a guide from another organization to lead the safari scheduled during your visit, so I could host you at the orphanage," he said as he scooted forward and took her hand in his. The sudden warmth gave her a jolt. "I just called him and canceled his services."

Leda took a quick, eager breath. "When do we go?"

"Tomorrow."

She added her other hand on top of his, resisting the little urge to squirm out of his touch, and instead leaning into its warmth. *Please,* she told the little monsters who were stirring awake, *please let me have this.*

By the time the cab dropped them off at the edge of Kibera, they were like two hot kernels about to pop. Leda paid the cabbie, whom they'd opted for over a *matatu* to accommodate the luggage, while Ita hoisted her suitcase on his back as if it were a box of feathers. Then they hightailed it home. Excited chatter had been replaced by sly backward glances and licking of lips, as Ita led the way back to the orphanage.

He couldn't get the door open fast enough for her. When he finally slung back the metal, she felt as if he was ripping off her blouse.

Sure enough, as soon as the suitcase was plopped inside and the gate closed behind them, he grabbed her by the waist with both hands and pulled her to him, their hungry hips slamming together. Leda gasped as he lifted both their shirts and smashed their naked stomachs together while his lips found hers again.

They kissed as if it was the end of the world, or the beginning, or as if the world didn't exist and who the hell cared. They kissed like seals, hot, slippery skin sliding up and down until the friction made Leda want to scream. She arched her back and his hands dipped into her pants, gripping her ass so hard the pain sucked the breath out of her, but made her want it all the more.

In a flash, he yanked his right hand from the back of her pants, drove it down the front, into her panties. His fingers dove inside her with such wet force that her feet nearly lifted off the ground. She squealed, certain she would faint from the searing fullness. Her arms wrapped around his shoulders as she raked his neck with her nails. He growled into her mouth, plunged deeper and rubbed her harder and faster, making her swell under the pressure and rhythm.

She nearly drowned in his touch, her warm response gushing out from her panties, down the insides of her legs. Dizziness mounted inside her until her knees buckled, her head fell back, and she rode his fingers like a rocking horse, gyrating atop his thrusting while he kissed her neck and her chest. He bit her nipple through the fabric of her shirt. She made a noise she'd never heard herself make before, a low growl to match his as he—

"Ita!" A yell came through the door as banging sounded against the metal. The boys were home with Mary. Inches away.

Their eyes flew open. Reality turned on them like a searchlight.

Ita withdrew his fingers, moved them, soaking wet, to Leda's waist until she found her footing. She swam in his hungry gaze.

"To be continued?" she whispered as the banging resumed.

Ita moved apart and adjusted his pants with a grin. Then

he kissed her cheek, slowly, savoring. When he pulled back, his eyes stayed locked on hers. She felt as if they were living in a snow globe, as though she was the only woman in the world, the only woman Ita would ever look at, ever love.

CHAPTER 16

January 1, 2008, Kibera—Ita

IT'S REALLY HER.

Kioni is really there, right before his eyes—her diminutive frame engulfed in a black cotton dress and shawl, clutching a laden bag.

Ita is too shocked to step aside, to let her in. So they stand facing each other, equally mesmerized, equally gripped by the bleeding fist of the past.

Kioni, the little girl in his dreams and nightmares, all grown up.

Her eyes brim with tears. She takes the first step, Ita steps back. And then she is in, slipped through the doorway like the shadow of a storm. She winds her arms around his neck, tightening her grasp like a garden snake, and presses her dry nose into his neck.

Then suddenly she goes limp, as if her spine turned to dust. She hangs from him like a collar of chains and he stumbles, trying to hold her weight. Her serrated breath darts in his ear, she's shaking like a baby bird flung from the treetops. Ita's eyes close automatically and his mind swerves back through

time, remembering the quick, trembling breath of a miniature Kioni dashing after him in the night, thrusting her fate
into his hands.

April 19, 1990, Kibera—Ita

"Don't look back," Ita says and clasps the little girl's hand
tighter, not sure if he's talking to her or himself.

The girl is lightning fast, he is glad to note. And she isn't
crying anymore. She speeds after him, barefoot, and Ita is
sure she is cutting her feet on the jagged night.

The slobbering men stay on their heels for three turns,
enjoying the sport of it, calling out the terrible things they
will do when they catch them. Ita's neck they will snap like
a chicken's, to the girl they will do much worse.

When the thunder of their footsteps slows, then stops, Ita
can hear only the panting of the fleeing trio. But they don't
stop. He and the little girl keep after Chege like a family of
antelope, squeezing between the houses of sleeping families,
ducking under jutting roofs and *duka*s, leaping over trash piles.

Ita knows where Chege is headed—out past the railroad,
to the landfill where they used to sleep when they first met.
It is the safest place.

When Chege leads the way into a ravine, he stops so suddenly, Ita nearly tumbles on top of him.

Chege bends over, heaving to catch his breath and Ita puts
his hands on his knees to do the same. The little girl, Kioni,
collapses to the ground, her body convulsing. When she starts
to cry, it isn't the mewling of a cat, it's full-size adult sobs of
misery that pour from the tiny creature.

"Make her stop," Chege says in between gasping breaths.

Ita goes to sit next to her. She doesn't even look over. She's intent on pouring all her soul into the wailing, as if she wants God to hear, the stars to see, the whole world to know her pain.

Ita feels a prick of fear—her crying could mean more trouble and they are all so tired. Soon, Chege's fury will turn squarely onto this little girl, and Chege's rage can be much like her crying in its fervor.

Ita digs into the little pocket on the inside waistband of his pants. His secret hiding place for the only precious thing he owns.

He takes out the necklace—the gold sparrow darting into the humid night air. He stares at the shimmering charm, always rousing the last memories of his mother.

He dangles it inches from the weeping girl's face, before her squeezed-shut swollen eyes, hoping to dazzle her out of the fit. With a sob, she opens them, and is instantly entranced, her crying corked like a bottle. For a moment, both she and Ita peer at the necklace together, the gold bird suspended between their faces.

Then Kioni reaches out, her tiny fingers yearning for the necklace, a smile curling on her lips.

But Ita yanks the necklace away, more viciously than he intended.

Chege cackles. "You can't touch it." He's been watching them. "He won't let anyone hold it, let alone sell it, like we should have a million years ago. He rather me knife an old man for his watch."

"You do that?" Kioni first trains her wide eyes on Ita. When she switches to Chege, then back and forth between them, reconsidering her saviors, the volley churning Ita's stomach into a cesspool. He can see it—her dawning realization that she's escaped the horsemen of hell only to meet their messenger boys.

Chege crosses his arms over his chest and huffs, making full use of his towering position over her. "He smart. He different. But what use we have for you, huh?" He looks at Ita. "She won't last a month."

Ita hangs his head. He looks at the necklace in his hand. "It was my mother's," he whispers.

Kioni peers into his palm, too, as though trying to read his future. "My mother's gone, too," she says, not because he hasn't guessed as much—a half-starved shoeless girl alone in the night—but more like she hasn't said it enough times yet to make it real. He knows the feeling too well. "Do you really do those bad things?"

She doesn't meet his eyes as she asks, and Ita avoids hers, as well. They both sit staring at the necklace until Ita folds his hand shut and tucks it out of sight into its hiding place. Kioni has her answer.

"Only when you have to," she says.

Chege's head cocks sharply, his face switching from ire to approval, and Ita feels a wave of nausea.

But it is settled. Kioni is one of them.

January 1, 2008, Kibera—Ita

Ita snaps back to the present when he hears Michael come up behind them in the courtyard, staring at the disheveled woman in Ita's arms, his eyes widening and narrowing with the rampant fluctuations of child emotions.

With Kioni still wrapped around his neck, Ita lumbers toward the stool. He sets her down, gently disentangling himself from her hot, dusty limbs. He nods at Michael and the boy padlocks the gate.

Slipping a finger under Kioni's chin, Ita lifts her head softly to peer into her eyes. They are exactly the same as he remembers—pupils big and shiny as an oil spill. When his gaze shifts to the scar beneath her left eye, he feels his stomach clench. Everything about her presence makes his body stiffen like a corpse.

"What happened, Kioni? Why are you here?"

She holds his gaze, her lips pursed as if her next words have been rehearsed, likely a thousand times or more in her journey from her faraway home. But under Ita's eyes, her courage turns to leaves curling in a fire, her words crackling embers that singe his skin.

"They burned everything," she says. "The school. My house. Everything. And what the men did to each other... and to children." She shakes her head at the images seared into her mind. "I took a bus as far as the money lasted. And then I walked. I've no one else—nowhere else to go."

Kioni gives out, like an exhausted battery. Ita can only imagine what she went through to get here.

But the thought of her being here, staying here, being so close to him—it makes Ita recoil, makes him want to throw himself to the dirt or jump into a fire.

But we are already in the flames, he thinks. *And Kioni is where the fire started.*

He has outrun the blaze all this time, thinking he could avenge his regrets with a good life, but that was a lie. Divine retribution doesn't follow man's rules. He will pay for his mistakes, his failures. If Kioni has nowhere to go, then she has not made a family. In the fourteen years since she fled, grew into a woman, she has not found a husband. And if that is true, whose fault is it but his?

Ita nods at the night sky, knows the stars are watching, his payment due.

"You're safe," he tells her. "You will stay here with me. With us."

He turns to Michael. With a reassuring smile and a wave of his hand, he sends the boy back to his room.

The decision is made, was made long before she got here. "Thank you," she says softly.

Fetching another stool, he sits, not too close and not too far. "Ita?"

"Yes?"

"Where's Chege? Is he okay?"

His teeth clamp together, it feels impossible to force the words through them. "I don't know where Chege is."

She looks down at the ground, at the bag by her feet, snatched as she fled a smoldering life. Finally, the tears spill down her cheeks. There is no sound, just tiny rivers dripping off the cliff of her chin.

Ita scoots his stool closer. When he rests his arm around her shoulders, he can't help but think of the days and nights and years they huddled together like this, against the rain, against the dogged hunger, against injustice and hopelessness and a horde of constant threats. But instead of giving comfort, touching Kioni now makes his insides squirm like worms in mud.

CHAPTER 17

December 18, 2007, Kibera—Leda

LEDA WATCHED THE SAFARI TOURISTS SNIFF out the orphanage.

It was a brilliant business move on Ita's part, she thought. Let them see where their money was going.

But it made her feel strange, wondering what her role was now, the day after their perfect lunch and their steamy kissing and groping session in this very courtyard that now held six waddling tourists (five adults and one child) making wide eyes at the open-fire kitchen, the single room for seven boys, the outhouse space for bathing.

Leda sized them up from the sidelines. There was an older American couple, fiftyish, dressed head to toe in safari-themed gear, as though chosen excitedly from a catalogue. There were two women from Dublin—loud, exuberant best friends in their forties. Leda would have expected herself to shy away from them, but somehow she knew they would be her favorites. Last was an English father and his ten-year-old daughter, an awkward pair, as if maybe the father wasn't her primary caretaker, perhaps a birthday present from an estranged parent, one not thought out too well. The girl snuck peeks at the boys waiting on the mat, and they eyed her back, just as curious.

The tourists followed Ita dutifully on the tour, asking polite questions about the orphanage, like a group visit to a museum or worse, a zoo. Exactly how she must have looked when she first arrived, Leda realized.

And how strange she must seem to them. Ita introduced her as a volunteer, but the looks the adults gave her made her think it was clear as day that she and Ita had been making out like horny teenagers and couldn't wait to do it again. *A hundred-and-fifty percent true,* Leda thought with a grin. If this group weren't here, they would wave the children goodbye, off to school, and send Mary on an errand a hundred miles away.

Ita looked over from his tour and winked. Nearly melting off her stool, Leda uncrossed and recrossed her legs.

Finally the group came over to meet the children. The boys had obviously been through these tours before, likely coached in Ita's thorough way on the importance of their role. Ntimi shook hands like the perfect gentleman and wished them lots of lions on their safari.

Michael asked if they'd had a good journey here.

Mary asked if they would like some tea.

So, for the next bit of morning, everyone piled onto the mat and sipped milky chai, asking each other questions that made both sides of the divide laugh at their strangeness. *How many toilets do you have in your house? You boys have never been in a taxicab? What is a hamster?*

It made Leda realize how much she felt at home here now, how the strangeness had worn off and become appreciation. But some of the questions were for her.

"Are you a journalist?" the father asked.

"She's a photographer, a chef, and she has three degrees," Ita answered for her.

"How long are you here, dear?" one of the women asked.

"If the children had it their way, forever," Ita said.

"You're pretty," the little girl said.

To this, Leda said, "Thank you," and Ita looked at her as though she was a sunset over the Serengeti.

December 18, 2007, Kibera—Ita

Ita loved almost every part of safari, but sometimes this— the drive to get started—was his favorite. He had the tours down to a science, a routine that gave him both the comfort and confidence needed to be a good guide.

After the boys left for school, Ita shepherded the group out of Kibera, shuffled them into a *matatu* and got them safely to the car-rental place where he hopped into the beige safari jeep that would take them the rest of way.

This part, with a full tank of gas and the road before him, was when he began to breathe deeply again and relax. Still, he must focus. He must be charming and knowledgeable, must establish a position of authority, dazzle them with information about Nairobi, Kenya, and their voyage ahead.

They would arrive at Amboseli Park by late afternoon, but for some reason, even after studying their maps, tourists never seemed to expect the land to open up so soon to the golden savannahs and Maasai children tending cattle in bright clothing under a blue sky.

It never failed to make Ita happy—the tourists' gasps and clicking cameras as each of them was forced to scoot aside their gritty mental pictures of his country to make room for the vistas of red coffee-berry bushes and the lushness of the Rift Valley.

His second favorite part was getting to know the travelers. It was a fun game, trying to fit their conversation puzzle pieces about their homes and lives with the encyclopedic facts he'd read about their countries' politics and statistics.

Sometimes his charges napped or read, sometimes they asked him endless questions about himself and the children, sometimes they talked only to each other and ignored him completely. No matter their behaviors, Ita liked to sit and drive and soak it all in, storing away the tidbits about small towns, towering cities, the phrases they used, the dynamics between fathers and children or sisters and sisters.

Just now, the Irish ladies snapped pictures of Maasai herdsmen, the father instructed his daughter coolly on the history of Maasai warriors, and the couple wielded phrases entirely new to Ita, like "holy moly" and "god blarnit."

But today was definitely different.

Today there was Leda.

The whole time while the Irish women said funny things in their funny accents, overpowering the conversation of the reserved father and daughter from London, and even the loud couple from a place called Houston in Texas, Ita let them be without interjecting his tour guide script.

Because all he cared to do was stare at Leda.

She seemed to be using the same method—sitting back and observing these strange creatures unnoticed. He could tell by her posture that she was listening, but she faced forward in her seat, eyes turned to the window, seeming to find the easy chatter of families and lovers even more unfamiliar than he.

Her stories about her home and childhood—they didn't tumble out of her like the two Irish women or countless travelers Ita had met. Leda's stories came terse and meager, as though she was more interested in *not* remembering than in telling. But yesterday, she had revealed much, and Ita pictured a life strung together of silence and solitude and a secret suspicion that her mother hated her. Of course, now she was a woman in her own right, who had built a life in a mountainous place called Topanga, and filled her mind with knowledge Ita esteemed. That she could smile at the stars over the slum and laugh as she bounced Walter on her lap meant that she was happy here. Certainly, she brought sunlight to all at the orphanage. That is why glimpsing her sadness made Ita want to wrap her in his arms and hold her there forever if it meant she would never be sad again.

Now he admired her long brown hair cascading in layers like eagle feathers. He knew if he stared too long she would meet his eyes, smile at him longingly and mean it, and that would send Ita back into a replay of yesterday, remembering the taste of her lips against his, how she felt and sounded as his fingers slipped inside her—memories that had kept Ita tossing awake half the night.

He turned his eyes back to the road.

"I'm glad you came," he said softly so only she could hear.

"Me, too."

He looked straight ahead, but he couldn't help himself from smiling as he felt her eyes stay on him.

December 18, 2007, Amboseli Park—Leda

Leda watched the lushness give way to the dry expanse of the reserve as the jeep pulled into the entrance to the park. She stayed in the vehicle with the crew while Ita went to pay the fees and fill out all the paperwork.

"Golly gee, my bum may not be the same after this trip," one of the Irish women, Esther, said to the other.

"Our bums haven't been the same in years, Esther m'dear. I think it quite smart we added the extra padding," her friend, Martha, replied with a wink. "Leda, on the other hand, we best find that gal a pillow, no?"

Leda laughed. It really had been a bumpy ride so far.

When Ita returned, his arms were stacked with boxed lunches.

"Hey, I could've helped," Leda said. She hopped out of the jeep.

"You are on vacation," he replied. "Your lunch, m'lady," he said and handed her the top box.

"Such a gentleman," Esther said, taking a lunch box next. "Should have brought the husband just for a lesson."

"Oh, Lordy, no, wouldn't do the lug a bit o' good," Martha said. "And then you might have missed the view." She pointed at Ita's backside as he strode away from them toward a picnic table.

Leda couldn't stifle a snigger.

Ita heard and turned. Puzzled, he smiled. "Oh, yes, the view," he said and motioned into the distance.

Majestic Mount Kilamanjaro towered before them.

The peak—covered in snow above a sea of clouds, above a plain of acacia trees—sucked every bit of air out of Leda's lungs as she stopped to stare. Ita stood beside her and looked, too. "One never tires of it," he whispered.

The blue sky, the expanse of clouds, the shadows of animals in the distance—all were stunningly beautiful, but nothing could compete with the vision of the mountain.

On the drive, Ita had told them how centuries of people worshipped the mountain as a god. At the time it had seemed quaint. Now it seemed like the only natural reaction a human being should have. Leda felt like bowing.

"And I never tire of seeing people's first sight of it," he said.

After a lunch of turkey sandwiches, potato chips and carrot sticks, everyone piled back into the vehicle, excited for their first real step into safari.

The second the jeep started down the red dirt path, Leda felt her cares vanish into the blue sky. Off to the left, in the not-so-far distance, a line of elephants moved gracefully across the horizon. Ita pointed but said nothing, letting the moment wash over them all. They were getting a late start, so there were no other buses in front of or behind them, and they had the endless expanse all to themselves.

Nothing could have prepared Leda for how it felt. In the modern world of Google satellite maps and travel blogs, there were few things that exceeded expectations or felt like something entirely new. Safari was one of those things.

"You should go up there," Ita said, pointing. The top of the jeep was open and the group stood on their seats, faces in the wind.

Esther caught Leda peeking. She held out her hand. "Sure, honey!" she shouted over the noise. "Come on up with us!"

Leda moved to the bench seat and stood up between Esther and Martha.

The mix of the wind, sun and mountain view took Leda's breath away. The peak reigned in the distance, dwarfing jaunty acacia trees and a pack of ten, eleven, twelve antelope, Leda counted. Wide swaths of golden grasses ran up against fields of lush wet green. Up ahead, water shimmered in the late-afternoon sun. As the wind stroked her hair, Leda scanned the land stretched wide like hope, like possibility, like nature's portrait of freedom.

From her new vantage point, she could see the path winding in front of and behind them. Martha gasped in her ear as they veered to the right. Ita slowed the jeep, and seven gaping tourists stared in amazement at a herd of zebras, striped fairy-tale animals clustered less than twenty feet away.

Once Ita sped back up, Leda, feeling tipsy, tilted her head back and gazed at the sky. It was as if she'd never seen the sky before. Perhaps she'd seen pieces of it in between the mountains or framed by backyards or skyscrapers. She'd seen it hanging out behind the trees or stretching its legs for a sunset. But out here—this was where the sky came to vacation, to show off, to retire and reflect on its legacy.

There was no sense shouting over the roar of the wind, so the travelers all enjoyed their own private magic show, Ita slowing the jeep when animals appeared, but never stopping.

Leda's whole soul sighed. And beamed. There was no place else she would rather be.

She ducked her head back inside the jeep and said, "Thank you."

"What?" he called back.

"*Thank you!*" she cried out. *Thank you for this, for everything, for so many other things I wish I could tell you.*

He couldn't turn from the wheel. But he reached his hand into the air behind his head. Leda took it.

She squeezed, feeling its warmth and strength, like passion and love on balanced scales. On impulse, Leda kissed it, lingering while she admired Ita's strong neck, the way the sunshine highlighted his cheekbones and jaw. Then she bolted back up between the two plump ladies. If she lingered any longer, she was afraid she would blurt out something ridiculous. Like *I love you.*

So she stood and let the wind caress her instead. Let the

wind whip her hair around her shoulders, let the golden dirt dust her face like glitter, let the sun sparkle in her eyes like fireworks.

She had one distinct thought, once, then twice, then over and over: *Why should I ever go home?*

CHAPTER 18

January 1, 2008, Topanga, CA—Leda

LEDA STARTS HER CAR, THE STRANGER-IN-A-strange-land feeling creeping back, as she goes through the motions of reversing then snaking along the hairpin mountain roads of Topanga Canyon. She tries to imagine what she will say to Estella to comfort her. *You've beaten it before,* she'll say, *you'll beat it again. You'll be okay,* she'll say. *You've got the best doctors, the means… You are so lucky, you don't even know.*

Her hands curl like a skeleton's on the steering wheel. She still hasn't heard from Ita. Any thought of him wrings her stomach like an ice-cold washcloth. She pictures him bleeding, moaning in pain and almost veers off a cliff. But she can't stop—she pictures the children cowering under flames, Ita's dead body on a pyre, until a wave of sickness brings a cold sweat to her brow. When she reaches the ocean, all she sees is Ita's face as the police dragged her away—swollen and pulpy like a trampled orchard plum.

Leda implores the sea, the sky above. *Please, please, please let him be okay.*

She stabs the button to lower her window, begging the

cold winter air to whip away her thoughts. He's a doctor, he can mend himself. Or maybe the doctors at the clinic can.

And he has the envelope I gave him. They will be okay.

It's ten hours later in Kibera. Nighttime. If he hasn't called, it's because he can't charge his phone, but he's okay. *Or he doesn't want to talk to you.*

Leda bites her lip.

Tears sting her eyes, blurring her vision of the highway. *In any case, I will tell Estella nothing.* Leda has to pull it together, push Ita from her mind somehow. There would be no point in telling her mother anything, anything that could be wielded against her later, to bribe her, hurt her.

As if she'll ask.

Leda sniffs and shakes her head as she flies down the road through the gray mist. With the holiday, there's less traffic than she's ever seen. The emptiness feels appropriate, but it means she will arrive all the quicker. She puts a hand on her queasy stomach.

She's been through cancer with her mother before, five years ago. It involved a lot of secrecy and awkward conversations and exhaustion on both their parts. Leda could never say whatever it was her mother wanted to hear, which she should have long ago realized was nothing.

Just before the bend up ahead, there's a glimpse of the house, towering over the sea, imposing palm trees adjacent to imposing glass. Then, immediately the house is blocked by the massive wall and gate.

Leda pulls up in front of the gate. She still has the opener, only because Estella isn't much of a greeter. The door swings open and there it is. The silent house of glass and sea.

No lights are on. Just the gray mist trying to get inside.

Leda pulls her car into the driveway and parks. When she tries the front door, it's locked. Taking a deep breath, trying to ignore her shaking hands, she knocks, lightly. She waits but when no answer comes she knows she's not meant to knock again.

She turns the key in the lock. Inside, the house is quiet, the hum of central air and nothing else.

"Mother?" she calls up the stairs.

"I'll be down in a moment." Estella code for *I am not ready to see you yet.*

Leda puts her key on the marble table and looks out the glass at the careful hedges, the empty yard, then back inside, down at the marble floor. But when she closes her eyes, all she sees is fire and smoke and screaming women and the shuddering bodies of children too scared to cry. She sees the red dust smeared across her bare stomach, Chege's hands smearing the color across her thighs like war paint. His breath hot and fast, the screams that seared her throat—

"Hello," Estella says.

Snapped back, she answers, "Hello."

Leda looks down as Estella descends the stairs and passes her in the foyer, mimicking her mother's aversion to eye contact. Leda's not surprised to see Estella's hair freshly dyed red, her skin powdered, her eyebrows drawn. As she trails her mother's silk robe to the kitchen, she keeps the flashbacks at bay by cataloguing the house floating past. Velvet drapery in beige, vases with swirling Asian designs she traced with her fingers as a child, wallpaper embedded with gold thread, furniture oiled a dark cherry.

There's not a single piece of evidence of Leda's childhood.

No framed photos, no handmade art projects. No trace of anything she ever chose, her preferences, her existence.

"So, there's not a lot more to say, I'm afraid." Estella sighs and sags into a chair at one end of the long polished table. Leda notices how she winces, how her fingers grip the edge of the wood.

"What do the doctors say?"

"I told you. It's back. I always figured it was coming back."

"Okay. So then what's the plan? The doctors', I mean."

"No plan." This time Estella's eyes nearly catch Leda's. But, instead, they come to rest on her jaw, on her scar. "Just time to pay the piper."

Leda sighs, in reflex, but the air hiccups halfway. She hadn't really considered her mother dying. Not really. Not at all. She feels dizzy. "Wait. What are you talking about?"

"One kidney, Leda," she snaps. "If it's shot, there's not much else they can do. Surgery is pretty much it for renal cancer. You remember. Radiation, targeted therapy—this time it would just be to prolong or palliate." Estella looks exhausted from the effort.

"Then can't you get a new kidney? A transplant?"

"Not if the cancer has spread."

"Has it?"

"We don't know yet. That's why I told you you didn't need to come over here."

The words sizzle like acid on Leda's face, spit with such force she flinches.

"Okay, I'll go."

Estella sighs. She puts both hands on the table, stares at them.

Leda doesn't move. She's not sure what to do. But there it is—the sinking, itchy feeling her mother's presence inevitably arouses, turning Leda back into a timid, scurrying child. Is she silently willing her to leave?

"The kidney donor list doesn't cater to old ladies with cancer. Even rich ones, apparently. My doctor asked if I had any loved ones."

Leda wonders briefly if she will throw up. Everything about the moment makes her skin prickle just like it does before she vomits. *Loved ones.* What an ironic turn of phrase.

"Well, I suppose I have my answer," Estella bites out. "Not that I asked, mind you."

"No, you didn't. Maybe give me a minute to—"

"Take all the time you need." Estella jumps to her feet. Too fast, though, and she wobbles. The color drains from her face and Leda steps forward, her arms open. Estella puts out both hands to prevent her daughter from coming closer. "Well, maybe not that much time."

"That's not funny," Leda says.

Estella shakes her head. "No," she says as she trudges past Leda out through the kitchen archway. "It's not."

Alone in the kitchen, it's Leda's turn to slump into a chair, grip the table's edge and feel herself tremble.

Time to pay the piper.

She looks around the kitchen, remembering how Estella had looked at her scar when she'd said it. Could her mother regret anything? In Leda's opinion, Estella wasn't cruel by intention, more by complete indifference. Would it be worse or better if her mother had done all those horrible things with intent?

Leda looks to the stove. They never spend much time in the kitchen, neither she nor Estella, because it's inevitable that eyes will drift to stare. To remember.

She drops her head into her hands, but it's too late. The

memory always comes the same way, floating on the sound of a little girl humming "Somewhere Over the Rainbow." She's eight years old, barely the height of the counter. Estella's been away for days, having left with a man. Leda's hungry, boiling water for macaroni and cheese. One minute she's singing, then as she reaches for the handle on the pot, tipping its contents, her song turns to screaming....

In the empty kitchen, Leda strokes the scar on her cheek, turns her head away from the stove.

She was unconscious by the time her mother returned, later that day. They sped to the hospital in an ambulance, Estella whispering in her ear. Leda told the social worker what her mother had coached her to say: her mother was home when it happened, with a migraine, sleeping upstairs. And Leda hadn't screamed, hadn't wanted to wake her.

But she had screamed.

Leda looks at her hands on the table.

For a long time, she's been able to see the memory through adult eyes, see Estella for what she is.

It isn't the only memory, maybe not even the worst. There was the day Estella passed out before noon and dropped her glass of vodka, and Leda ran right through the shattered glass in bare feet only to get smacked when her mother saw the blood on the hardwood floor. There was the time Estella locked her in her room when one of her boyfriends had come over, forgetting about her for two days, two whole days without food or water. There were the nights Estella shut herself in her own room before Leda got home from school, leaving her to fend for herself—so many instances it was hard to count them.

Looking around the house, listening to the echoing memories, Leda can't help but ask herself, Is this the kind of mother you give a kidney to?

CHAPTER 19

December 18, 2007, Amboseli Community Campsite—Leda

SAFARI WAS MOTHER EARTH'S BEST PHOTO shoot, it was seeing her in her prime. Their first game drive coming to an end, Leda marveled at acacia trees basking in the sunset, branches waving to the sky, thanking it for warming their tops as the evening cooled off.

From their perch in the jeep, Leda and the group watched all kinds of animals following the trees' lead—enjoying the end of the day, tucking in for the night. They passed hippos slathering themselves in a mud pond like gossiping women at a Roman spa. Esther belly laughed at the sun dipping behind a family of giraffes, babies nuzzling their parents' knobby knees. The sweeping gold plains waltzed with the blazing sky. Birds swooped and surfed the wind. Zebras lollygagged like teenagers at the mall.

As the travelers gazed in wonder, Ita drove them, zipping along the red earth road back to camp, racing against the setting sun.

Ita built them a campfire before he went off to prepare dinner. Leda settled comfortably into the chair he'd unfolded for her in a prime spot with the best view of the mountain. Again, he refused to let her help with the meal preparation. She would have protested more, except that she was wiped out from the drive, and he seemed so happy to pamper her. She figured they'd have more sandwiches from that big, lit wooden building over past the showers.

Other groups could be heard merrymaking nearby. Campfires dotted the grassy hill they occupied. But no amount of human flame could blot out the stars that twinkled above them. It was like viewing a sea of diamonds from beneath the surface. Leda floated happily on the vision.

As Esther and Martha chattered sleepily to each other, the father/daughter pair sipped hot tea, and the couple discussed the restrooms, Leda wrapped herself up tight in the red Maasai blanket Ita had given her and imagined it smelled like him, the same earthy scent of the blanket on her metal table/bed at the orphanage.

"How many hippos would you say that was, Sarah?" the father asked his daughter.

"A thousand?" she replied and everybody laughed.

"But it did seem like that many, didn't it?" Esther said. "And those hyenas. Wretched little creatures, lying about in their own mess, cackling the day away. They remind me of my husband."

"And those zebras," Martha broke in. "Like a Missoni fashion show…" Around and around they went, discussing their impressions of the day's sights, until Sarah dozed off and her father saved her mug from spilling out of her lax hand just in time.

Leda was feeling as though she might doze off herself when Ita reappeared. He carried an enormous tray of plates piled with steaming food.

"Would you look at that spread!" Esther said, licking her lips and getting up to help Ita serve the food.

Leda took her plate, surprised at the gourmet meal that was to replace her expectation of sandwiches. Each plate held a cup of soup, pan-fried chicken and vegetables, and mashed potatoes on the side.

Esther was right—this was luxury camping. Everyone dug in with a chorus of "oohs" and "aahs." Leda slurped up some heavenly soup—homemade celery and onion, creamy and buttery.

When she opened her eyes, she saw Ita watching her expectantly.

"Wait a minute," she said. "Did you cook all this?"

Ita grinned and nodded, then he turned and headed back toward the kitchen, leaving her stunned.

"A gourmet chef to boot," Martha cooed. "I do believe I'm in love."

When Leda's spoon splashed down in her soup, Martha looked over and caught her blushing. "Too bad he's taken," she said with a wink.

Ita returned with beverages. "Anybody need anything else?" he asked. He handed out the sodas, then put his hands over the fire to fight the evening's dipping temperature.

"Oh, no, dear," Esther said. "Lordy no. Look at all this grub. You just sit your skinny arse down, it must be foundered." She shivered, so Leda guessed she meant Ita's skinny arse must be cold.

Martha pointed at Sarah fast asleep in the chair next to Leda. "Reckon you can take her seat. Tuckered out, that one."

Sarah's father took the hint and scooped his daughter from the chair into his lap.

Ita smiled and sat down shyly next to Leda. They weren't fooling anybody.

Martha piped up. "There is one more thing we need, dearie. You can tell us a story. A story fit for a campfire."

"Like a fairy tale?" Ita asked.

Esther swallowed a loud gulp of soda and smiled. "You must know plenty, what with the lads you tuck in every night."

Ita nodded. "You want to know how elephants came to be?"

"Yes!" Leda said, too loudly.

Ita cleared his throat. "One day," he began, "a poor man heard of Ivonya-Ngia, which means 'The one who feeds the poor.'"

Leda watched his face as he spoke, envisioning the boys at the orphanage enchanted by his voice.

"He set out to find him, and did, discovering a land of green pasture that held a million cattle. Ivonya-Ngia offered the poor man one hundred cows."

Leda imagined Ntimi trying to picture a hundred cows, let alone a million.

"'I want no charity,'" Ita said in a booming voice, imitating the poor man's refusal of the cows. "'I want the secret of how to become rich.'" He looked around the circle as he spoke and began to mime the story. "Ivonya-Ngia answered by taking out an ointment. He told the poor man, 'Rub this on your wife's upper teeth. When they grow, sell them.' The husband persuaded his wife to comply. Her canine teeth grew into tusks as long as his arm. He pulled the teeth and sold them and they had lots of money. But—" Ita paused for drama "—the next time his wife's teeth grew, she would not let her husband extract them. She gained weight, her skin grew thick and gray. One day she left for the forest, where she gave birth to their son, who was also an elephant. The husband found her in the forest, but she would not come back to him. She was happy, she said, being an elephant."

Be careful what you wish for, Leda thought. Or was it *money isn't everything?*

"Was that a Kikuyu story?" Sarah's father, Tom, was intrigued. "It sounds like a story I read."

"It's from the Kamba," Ita replied. "They are a similar tribe to Kikuyu. Neighbors. They share many stories and religious similarities." He looked into the fire as he spoke.

"Are you Kikuyu, Ita?" Tom asked, craning forward over his sleeping child. "I've been following the elections. The sitting president, Kibaki, is Kikuyu. Do you think Kibera residents care more about politics or tribe? Would a Kikuyu consider themselves Kikuyu first? Or from Kibera?"

Ita squirmed in his seat, all eyes on him, but differently than a moment before, when he was their handsome storyteller.

"I am as Kikuyu as I am Christian," Ita said softly as he stood to tend the fire, obviously wanting to be done with the conversation.

Tom laughed. "Touché."

While the rest of the group pondered Ita's statement, Tom kept at it. "You mean tribal affiliation is complicated, just like religious identity is…everywhere."

Ita sat back down, straight backed. "I meant that tribal identity is woven into a person's soul from birth, the same way a child is exposed to religion—through holidays, rituals and formative memories. It is not something you think about until it is threatened or viewed by an outsider."

Ita didn't look directly at Tom, but his audience was clear what he meant. Leda was proud of him. And impressed.

"Indeed." Tom looked at Ita appreciatively, too. "Well, I would love to hear more folklore. Anyone else?"

"If Ita wants to indulge us, yes, please," Esther said.

Leda looked at Tom and the Irish ladies, smiling in the glow, and decided they weren't very skilled at social cues. Ita sighed, almost imperceptibly, but Leda felt it. As if suddenly remembering who was footing the bill, he resumed the role of obliging guide.

"Kikuyu means fig tree, fertility," he said, and Esther and Martha poked each other, watching Ita's handsome face in the firelight. "Kikuyus call God *Ngai,* The Apportioner, because God gave gifts to all the nations of the earth. Kikuyus received the skill of agriculture. God controls everything, including the rain and the thunder, which he uses to punish evildoers." Ita looked to the sky ominously.

He's a natural, Leda thought.

"Every person has a spirit, *ngoma,*" he continued, gazing around the circle, "which after death becomes a ghost. The *ngoma* of a murdered man will hunt his murderer until he confesses, preferring prison to the relentless ghost."

The chill in the air made a ghost story all the more fitting for their campfire. Esther made a *wooooo* sound in Martha's ear, making her jump.

Ita lowered his voice another notch. "Burial rituals must be observed, because spirits are to be feared. They live in the trees, and you must feed them—"

Leda recalled piles of food she'd seen one day in Kibera. Too tidy to be scraps. *Offerings,* Ita had said.

"—or else Ngai will punish you with lightning. But—" He broke off. His gaze landed on Leda. "Kikuyus believe that a man's character is decided by God. He cannot help what he is. And his life—rewards or punishments—is predestined."

Leda looked back into Ita's eyes, hypnotized by the shadows dancing over his face. How handsome he looked, bathed in the fire glow. But haunted. Leda could sense the ghosts that swirled around him, followed him. She shivered and wrapped her arms tighter around herself to listen to his next tale about destiny.

Eventually there were no more requests from the sleepy audience. The group splintered off for bed, in pairs, to their tents. Leda had her own tent, as did Ita, far off somewhere, apart from the group's circle.

Ita made the rounds, making sure everyone was comfortable, had everything they needed, while Leda slunk nervously off to her tent.

She stepped in and sat down, breathlessly debating what to do. Undress? She'd worn matching lace panties and bra under her safari clothes all day, but, come on, it was freezing. Her skin prickled with gooseflesh as she deliberated. All day, she'd been waiting, all night, waiting to touch him, kiss him, feel those hands run over her skin again.

Finally, Ita's footsteps stopped outside her tent. "Everything okay? Anything you need?" he asked loudly.

Leda smiled. She poked her head out, and he looked down at her.

"Later," he whispered. He looked left and right, before placing a warm, soft kiss on her forehead. "Soon."

She zipped up in her tent and endured the longest wait of her life, all thirty minutes of it. Nervousness unfolded in her stomach like tulips shivering in a breeze. Ita was so tender, it disarmed her. The electricity she felt around him raised every hair on her body, but it was about to set her on fire. Whoever first said the thing about the butterflies, Leda decided, they weren't a genius. They were stating the obvious.

"Leda," a whisper came in the night.

She jolted in her tent, trying not to pant. She heard Ita's shuffling feet on the ground just outside. With trembling fingers, she unzipped a tiny gap in the entrance to the tent, granting herself a breathtaking view of the moon and Mount Kilamanjaro. But even those were dwarfed by Ita's smile.

"May I come in?" he whispered, hunched over in the dark, cold night like a naughty teenager sneaking out.

She nodded eagerly. As he slipped in past her, she zipped up the tent against the last sliver of the sea of stars.

She scooted on her knees to meet him in the middle of the tent. Gently, he pressed their foreheads together so their smiles could look themselves in the mirror. It was such an innocent gesture, it warmed Leda's skin in the cold air.

He put a hand to the small of her back and pulled her in. His lips found hers and she dove into the softness. His hands caressed her back and flank, and hers went exploring, too. They kissed, grasping and breathing and stroking, until the desire built up between them like an underground spring.

Leda untangled herself. She lay down, stretched out on the sleeping bag, and Ita snuggled in beside her. He didn't jump on her hungrily as she expected him to. Or as she wanted him to. He traced his fingers over her face and brushed back the baby hairs from her temples.

"It is as if you came from the stars," he said.

But she didn't have a chance to respond, because he kissed her, first her eyelids, then her cheeks, her earlobes, her neck— in a slow procession that made her arch and squirm and moan.

He took his sweet time with her body, his hands taking laps like a runner pacing himself around the track. Off came her shirt, so he could kiss her collarbone, tenderly kiss her healing henna marks. For a moment, he held her hand to his cheek.

Next, he kissed her sternum, then just above and just below her belly button. After he tugged off her pants, he kissed each of her hips and her sides and the tops of her knees.

Then he stopped, looking up, pausing to catch his breath, or else for permission. Whichever it was, Leda nodded. *Yes. Please.*

He pulled down her panties and nuzzled his nose in the un-covered triangle of hair, the most endearing gesture. What he did after that, however, was hardly so innocent. He stripped off his own clothes, giving Leda a view of muscle and girth that made her moan, then he dove down on her, his mouth a magical combination of softness and pressure—urgency mingling with relish.

Leda lay splayed like an anemone and Ita washed over her like the sea. She let herself be nourished, by his touch, by his tongue, by the way he looked at her as if she really was a shooting star falling from the night sky.

And then, after he retraced his path of kisses from her hips to her neck, he kissed her, achingly hard, as he readied him-self, then thrust inside her in one deep swoop from tip to base.

Leda cried out beneath his lips. She arched into him, her back like the crescent moon, then curled up her hips, forcing him in even deeper, allowing it, needing it, so thick and so hard her body squealed against the fullness, but begged for it.

Ita groaned. He plunged into her, harder, faster. He grabbed both her hips, pulling her to him. When he reached beneath her, gripping her ass, Leda bit down on her fingers to keep from crying out.

Suddenly, smoothly, he rolled her, pulling Leda on top. With her breasts in his hands, he squeezed shut his eyes and let her ride until she came. The first orgasm was a torrential surprise, the second a cresting wave, the third a rocking hurricane, whereupon she collapsed into his scent and skin, consumed by pleasure. Once she'd exhausted herself, Ita rolled her over again, flipped himself on top.

His eyes searched for hers. Even in the near darkness, she could see his gaze, loving, hoping.

This time as Ita entered her, it was slow as honey drizzling into tea. He kept his eyes locked on hers, in and out, in and out, until Leda felt tears well in her eyes. He put his hand to her cheek, on the side of her scar. First he wiped the tear with his thumb, then he caressed the wizened skin at her jaw, as if he could smooth it away—the memory, the pain, the hurt. By the time he leaned forward to kiss her, by the time his lips closed over hers, they were both coming like the rumble of a crumbling dam, wrapping their arms tight around each other once the gushing broke through and overtook them both.

Ita lay with her for a long, long time, staring into the dark. Playfully, they whispered little dreams back and forth, each starting with the magical phrase *we could*.

"We could take the boys on safari," Leda said, picturing them piled up in the jeep, pointing out elephants. "Or we could go other places in Africa. The pyramids. Egypt. The Nile."

"We could visit your home," he said.

She sucked in a breath. It was the sound of the cartoon dream bubble above them threatening to pop. "We could."

She tried to imagine Ita in Topanga. It wasn't that hard, actually. She saw him scratching Amadeus behind the ears, looking through her bookshelves, lying beside her like he was now. Maybe he was what had been missing from her home. He would fill the airy rooms with coziness, warmth, laughter. Happiness.

He kissed her earlobe, ran his hand along the curve of her hip. "It is difficult to imagine giving this up now that I have tasted it."

Leda sighed. *You took the words right out of my mouth.*

CHAPTER 20

January 1, 2008, Kibera—Ita

IT'S NEARLY MIDNIGHT WHEN ITA LEAVES THE boys' room, letting the sheet fall, wishing they had built a door along with the bunk beds. Slinging the rifle over his shoulder bangs the stitches he gave himself and he winces as he makes his way to Kioni's post near the orphanage door.

Outside, close, a baby's been crying for hours, since before the sun dove into darkness. The sound is broken periodically by other screams, louder, higher-pitched—mothers and children too old to be crying like that.

Ita listens, feeling every muscle in his body pulled taut as though jerked by a puppet master. His mind races, considering the crying anew, deciding if there is a threat.

Now Ita knows the stories. Earlier this evening, he and Kioni snuck into his office to listen to the radio. The things they heard—women raped in front of their husbands, children trampled and killed, men with panga wounds to their skulls, left to bleed to death in the street—he and Kioni could only stare at each other in disbelief. Next came the dawning understanding that they would be barricaded in the orphanage, under siege for who knew how long. The announcer's voice sounded scared as he rushed on. Live TV coverage suspended. Riots everywhere, not just in Kibera, but even in the tree-lined streets of Nairobi. Thousands fled, thousands more hiding—no one to clear the bodies. Raila's supporters, Luo protesters, now feeling the full vengeance of Kikuyu.

"They asleep?" Kioni turns, sees Ita standing there, frozen.

"Or willing to pretend," he says.

"They are good boys," she says as he sits down stiffly beside her.

Each point of contact sends pain shooting through his nerves. He can feel Kioni watching him, noting his wounds but saying nothing.

They took turns that day tending the children. Kioni moved her things to the boys' room and slept some. Then she served the boys lunch while Ita chased sleep in his stuffy room. It was a futile endeavor. Every time he closed his eyes, buried memories of Kioni and Chege mixed with more recent nightmares until he became paranoid that something bad was about to happen with Kioni on guard.

Like a gullet full of lead, Ita still feels the conditioned urge to protect her. But her silence fills him with dread, not to mention a running tally of his faults.

Now that the boys are in bed, the reviled feeling comes stronger, as much as he tries to shake it—he should feel grateful for her help, not this pinching desire for her to leave.

Side by side, they sit and listen to the horror movie playing just outside. Ita keeps the rifle in his lap, his fingers already stiff from clenching the metal. His whole body is tense, ready to fight the world and knowing that eventually he will have to.

"The boys, they talk about a white woman. Leda."

Ita's heart nearly stops at the sound of Leda's name on Kioni's lips.

"They think she is coming to save them."

Ita opens his mouth, but finds no words to respond. Even though both women sat here in this very spot, destined to share the same reservoir of regret in his heart, Kioni and Leda in his mind are like two continents crashing in the ocean.

"Her things are here. They showed me. Is she coming back?"

Kioni's words lance his heart, especially the boys' impossible fantasy that Leda will return.

"Ita?"

He still can't bring himself to answer.

"Well, they are right to worry," Kioni says. "There is not nearly enough food. Supplies. Water. Do you have money to last—"

"Very little." He'd paid most of the safari money toward bills when they came back through Nairobi. And on Christmas presents.

"Ita, what happened here? To her? To you?"

He clenches his teeth, says finally: "She's gone. Leda left the night of…of the riots."

"As she should have. This is no place for a *mzungu*."

"Stop. Please. Just—" Ita's teeth feel as if they will crumble into his jaw.

"Leave? Do you want me to go?"

Yes. "No, you cannot go back out there. You have to stay."

Silence.

Silence and screams in the night.

"If she isn't coming back, maybe we should sell her things."

"No!" The volume of Ita's voice startles them both. He frowns—doesn't Kioni think he would have considered that?

Even if it would kill him emotionally, he would do it for the children. "It's impossible in Kibera now. And unsafe." So many things were impossible now. Ita sighs. "Please," he says softly, "please do not speak to me of her again."

Kioni is studying him, her eyes boring into his skin. "Ita, it's not your fault she left."

A bitter snort escapes him. "I could have protected her. It *was* my fault she got hurt."

The statement hovers in the air between them, accusing and remembering, growing like a monster under a full moon. Until they have to look at each other, hear the echo of his words dripping with regret, swollen with the sorrow that belongs to the memory that binds them, the one that drove them apart.

"Oh, Ita," Kioni says. She lays a hand gently on his shoulder.

He flinches as if she struck him.

"Ita!" The front door rattles like a demon banging from the underworld. Kioni and Ita jump to their feet, terror lighting their faces on fire. Ita aims the rifle at the door. Kioni backs away.

"Ita," the voice comes again. "Let me in!"

Ita and Kioni look at each other, each registering the voice at the same time. Chege.

Ita hesitates, keeps the rifle where it is, jabbing the air. Kioni looks at him strangely, back and forth between him and the door, hearing the frantic shuffle of Chege's feet, his desperate banging.

"Ita," she hisses. But she doesn't know. She doesn't understand.

"Shhh," he says. But the knocking only intensifies. Chege

begins hollering nonsense, his words spraying the orphanage like shattering glass.

Ita lowers the rifle. He will tell him to go away. Forever. To go away forever or he will kill him. He undoes the lock, slides open the rusted metal and meets Chege face-to-face.

"Go away," he says through closed teeth.

Chege stares, his eyes like a wild animal in flight. He shifts back and forth on his feet, looks behind him worriedly, back at Ita, then back into the street. His clothes are torn and filthy. His right eye is engorged with blood, his nose swollen monstrously where Ita punched him. He's barefoot, with more bloody cuts on his arms and legs. In one hand dangles his machete. "Please, they coming. I have to come in. I have to tell you. You don't understand. Ita—"

Chege tries to worm his way in, then glimpses Kioni in the shadows. His desperation flips to confusion and he stares at her as if she's a ghost fluttering down from the sky.

She, too, is stunned, but her lips curl in disgust at his appearance. "Chege. Yes, it's me."

While they stare at each other, Ita peers into the darkness behind Chege, realizing in an instant what might be following him. Ita remembers the police that dragged Leda away, the look on their faces that said they'd been given free reign to murder at will in the name of the law, how lucky he was to escape that fate at their hands.

Lost in the memory, Ita is caught off guard as Chege rushes the gate, knocking him off balance and squeezing his way inside.

"Ita," he says and stops. "Ita," he begins again and stops. It's as if he's short-circuiting. He drops his machete to the ground with a clatter, pulls at his dreads, rubs his eyes, scratches at his shoulders.

He is like a dog gone rabid. Ita feels ready to shoot him if he bites.

But then Chege does something wholly unexpected. He slumps to the ground, between Ita and Kioni. He reaches out and grasps both of their legs at once, with such force that they slam together. Chege starts to sob uncontrollably.

Ita and Kioni find themselves face-to-face, inches apart and quivering with Chege's cries. And Ita knows if anyone could understand his twin hatred and loyalty to Chege, it is Kioni. If anyone has reason to hate or love him as much as Ita, it is she.

But where does loyalty end?

Chege staggers to his feet, thrusting them apart. Kioni and Ita stumble backward. Chege is up, weaving like a boxer about to go back down.

"Oh," he says, and starts to moan. He looks back and forth between Ita and Kioni. Then he takes his head in his hands and swings back and forth. "Oh, oh, ohh. I'm sorry. Ita. Brother."

Kioni stares.

Ita's heart goes cold.

"I'm sorry," Chege whispers, his eyes closed.

Ita looks away, disgusted. But Kioni's eyes fill with tears. Her brown eyes, all grown up, force Ita to remember. Remember when things were different. Remember when they were a family.

November 29, 1991, Kibera—Ita

"Get closer!" Chege barks, pushing Ita and Kioni deeper into the scavenged crate, so his head is the only one that sticks out in the storm. Ita can feel Kioni shivering, so he wraps his cold arms tight around her, as if he can hug warmth into her by sheer force of will.

Chege spends equal time on the lookout for thieves and gazing upon Ita and Kioni as if they are a riddle he is trying to solve.

The smell is even more awful than usual, and Ita knows it is sewage that runs into the crate. They're downhill from the biggest latrine in the ward, and Ita now sees why this area was clear to set up camp.

"We should move," Ita says between chattering teeth. "To a hill." It isn't that cold, and he wonders briefly if he has a fever. He presses his forehead against Kioni's cheek to see if he can feel a temperature difference. Trying to still both their shivering, he watches the brown liquid seep over his sandals.

Chege frowns and Ita knows he realizes the error of their position, too. But since Chege always acts as leader, he wants to be the one to decide.

Kioni starts to weep. Silently, but Ita can feel it eclipse her shivering.

They sit like this for some time before Chege starts to sing. It is a folk song, but Chege always sings it like a nursery rhyme.

Hakuna matata, Kenya nchi nzuri, nchi ya maajabu, nchi ya kupendeza, hakuna matata…

The lyrics would be funny enough in their situation—*no worries, Kenya is beautiful and peaceful, there is no cause for worries*—but then Chege would always break off into his own lyrics, whatever fit. This time, *shit running between our toes and Kioni shivering like a wet cat.*

For once, however, Kioni doesn't smile at Chege's off-key singing. She lifts her chin off Ita's arm and stares at Chege, dead-on.

"I can do it. That girl Maryham, she told me how. She made it sound nice. A meal first and a dry room. I can help us—"

Chege cuts her off with a grunt and a wave of his fist. Then his fist becomes a pointed finger and he angles it straight at her. "Listen to me, little sister. You will never do those things."

"I can change all of this," she says in a firm voice that falters with the dawning realization that she is defying him. But she finishes by sweeping her arm over them—their ragged clothes and the filthy ground.

Chege leans into their makeshift shelter, close enough that Ita can feel his breath hot on his arm. "But you will kill us all with your shame."

Ita looks up, surprised. They do twenty things a day to be ashamed of—stealing, begging, dodging police. Ita knows Chege sniffs glue, too, although he tries to hide that from them.

Watching Chege take heaving breaths, Ita thinks he is thinking the same thing, his faraway look watching a movie of the bad things he's done.

"We are a family," Chege says. "Hustling, stealing—these things you will pay back when you get out of Kibera, go to school and work. But you, Kioni, your body, your soul, we cannot get back. And Ita's heart would turn black along with yours. It would be better to die right now, in a river of shit, than to send you to hell for us. You understand?"

Kioni nods with a whimper and burrows her chin into Ita's arm for comfort. When Chege turns to him, Ita nods, too. Then he finds Kioni's big brown eyes carrying the weight of the world like a sack of coal with no way to burn it.

January 2, 2008, Kibera—Ita

"Chege, it's okay. Come here." Kioni opens her arms to him, but they stick out like bare branches. Chege paces just outside her reach.

"They're coming. They're coming for me." He crouches down on his haunches and rocks himself.

Ita can't move. It's all he can do to stay upright in the waves of feeling crashing over him. His blood still boils, but it isn't as simple as fury. He loathes Chege, he loves him, he yearns to see him beg, cry, grovel…so that what? He can forgive him? How could he ever forgive him?

Ita looks to the door, up to the night sky. When the police come, can he really turn Chege in? Let them lock him away? Isn't that everything Chege deserves and more?

Chege looks up from the ground. "Ita. Listen to me—"

"No!" Ita shouts, finally finding his voice. "You listen. Always, I have acted like I owe you my life. But you—you ruined my life." He points at Kioni. "You ruined all of us. Kioni. And Leda—" He looks away before Chege can see the tears welling.

It's then that he hears his name whispered in the distance. He turns and Michael's head hangs out of the boys' room.

"Go back inside!" Ita shouts. What is he thinking, letting Chege in here like this? He has to leave.

Ita turns back to Chege, heaped in the dirt. *This is where loyalty ends.*

"Chege, you owe me no confession. I saw what you did to her—"

Kioni's head jerks up.

"We are done," Ita says, nailing the coffin. "Anything I owed you is paid."

Like God echoing Ita's words, whispers ripple through the night. A legion of boots shuffles in the dirt outside, surrounding the orphanage.

Kioni's wide eyes register the foreboding sounds.

But Chege has eyes only for Ita. A look oozes down his face like acid melting iron. A noise utters from his throat—a whimper of pain.

"Go," Ita says.

Chege flinches. His moist eyes dig deeper into Ita's, but not to plead. He is stone crumbling to dust. The wildfire in Chege's eyes goes out, his twitching ceases, his limbs hang limp at his sides.

When he finally nods, slowly, Ita feels a twinge in his stomach. Followed by a chill that whips through him like the premonition of a storm.

Then Chege's up, springing for the gate. He slides it wide open.

His sudden appearance catches the police by surprise. Four officers gape as he charges past the muzzles of their guns.

There is a second where everything slows to the speed of honey and Ita watches with his heart rising into his throat. He sees Chege, the eleven-year-old boy slicing his arm with the machete, smearing his face with his own blood.

The officers raise their rifles as Chege fumbles with his belt.

Ita hears the songs Chege sang, his laugh in the night, teasing him, pushing him to study.

When Chege reaches the dirt road, he thrusts his arms out to either side, Christ on the cross, lit up in the red dust by distant fire.

In his right hand, glinting in the moonlight, is a gun.

Ita squeezes shut his eyes. He hears himself and Chege

playing kickball in the alley, Chege making jokes to pretend they aren't starving.

One shot.

Chege fires one shot into the night air, inciting the officers to fire at will. They gun him down like a sack of flour, like a paper target.

So many bullets mow Chege's back that he flails in the air, suspended like wet, heavy laundry pinned out to dry. But when the shots cease, Chege's body drops to the dirt.

And Kioni does the same, falling atop Ita's feet, dissolving into the cloud of fiery dust that rises around them both. She clamps her hands over her mouth, biting down on her screaming heart.

CHAPTER 21

December 24, 2007, Kibera—Leda

LEDA AND ITA RETURNED HOME TO THE orphanage like two birds swooping in to nest. The taxi dropped them off at the edge of Kibera, and they walked back laden with packages.

It was Christmas Eve, and Leda wouldn't want to be anywhere else in the world. She couldn't wait to see the kids.

It had taken forever in Nairobi—wrapping up the safari, making sure all the tourists got off on their way safely. Then Ita had had stops to make—paying bills with practically all the money he'd just made on safari, further solidifying Leda's planned Christmas gift to him and the boys.

When Ita knocked on the gate, Michael tugged it open not a second later, and the seven boys Leda had been missing so much swarmed around them like they were an ice cream truck.

"Krismasi Njema! Heri ya krismas, Leda!" they chirped like baby birds at the return of their mother.

"Merry Christmas!" Leda shouted back, kissing their dusty heads and cheeks. "Oh, we missed you!"

The children asked what they'd brought them, eyeing all the packages. Ita spread his arms wide and told a story so animated even Leda could follow the Swahili: how all their presents got eaten by hippos, that he tried to fight them off, but it was Leda who banged a hippo on the head (an image that made them grab their bellies with laughter). Then an ostrich came along that was *this* big and… Leda laughed along with the kids, about the flamingos and the zebra and the monkey that stole the rest of their Christmas presents.

Watching Ita tweak their cheeks and tug on their ears, Leda was struck by how much he loved them. And vice versa. Each boy strained forward until Ita's eyes focused on him individually, then they shyly murmured *karibu* and *nakutamani. Welcome home. I missed you.* Even Jomo hovered, his eyes down, but his heart open.

Something about the scene made Leda sad, though. When she was little, she'd always secretly yearned for a Norman Rockwell Christmas—one she'd never had. She'd collected the Realtor Christmas cards that were sent to their house every year. Here she was, past thirty and in Africa, and watching Ita with the orphans was the closest she'd ever come.

"Okay, little brothers, okay," Ita said, laughing heartily. "We need to eat before church. *Msaada* Mary?" *Did you help Mary prepare?*

Leda tried to shop for the boys in Nairobi, but Ita had protested that he already had clothes for them—what children got for Christmas in Kenya. He'd flat-out refused her plan to buy toys. Leda respected him for it, but couldn't help feeling a little judged and reprimanded.

She consoled herself that she'd loaded up on as much Maasai jewelry, candy, nuts and seeds for them as she could while on safari. But now, looking around the orphanage, all Leda could see were the things they *really* needed—paper and pencils, medical supplies, cooking utensils, books, blankets. Which made her feel all the better about her plan, which would include all those things, for starters.

Ita took Leda by the hand, as the boys dispersed to clean up, and pulled her into his arms. They stood nestled against each other, united, absorbing the excitement of the boys' chattering as they walked off.

When Mary stepped from the shadows and saw their embrace, Leda thought she detected a frown, but the older woman beamed as she got closer.

Ita and Mary conversed in Swahili in an ebullient tone, far too rapid for Leda to follow, but she imagined that Ita, with his hand gestures and smile, was regaling Mary with tales of their safari.

"Yes, it was magical! Truly," Leda chimed in.

They both stopped mid-sentence and turned to her in confusion.

"What?" Leda asked lightly.

"We were talking about the elections," Ita said. "Sorry. The election is in three days. At dawn. I'm taking Mary to the polls with her friends. They are very excited." He smiled at Mary, then turned to watch two of the orphans scampering in the courtyard. "Mary is Luo. She thinks Raila is what he claims—hope for her, and—" Ita nodded at the boys "—for them."

Mary left for Grace's house in a different part of Kibera. They would all meet later at church. That gave Leda and Ita a few precious hours alone with the boys, eating the meal Mary left for them and drinking steaming hot tea while telling safari stories. The boys must have heard the same tales from Ita a dozen times, but still they listened, rapt. It was probably very different, Leda realized, to hear *her* rendition of the baboons and the baby elephants and the hippos. Leda told them she had a surprise for them on Christmas. Intrigued, they swam around her like a school of nibbling fish. Leda looked up and caught Ita watching her with the same warm look she'd given him earlier as he greeted the boys.

Before long, it was time for church. Ita lined the boys up near the front door. Leda's heart sang, seeing the little angels arranging themselves by height, Michael taking his guard post at the back of the line.

Leda slipped off to change into the dress she'd chosen for church—an intentionally long one that brushed the dirt. A matching navy shawl added even more modesty. But when she came outside, the boys hooted and clapped in appreciation, as if she'd donned a sequined gown. Leda played the part, catwalking down the line, waving and blowing them kisses like Marilyn Monroe. At the front, by Ita, she made a curtsy and everyone laughed aloud.

It was time to head out; Ita opened the door and the night loomed before them. Leda was nervous about going out in Kibera after dark. Ita had always warned against it. But the boys pranced out the door in single file, and plenty of neighbors moved through the streets, their silhouettes sporting the same sprightly gait. No streetlamps and no one carried flashlights—Leda wondered how anyone could find their way in the dark. She suddenly felt sure she would arrive at church splattered in mud and sewage.

But in she plunged, and Ita locked the gate behind her. They walked slower than usual, winding through the rows of mud houses, radios blaring reggae music and BBC and Christmas songs and what sounded like a Bruce Lee movie.

They passed so close to homes, Leda felt as though she was walking through someone's backyard, which they were. She could hear conversations perfectly, if only she understood Swahili better.

Farther ahead, the road opened up and a few scattered electric bulbs illuminated storefronts. First, they passed a butcher with meat strung in the air, flies buzzing about. Then they passed cart after cart loaded with fruits and vegetables, dried fish, soap, batteries, phone cards, charcoal—many of the stands lit by flickering candles in each corner or a liquor bottle with a burning wick.

They passed the movie theater, a show flickering to a packed crowd inside. Leda inquired about the carts men clustered around. *Bars,* Ita told her in a tone that sounded like *duh.*

One section of the road was lined with what looked like hot dog stands—which, as Leda got closer, she saw was exactly what they were. Steaming skewers of meat and seafood were set out for sale.

The next strip held no more carts, just rows of women, shoulder to shoulder, bent over charcoal fires and sizzling pots. Everything it was possible to fry in Kibera seemed to be bubbling away in their kettles.

The children piled up in their line, swelling into more of a mob, and tugged at Ita's shirt. They'd stopped before a woman frying potato dumplings and sugared rolls. Ita gave in and bought them the treats. Here the crowd was the thickest, and Leda bounced off people as though she'd been dropped into a pinball machine. Many people called out greetings to Ita and the boys, all of whom looked at her in surprise, especially when she offered them a smile.

The church was a concrete structure at the end of the road. She and Ita and the boys filed inside along with everybody else. Nobody stopped her, which Leda suddenly realized she'd been half-expecting.

Sandals were deposited around the edge of the room, as people stepped barefoot onto straw mats. Mary was there, with Grace and her husband and children in tow. Leda was happy to meet Paul and the little ones; together they made quite a crowd.

Once everyone arranged themselves on the mat, the preacher began shouting, urging everyone to sing. Leda looked around for any sign of hymnals, but everyone just threw their head back and belted out songs like a theatre troupe who'd been rehearsing for months.

She closed her eyes and let the sheer volume of it wash over her. Then she tried picking out single voices—Ntimi, the loudest, alongside Michael's more somber tone. But eventually she resumed blanket appreciation of the harmony created by men and women, young and old.

Ita didn't nudge her to sing, and she loved that about him, that he didn't push her, seemed to understand her.

So Leda allowed herself to let go, get lost in the spectacle. The singing and sermons continued for many hours and left everyone sweaty, winded and divinely happy.

December 24, 2007, Kibera—Ita

Ita couldn't believe how late it was when they finally made it back to the orphanage. He felt as carefree and light as he'd ever been in his life, truly believing things were going to get brighter finally, easier. As he watched the boys file through the door, barely able to keep their eyes open, he remembered the prayers he'd said in church. *Please, God, watch over these boys. Help them grow strong and good.*

He decided to let them go off to bed without washing, even as he saw their sticky *mandazi* fingers and powdered sugar lips. Mary was spending the night with her family, and Ita wanted as much alone time with Leda as possible.

Leda escorted the sleepwalking children to their room and Ita remembered his prayer for her—*Let her heal and be free.*

He'd prayed for Mary, too, of course, and his neighbors, and the doctors at the clinic.

And he'd prayed for Chege, as always. Ita prayed that Chege would find the strength to believe in the good in himself, believe in the good in others and the world, so that he could pull himself off his dark path and remember the true self that Ita loved, that was still there, buried inside him.

"Did you have fun?" Ita asked as Leda returned from the boys' room.

"Are you kidding? This is the best Christmas Eve I've ever had," she said. "Thank you."

They stood in the courtyard, under the stars, her skin glowing like the moon.

"I—" He took a step closer. "The truth is—" But Ita stopped himself before saying it. In his experience, wanting something too much, out loud—it only let the devil know what to take away.

"Me, too," she said. She took one step closer and held out her hand.

Ita's heart soared. He interlaced his fingers with hers, all the whispers they'd shared through the late nights of safari rushing through his mind. Would Leda really stay? Would she return? She had admitted she didn't have a job at home. And yet she'd spent the money to come here to help, to volunteer. It meant she cared, she was compassionate. Ita had dreams, for the orphanage, for Kibera. And dreams for himself he'd locked away. But if she came back, they could do it together. It was crazy, he knew, but this was the fire she'd lit in him, one he was unaccustomed to, one he never let himself feel. Because it was dangerous—this burning feeling, the very emotion Ita decried in Raila's supporters. Hope. Fiery hope that things could be different. Better. Hopes let the devil know what to take away.

Leda took his hand. She was strong, but at the seams she was fragile. Ita yearned to take care of her, protect her. He would happily spend the rest of his days trying to make her smile.

He clenched her pale fingers in his. He took one step and she took another and then they surged together, kissing, their mouths open and sucking, bent on swallowing each other whole.

Ita knew how a rocket must feel, lit and ready to fly. They ran their hands over each other's hot skin and panted and slurped so loudly he had to pull away. He gasped for air, stared into her hungry eyes. With a moan, he spun her around, bent her over and lifted her dress. One hand undid his pants while the other moved her panties to the side and gripped her hip. He grabbed hold of her shoulder for balance and entered her, all the way to the hilt, which sent lightening shooting through his body. The way he fit inside her, the way her body responded, it made Ita want to do this forever.

Afraid he would call out, he buried his face in her hair, growling into her neck while he reached around to pleasure her. He felt Leda come, clenching him in waves, her thighs quivering, her orgasm fueling his.

"I'm ready," he breathed into her ear.

She clenched him harder, reached back to pull him deeper inside her.

When he came, he nearly pitched forward. He saw the stars swim above him, felt as if the whole universe approved of their union.

Leda spun around and kissed him, laughing.

"Was it too fast?" he asked, made self-conscious by her amusement.

"No," she said. "God, no, I can barely stand." She pointed at her knees and they were indeed shaking. "I'm just happy. Very, very happy." She looked up at the sky and the stars and took a deep breath. Then she said it again, *"I'm happy,"* loud enough for Kibera, for the world, to hear.

Ita laughed. "Me, too," he said, feeling his smile strain at the edges, feeling the warmth of Leda's skin coursing into his. He wrapped his arms around her waist and nuzzled his head in her hair. But a worry crept into his stomach, tied a knot in his insides.

Now the devil knew.

December 25, 2007, Kibera—Leda

Christmas morning, Mary returned to the orphanage, so Leda and Ita could go buy the food. Once a year, Ita said, everyone had meat and new clothes. What the other 364 days brought was implied.

Leda skipped along the path, her footing sure as a doe in the forest. She smiled at so many residents doing the same, out to celebrate on a sunny day. Christmas and the coming elections—a cocktail for optimism.

Ita zipped ahead, in high spirits, skidding through the crowds like a water spider.

"This way!" He pointed out a *duka* ahead. "Nelson's," he said.

There were dozens of *dukas* in every quadrant, so no one had to walk far to get margarine, cooking fuel or tins of tomato sauce. Nelson's *duka* had the typical pack of kids playing out front with two matrons standing watch. The women debated and laughed in equal measure.

"Joyce!" Ita called out merrily and one of the women smiled and waved him over.

Joyce had a laugh like Mary's stew—rich and hearty, deliciously layered. A laugh like that could cure any of the world's woes, Leda thought to herself.

"Merry Christmas!" Ita said, and both women fluttered their eyelashes in response.

Leda had to admit, his looks served him well.

"What you come running up here for, Ita? You not yet bought all the meat, then, for them boys of yours? They been troublemakers this year?" Joyce's smile matched Ita's as she teased him. "I think we all out," she said, pointing. "Look, only onions."

"Oh, well, then I guess we'll be going round the way—"

"Brother!" A wiry old man appeared, waving his arms at Ita. He was strong looking in spite of his age.

"Nelson," Ita said warmly.

The man's eyes bore the yellow stain of hepatitis, but they glinted with benevolence. "Don't listen to that crazy woman." He grinned at his wife. "We saved the best for your boys. You'll see."

They waited while Nelson ducked back inside. He reappeared with three hulking parcels wrapped in newspaper. Ita took two and Nelson unwrapped one to show.

The contents made Leda's stomach churn like a cement mixer. A mound of meat, firm in places, squishy in others, ribbons of fat meeting jagged bone and matted clumps of hair.

"Goat," Ita said to her. Probably because her face exposed her thought: *human*.

Leda rearranged her lips into the best grin she could muster. "Yum," she offered. Sarcasm was an American thing, she realized, as both men nodded in approval.

Best damn barbecue Leda had ever been to.

They gorged themselves on skewers of magically greasy, smoky meat and ate as much *mandazi* as they could stomach. Grace clucked over Leda's henna scabs. Then she taught her to make coconut bread for dessert. Paul and Ita talked soccer while the women played with the children.

Watching Ita and the orphans and Mary's brood, Leda imagined they felt as she did—that the day was one big metaphorical exhale.

Late in the afternoon, Mary's family took their leave, hugging each of the boys and kissing the tops of their heads. After they'd gone, Ita clapped his hands together. Present time. The boys took their seats on the mat, wriggling like Mexican jumping beans.

Leda had seen the big bag of clothes. She was expecting a free-for-all. Instead, Ita called out each boy's name in turn and they approached like little graduates. Tears stung her eyes when she realized Ita had handpicked each boy's favorite color. Michael got a polo shirt striped red, black and white— Manchester United colors, which the boy favored over food and water. Jomo's shirt was electric blue, which made Leda proud that she'd noticed, too, that he always picked the blue cup for breakfast and the blue rag for washing up.

Once all the clothes were handed out, Ita looked at the boys expectantly. "What are you waiting for, little brothers?" he asked.

Like a surge in electricity, all the kids ran off to try on their new clothes.

It gave her a window of alone time with Ita. He led her by the hand into his room. When the door shut, he pressed up against her with a long, warm kiss while his hands slid up her sides like serpents. Leda disappeared into the rush and listened to their breaths spar in the hot room.

"Ita—" she said in between kisses that swept her away. She must focus. It was time to tell him. Why was she so nervous?

"Mmm—" Ita answered, his eyes closed. He moved to her neck, raising goose bumps down her body.

There was never going to be exactly the right time to tell him, she decided. She hadn't meant to mislead him. In the beginning it was about safety, on safari unimportant. Now it was different.

But suddenly the children's voices chirped outside, "Ita, look" and "Ita, *asante*."

Reluctantly and with effort, Ita pulled away. He reached out and smoothed down her hair. She melted at the gesture. Suddenly, she couldn't wait to tell him her plan.

Ita made a show of opening the door and gasping in appreciation at the boys' new outfits. Leda put a hand to her heart and gasped, too, but it was a hundred percent genuine. "Look at you!" She reached out and patted one shoulder after another while the boys strutted and posed. "*Nzuri sana!* So handsome!"

She ran off to get her camera as the boys assembled in the courtyard. Leda snapped picture after picture, viewing her adopted family through new eyes. For the first time in her life, her camera gave her not a sense of distance, but of intimacy. Through the lens, she saw the scar on Ntimi's ear she knew was from a dog attack. She saw the glint in Michael's eyes that betrayed the love behind his apprehension. In Jomo's eyes, she saw the seeds of confidence. She let Jomo take a turn at the camera, imagining him becoming a photographer. Why not? If she could help them, she wanted them to become whatever they wanted. She'd always been embarrassed by her wealth, but she realized she shouldn't be anymore. Money could do good things for good people. It could give them license to dream.

Ita clapped his hands together to get everyone's attention. "*Zawadi,* Leda! Time for Leda's present."

She turned in shock. "Oh no, Ita." She'd told him not to get her anything.

"Come here," he said with a grin. He held something behind his back.

The boys obliged, hurrying to sit on the mat, all eyes on Leda. Ita instructed her to close her eyes. In the darkness, she felt him step behind her.

"Merry Christmas, Leda," he said as he draped something light around her neck. A necklace.

Leda opened her eyes. The chain was short, but she could pull it out just far enough to see the delicate gold bird linked in the middle.

She inhaled and felt dizzy, off balance. How did he get this? It was so dainty, pretty. Expensive. How could he have spent that kind of money—

Ita kissed the nape of her neck. "It was my mother's." Leda tried to breathe and failed. "A sparrow. They fly free until they meet their destiny. Then they fly together."

Leda spun around. She looked into his eyes, wide and watery. When she fell into his arms and hugged him, she felt his heartbeat pound against hers.

The boys clapped and whistled.

"You're like a bird," Ita whispered. "Come from a faraway land." He touched the charm at her throat.

"Ita—" She was overcome. "I can't—"

"You will leave. But now, with this necklace…" He traced her collarbone, his eyes shining. "You will come back."

She closed her hand over his, over the little gold bird. "I will," she said, and she meant it. "I will come back."

He took her in his arms, rocking her to and fro on the sea of emotion between them. The children sprang from the mat, ensnared by the spirit, too. Ntimi hugged them first, and then Michael. Walter hugged Leda's ankles. It was such a perfect moment, Leda felt her heart start to race. The bodies squeezing her tight, the necklace pressed against her skin, it brought thoughts bubbling up unbidden. *This is too much—too good. I don't deserve it.* Leda tried to suppress the creeping thoughts, tried to allow herself this moment of bliss, of warmth.

But it didn't feel merely warm. Leda felt hot, suffocated, like she might faint. She pulled apart from Ita and cleared her throat. "I—I have something for you all, too. One second."

Leda went and got her bag, still packed from safari. She spilled out the candy and gifts onto the mat. The boys' eyes went wide at the cache and they all dove for the goods, scrambling.

Ita laughed. He wagged his finger playfully at Leda for disobeying him, but was obviously pleased. It buoyed her confidence.

"There's more," she said a little shakily. "There's something I have to tell you." While the boys were distracted with the treats, Leda stepped closer to Ita, pulled him aside. "The reason I don't have a job, it's not exactly what you think. I don't…need one."

The flicker in Ita's eyes made her gulp. *Just spit it out.* "My family, my mother, well, my father actually, who died, he had money. So…I have money. Lots of it." Ita took a step back. Leda attempted a smile. "And I'd like to help."

Ita stilled. He opened his mouth to speak, but said nothing, until finally, after seconds that wrung her stomach into knots, he put on a half-cocked, strained, non-Ita smile and said, "Okay."

"Okay?"

"Thank you."

Leda tried to stop her brow from knitting together. What had she been expecting? A ticker-tape parade for a superhero? A prideful refusal? She floundered, anger flittering into her mind. But then she remembered how Chege had taunted her, and Estella before him. *Off to save Africa?*

As her stomach sank further, Leda saw Ita trying to recover, trying to dig back up his true smile. But his eyes kept darting to the necklace around her neck. She touched it self-consciously. Did he finally see the truth—that she was unworthy of such admiration?

"Ita," she whispered, reaching across the sudden distance between them, but he made no move to meet her in the middle. He stepped out of reach of Leda's hands, still fumbling to smile.

When a banging sounded at the door, he turned and called out to Michael, as if grateful for the interruption. The kid darted off to see who it was as Ita stayed turned away from her.

Ntimi came to her side. He played with her hand, intertwining fingers, black and white. Leda watched the piano key pattern and felt as if the world had tilted, as if a story had been erased and written over, but she couldn't read the new ending.

Before she could ponder it any further, she heard a familiar voice and looked up in time to see Chege burst inside the orphanage.

She watched him meet Ita's eyes, Chege smiling ear to ear. Leda tried to imagine the river of memories between them, tried to understand their connection, their bond. But she couldn't. She had no frame of reference, nothing to relate it to in her life.

As Chege strode closer, he reached into his pocket. Leda stared as he pulled out a bulbous wad of cash and waved it in the air. "School money!" he shouted and whacked Michael over the head with the bills. "School money for Christmas!"

Leda couldn't move, her breath held hostage in her throat. Ita frowned.

Chege's wad of cash lowered to his side like a withering vine. "What?" he asked, looking around the triangle he formed with her and Ita.

It was Michael who spoke, with his characteristic calm. "Leda will come back to stay. With lots of money for us."

Ita closed his eyes, aware that Michael had been listening. Chege digested the words one at a time. Then he looked at Leda, Ntimi still holding her hand. His yellow eyes narrowed to slits, and she felt with a pang what he was looking at. She put her hand to her throat, covering the necklace. Chege stared another moment, his gaze a fire doused in kerosene. When he spun to face Ita, the icy glare made Ita flinch before he lowered his head, sheepish.

Leda dropped her chin in suit, wishing she could disappear. Wondering if Ita wished she would, too.

CHAPTER 22

January 2, 2008, Kibera—Ita

"CHEGE!" ITA'S SCREAM TRIPS OVER KIONI AS HE tumbles into the street. "Chege, no!"

Ita is running Chege's path, replacing Chege's tracks with his own. Under the eyes of the stunned policemen, he stutters to a stop.

Chege's body lies facedown, his T-shirt riddled with too many holes to count. Ita's nostrils burn with the sulfur smell of gunfire, blended with the sweet, rusted smell of blood. The gun smoke drifts to join that of the rioters' fires, still blanketing the sky above.

Ita can do nothing. No doctor in the world would try. He drops to the ground, rocks and shrapnel piercing his knees, his blood mixing with Chege's in the dirt, his tears following soon after.

Ita doesn't know the physiology of how a mind snaps. But he can feel it. He can feel his mind stretch to the limits of sanity, then snap like a rubber band. The sobs that gush onto Chege's body, they don't belong to Ita, they are not his to control. As he turns Chege over, he hears no sound, no groaning, no escaping breath—Chege has left this body behind. Ita peels the dreadlocks from his friend's face, but he doesn't move his hand away quickly enough to escape the blood that spills from Chege's mouth onto his fingers. Ita doesn't flinch—he lets his hand glisten in the night, moves it to cup the side of Chege's face, something he could have never done in life.

So calm. Chege's scarred face is slack, unrecognizable, peace smoothed across it as Ita has never seen, not even when they were boys, not even when Chege slept. Ita remembers in vivid succession the thousands of nights he took his turn at watch, over Chege frowning in his sleep.

"Sleep," Ita whispers.

In their world without mirrors, Ita knows Chege's face better than his own. Every scar, he knows the story. They are linked. He will never escape Chege. Something Ita has always known, and which is no less true now. In life or death, their fate was woven together long ago.

In the last few moments the world gives Ita to say goodbye, he sees their relationship clearly for the first time. Grief provides the clarity like water flattening into a reflective surface.

While Ita's face has stayed clear and smooth, Chege's is covered in scars. He took every one for himself. For every piece of knowledge Ita prides himself on, Chege traded a piece of his soul. For every indignity Ita was spared, Chege swallowed it whole.

Ita didn't ask for it, but he took it. Sometime, a long time ago, Chege made him believe that he was better, special. Chege decided to sacrifice, to give up the things he thought Ita could do better—school, legitimate business, charity. Love. The sacrifices created Chege's identity. *What did he see in himself?* Ita wonders. *What demons found him in the night? What did the little monsters whisper in his ear?*

Holding Chege's head in his hands, Ita knows that whatever his friend became, Ita played his part. His role, even if it was given to him freely. Every day that he accepted Chege's vision of what he could be, Ita let him be his painting and himself be Dorian Gray.

Chege was a murderer, a thief, a rapist. All the things that Ita could have become, but didn't.

"Ita." Kioni's voice echoes in the night.

He looks up. She peeks through a crack in the door, a crack too small for scared awoken children to see through. Her eyes look to her left. Ita follows them and finds the soldiers whirring into motion like puppets whose strings have been cut.

His moment to say goodbye is over.

The soldiers stand, converge all at once. Ita can sense the agitation in the scramble of their boots. They came for a manhunt, got tricked into this mess. Still, Ita knows the danger he's in if plays their fleeting sympathy wrong.

"Take him," he says. That is what they want, to be rid of the evidence. They want Ita to acquit them for their zeal, for their complicity in the sacrifice. He gives them what they want.

With his head lowered, he stands, hands out, palms down, away from his pockets. He backs away, keeping his eyes averted.

When he reaches the door to the orphanage, Ita slips inside and shuts the door. He doesn't look back.

Instead, he finds the children assembled, a line up of baby owls. Walter waddles to the front. When he sees the blood on Ita's hands and clothes, his lip trembles and his mouth opens to cry. Ita yearns to pick him up, but Chege's blood is still wet between his fingers.

Kioni scoops up Walter instead, fends off his wailing by bouncing him on her hip.

"Go," Ita says to the boys. He feels the sting when their eyes flinch, wounded. "It's okay. You're okay. But please, go." He sighs when they hold the line, stunned. "Michael."

Michael doesn't budge until Ita looks straight into his eyes. Then, with a clench of his jaw, the boy resumes his role. He herds the children back to their bedroom.

Ita slinks past Kioni into his room. He strips off his shirt, pours water over his hands, wipes them on a rag. Then he sits hunched on his bed, not knowing what to do next.

The med student in him knows he's in shock by his numb hands, his rapid heartbeat, his shallow breath. His blood pressure is sinking alongside his heart. But he is helpless to do anything about it. For the first time, Ita glimpses the minds of the ghost men who wander the alleys of Kibera, shells of fathers and husbands whose whispered grievances are like trash in the wind. Their wives and children, their youth and hope—all having slipped through their fingers.

Ita thinks he understands. He sees how loss can flood a mind, leave room for nothing else to matter.

When Kioni opens his door, he can't be bothered to look at her. His eyes are ripe with tears that cannot fall, tears he doesn't care to wipe away.

"Ita—" she says, but stops. Maybe she sees how words have lost their meaning, their purpose flittered away like everything else. But she's moving anyway, sweeping into the room like a storm cloud, misting down onto the mattress next to him. He is glad she doesn't touch him.

After a long drift of silence, out of the corner of his eye, he sees her open her arms. At first, he does nothing and Kioni leaves them be, a stone angel in a cemetery.

But then Ita feels something inside stirring, pushing him, nudging at what's left of his soul, until he lets himself fall into her lap.

Images of Chege saturate the air around them. Not just of tonight, of shots ringing out, of blood pooling in the dirt. No, not just that. Images of nights piled up through the years, from long, long ago—they dance around them in the room, cresting and falling on their twin strangled breaths, their crippled heartbeats.

Ita feels the roughness of Kioni's dress, feels the warmth and softness beneath, and he gets caught, careening from one memory into the next.

When Ita touches his cheek, the wetness of his tears slips between his fingers like blood. He feels sick inside, the acid rising up in his throat. He lifts himself away, away from her warm skin and the terrible visions it brings.

Her hand finds its way to his cheek, a mirror gesture of how he cradled Chege's face. She looks at him, mourning, as he did over Chege's body.

They cry together for their friend. No matter what he was, he was theirs. Their only family. And they cry for themselves, for the parts of them that died in the dirt with Chege.

Light is seeping into the room when Ita looks over and finds Jomo standing in the doorway, watching them. Their eyes meet and hold.

"Come in," Ita says, his voice thick. "It's okay. Come here." Jomo doesn't budge.

When Kioni raises her head, the three of them get stuck in a slice of time, like a fuzzy photograph. Ita imagines himself trapped inside a camera, and he wonders if he is destined to lose his mind in the coming hours and days.

Then Ita sees it—Jomo's big toe inching forward in the dirt. He approaches like a frightened cub, eyes averted. His little fist is closed tight over something.

Ita and Kioni watch, entranced. Jomo reaches the edge of the mattress, drops the thing onto the blanket, then jumps back and runs out of the room. Ita gets up to go after him, until a sparkle pulls his eye to the bed.

The necklace.

His mother's necklace. The necklace he clasped around Leda's ivory throat on Christmas. Ita snatches it up, closes it in his hand and hangs his head, eyes squeezed shut.

He sees Leda, tossing back her dark hair to expose the pale skin of her neck that seemed so naked to Ita, indecent almost, both in sensuality and vulnerability. He sees the light glinting off the necklace, the promise that would bring her back to him.

Ita opens his hand, stares at the gold chain with the bird forever imprisoned upon it.

How did Jomo get it? Did she leave it behind before she left? Ita can almost feel his heart ripping through his chest. The light catches the end of the chain dangling from his palm— it's broken. Snapped. Ita fingers the edge, his mind reeling, so much so that he barely notices that Kioni has seen what he holds. Her hand flies to her throat.

"I gave it to Leda," he says.

Kioni's face falls, her pupils swelling to spill their ink. "You gave it to her? To a stranger?" She scrambles off the bed. "After everything. After all those years. You gave it to a *mzungu?*"

Ita doesn't have a chance to respond before Kioni flees the room, vanishing into the night. He doesn't have the chance to tell her, *Leda wasn't just anyone. She was a chance at light, beauty, at peace. She was a chance for redemption. Redemption for what I did to you.*

CHAPTER 23

January 9, 2008, Topanga, CA—Leda

LEDA ARRIVES LATE TO THE DOCTOR'S OFFICE.
But the look on the receptionist's face, either from too much Botox or in response to Leda's haggard appearance, says she's forgiven. Or maybe, Leda realizes, the kindness is due to why she's here. Donor testing.

"Have a seat, honey," the receptionist says. "Dr. Gordon will be with you just as soon as he can."

Leda feels as if she's moving through a haze, as if she should put her hands out to clear the fog. The cumulative noise—the beeping, the incessant ringing of the phones, the loud typing, the rampant whispering—it all feels choreographed, overdone. Chipper. American.

She sits down to wait. Her mind's swimming like a dunked feline. She hasn't been able to drag herself from her bed for over a week. Her phone hasn't rung once, despite her constantly, desperately, willing it to. She finally decided the only way to rise from the rumpled sheets was to promise herself not to think. Promise to avoid the wide swath of things tearing apart her mind—Estella's cancer, today's tests to see if it will fall to Leda to save her, the dreams that plague her, of fire and blood...

I'm thinking about it.

She snaps the rubber band on her wrist. She slipped it on this morning and anytime thoughts creep in, she snaps it, a psychological trick. A weapon. She has already snapped it seven times in the car ride over, twice since she's entered the office. So far she doesn't think the receptionist has noticed.

On the table in front of her are the usual assortment of women's and men's magazines, and a newspaper. Leda knows she should snap the rubber band, but she picks up the newspaper.

It's not on the front page. She has to flip two pages to the World section, but there it is, from a bird's-eye view.

The newspaper says that in the months preceding the December 27 presidential election, clashes in the western part of Kenya killed hundreds of people, although this was not as bad as previous election years. The article blames politicians for stoking ethnic tensions, saying anyone could have foreseen that a narrow victory for either candidate would mean mayhem and riots.

Leda looks up, the paper extended, open. *Idiot.* That's what she was, an idiot. Acting like a love-struck teenager frolicking on a beach while a tidal wave rose offshore. The tsunami was there the whole time, steadily positioning itself to drown Kibera and everything contained within. She pictures the shops, the blur of faces, children running through the alleys. The orphans. Ntimi, beaming, ever the gentleman. Michael, the martyr. Walter with his chubby exuberance. And Jomo, his watchful eyes, just starting to come around to the idea that maybe the world wasn't so horrible.

When all along, Jomo was right.

Leda's eyes return to the newspaper.

At first, the article says, Raila Odinga was reported in the lead. People celebrated in splatters. But when the official election results were withheld, people got antsy.

Leda sucks in a shaky breath—she knows what's coming next. What will the newspaper say? About December 30, the night Kibaki was hastily sworn in. The paper says Kibera went mad. Thwarted Luo men took to the streets, hell-bent on hunting Kibaki's long-privileged Kikuyu. After, during the night and day Leda spent on a plane, government security forces flooded the slum, and live TV was cut. Police rounded up protesters and took the opportunity to kill dissidents and Mungiki gang leaders, too.

New Year's Day, while Leda sat at Estella's kitchen table, public accusations were made of mass killings by Kenyan government forces. The same day, a mob set fire to a church full of women and children. The next day, President Kibaki accused Odinga's Luo protesters of "ethnic cleansing" as the death toll rose. Odinga followed with a Nairobi rally that police squashed with tear gas and water canyons. By the fourth, as Leda tossed in bed, the United Nations announced their estimate that the violence had uprooted 200,000 people.

And who would've thought this would happen, the newspaper muses, when December 27—voting day—was such a relatively peaceful event? Millions turned out, hopeful and in good spirits, Luo and Kikuyu neighbors side by side.

Leda's eyes drift from the page. *Voting day.*

The day the little monsters came out to play.

"Leda Walbourne," the nurse calls out.

Leda looks up.

"We're ready for you," the nurse says with a smile. "We need blood and urine samples, then Dr. Gordon will see you."

CHAPTER 24

December 27, 2007, Kibera—Leda

AFTER LEDA'S ILL-FATED ANNOUNCEMENT ON Christmas Day, the bliss between her and Ita sputtered like a car running out of gas. He was as polite and kind as ever, but somehow that made the distance more pronounced. If falling in love meant turning a stranger into something as familiar as oatmeal, then falling out of love... Was it this? Watching Ita turn back into a stranger one hour at a time? Leda sensed him rewriting her, sketching a new image of her in his mind.

He asked her a few questions about the money, what Leda wanted do with it. But each time, his questions and her over-eager answers wedged them further apart.

She didn't understand what had happened, not really. Did he feel betrayed? Emasculated? Suddenly indebted? Or was it just that she had suddenly become a stranger, a rich foreigner, a *mzungu,* in his eyes?

He needed help for the orphanage. She wanted to help. Why did this have to become a mountain between them?

That morning, Ita and Mary had left for the voting station before Leda even emerged from her room.

The night before, she'd asked to go with him to the polls, but Ita had said no. "Optimism," he'd said, "does not negate caution." Plus, he needed her to watch the boys.

When Leda joined them, the boys were already eating breakfast. They were riled up as if it were Christmas morning—infused with frothy excitement. They must have caught it from Ita and Mary before they'd left.

Leda tried to feel excited, too. This could be the day nefarious leaders toppled, replaced by saviors. The day when life in Kibera got better.

But Leda couldn't. She couldn't rise above the unease caused by the rift between her and Ita.

As she played with the younger children, who understood neither English nor her butchered Swahili, Leda felt her anxiety increase. On safari, she and Ita had been a romantic fairy tale, reveling in their impossible love. But in Kibera, the vivid dreams they'd whispered in the dark became chalk drawings in the beating sun. Had she been honest, telling Ita she could live in Kibera? Although he might see her life in California as wasteful, idle or shallow, at least he could go to med school there. Follow his dream, because he had a goal. But what would she do there? Maybe staying in Kibera wasn't ridiculous. Here, at least, she felt as though she had a purpose, as though she could help. Or at least she *had* felt that way. Did Ita even want her to return anymore as his benefactor, if it meant this unease between them—tiptoeing around their love like a shattered vase hastily glued?

Leda gathered all the boys in the courtyard and vowed to stop thinking about it. She would just have to talk things out with Ita that night. It would be fine.

For a few hours, they played Duck Duck Goose and Red Rover, Red Rover. Leda taught them how to patty-cake and they showed her how to use the wooden Bao board she'd been curious about. It was like a cross between checkers and backgammon, with dried seeds as playing pieces.

Afterward, Leda heated the lunch Mary had left for them— chapati and salted cassava with peas.

After the meal, and after all the dishes were done, Leda announced it was story time. She stuck to the simplest one— Shel Silverstein's *The Giving Tree*. The boys traced their fingers over the shiny pages, laughing at the little boy picking apples. They felt sorry for the wrinkled old man the boy becomes, with only a tree for a friend.

After they read it through three times, Leda could tell they were losing interest. Jomo was the first to get up and leave, ducking away without so much as a glance. Could he sense the shift that had happened, too? Would they all treat her like an outsider now?

Leda was continuing with the story—pointing out the apples and the trees, imagining her voice sounded boring and screechy—when there was a loud knock at the gate.

Her hands froze, clenching the book like a baseball bat, as the boys jumped up and dashed toward the sound.

"Wait!" she called out.

But overlapping her voice was another—Chege's, coming from the gate. *"Ita! Sasa?"*

Michael grinned and unlocked the door before Leda could stop him. Her stomach twisted like a balloon animal, but with nothing funny about it. Every single thing about Chege made her uneasy.

She jumped up and scurried to the door, hoping to block his entrance. Chege stopped, surprised, and peered past her as he asked, "Where Ita at?"

"Voting with Mary," she said, and instantly regretted adding the Mary part, as Chege's snarl curled into a sickening smile.

"Just you? Alone?"

"Ita will be back soon," she said, her hand resting on the door pointedly. "I'll tell him to call you." She tugged on the metal.

Chege chuckled as he reached in and put his hand on Michael's shoulder. "Nah, I just play here till he come back."

Michael moved aside, allowing Chege to slip in. Leda looked at Michael in anger. Traitor.

She stood awkwardly in place as Chege strutted past her to the mat, pied piper to seven pairs of pitter-pattering feet. He wore jeans and a shiny red Fila athletic shirt. His dreads snaked down his back, loosely gathered by a red piece of cloth.

For a split second, like the first time she'd laid eyes on him, Leda was struck by an unwelcome thought: Chege could be handsome. Not at all like Ita, who was smooth and solid and chiseled. No, Chege was both jagged and lithe, his allure like that of a lizard or a snake.

As if he could feel her studying him, he turned and winked. It caught Leda so off guard, she turned away, pretending she'd heard a noise outside and needed to shut the gate, fast. Her cheeks burned with shame.

Ntimi noticed her hovering near the door. "Leda, play! Come here, play!"

Chege smiled, showing his teeth with the brown streaks. Ita told her it was from chewing *miraa,* a twig with an effect like cocaine. "Yes, Leda," he purred. "Come play."

Leda's general nausea about him returned, and that was comforting somehow. She went and sat down next to Ntimi on the mat.

"What you boys reading today?" Chege picked up the

book and ran his hand seductively over the shiny cover. He didn't open it, Leda noticed. She wondered if he could read.

"The Giving Tree," Ntimi said. "By Mr. Shel Siverstein." He pronounced it perfectly. Leda smiled at him proudly.

Chege chuckled. "Yeah? What the trees giving us today? I thought you don't need a giving tree anymore, now you got Leda. Ita's angel. That what he think. You boys, too?"

Leda's smile faltered.

He laughed. "Aw, come on. Let's be friends, Leda." He pulled up his shirt enough that she could see his stomach. She expected to see a weapon, a machete, but instead he took a flask from his waistband. "Share a drink with me. For voting day. You American girls like to drink."

"No, thank you," she said.

He shrugged his shoulders and took a swig. With wet lips, he studied her. "You know *changaa?*"

She knew he meant the liquor. Slum moonshine, brewed illegally at great penalty. "No," she said.

Chege's face softened. "It not your fault, you pretty thing. You from the other side of the world."

Leda felt heavy, like an anchor sinking to the bottom of the sea. She wished she could go hide in her little room. She felt exposed before Chege. Naked. But daring to look in his eyes, she was surprised at what she saw. Not the judgment she imagined, not at all. He looked at her with something like sympathy, understanding.

"Anyway," he said. "That not your real problem, is it?" He took another swig from the flask. He closed his eyes as it went down and brushed sweat from his forehead. He looked tired, suddenly. Beaten down. When he opened his eyes, he stared straight ahead, not at Leda. "You no angel. Nobody is.

Not after what the world done with us. Nobody an angel."
Now Chege looked over, extended the flask. "Except Ita."

Leda didn't say a word. The image of Ita's face loomed
between them, his eternally kind, patient face, loving her so
innocently, so unconditionally, the same as he loved the orphans, same as he loved Chege. Not believing that anybody
could be undeserving of his love—

When Leda's eyes met Chege's, she saw herself reflected
in them. She reached out and took the flask.

The fluid that gushed down her throat was liquid fire—
possibly gasoline—and she imagined it scarring her insides
as it went. Not warming them, but harming them—rivers of
burned tissue. She liked the feeling, liked the dull wave of
fog that followed.

Chege watched her face as he took back the flask. But he
didn't say another word.

Instead, he seemed to relax. He turned away from her and
started jabbering to the boys in Swahili. Leda sat weaving in
place for a few moments, a balloon tied down in a breeze.

Chege smiled when Walter waddled over and sat in her lap.
Leda kissed the top of the toddler's furry head and gave him
a squeeze. She felt so much better after the drink.

All of sudden, Chege drummed out a beat on his knees
and right away the boys copied it. Ntimi thumped his knees
next, faster, and ended with a loud puff of his cheeks. Everyone imitated, laughing. One by one, each boy took their turn,
adding their own flourish, like a King Kong chest-beating
or an arm flap accompanied by the squawk of a chicken.
Ntimi's second turn, he jumped up and did a little dance.
This time, Leda popped up with Walter in her arms and ap-
proximated Ntimi's wiggly jiggle. Everybody laughed appreciatively, Chege the loudest.

★ ★ ★

After playtime, the group stretched out on the mat to rest.

"Now I want to hear the book," Chege said, sprawled out opposite Leda.

She hesitated shyly, but Chege pressed the book into her hands.

Ntimi scooted in. "I start," he said, and opened the book on Leda's knee.

Each of the boys found a way to participate in the story, pointing out an apple to Chege or the old man's glasses or the carving on the tree. Leda applauded their efforts and their English. She was thrilled to feel the ease between her and the boys had returned—it made her feel drunk on contentedness. Or *changaa?*

Chege looked at Michael, sitting, watching as usual. "Is it teatime?" he asked. "Huh? Teatime, brother," he said when Michael didn't answer. "Take them."

Michael looked at Leda and the intensity of it unnerved her, made her feel suddenly guilty somehow.

"Go on," Chege urged and then rattled off a string of Swahili. The boys got up at once, Ntimi taking Walter, and headed for the kitchen.

"Hey—" Leda said, the word cottony in her mouth.

"I want to talk to you, Leda."

The cozy feeling began to dissipate. "I should go help them."

Chege laughed. "You think they need your help?"

Leda felt the sting, but dulled.

"Do you think Ita needs you now?" His voice turned soft again, low. "You want to help, I know."

"Why is that so bad?" she asked, thinking of Ita, of the way he looked at her now—warily.

"What are you gonna do, Leda? Live here? Mother those little black boys?" He snorted, his dreads trembling. Then he got serious, looked her dead in the eye. "Or you plan to take him away? Save him from Kibera. From *me*."

"We don't know yet," she said, trying to match his tone. But her voice wavered.

"Oh, Leda," Chege growled. "Those things ain't going to happen. This—" he gestured around the orphanage, but kept his eyes glued on hers "—is not your home. And you are right that Ita don't belong here. But—"

He didn't have to finish. As he reached inside his pants for the flask, she heard the rest in her head. *But he doesn't belong with you, either.*

Chege leaned in closer, so Leda could smell him—smoky and earthy. "I did something," he whispered, "that Ita will never forgive me for. Never. No matter what I do."

She searched his eyes, expecting to see a monster, but all she saw was pain. Regret. Shame.

"And one day," he said, "you will, too."

Chege moved in slowly, put his forehead to hers, so that his dreads swung forward and made a tent of privacy. His hand gripped the back of her neck.

When his lips met hers, sensually, softly, deeply, Leda expected herself to recoil instantly.

But she didn't. She let him kiss her.

He was right, she thought. Chege was right.

CHAPTER 25

January 9, 2008, Topanga, CA—Leda

WHEN DR. GORDON OPENS THE EXAM ROOM door, it cuts through the memory so sharply, Leda puts a hand to her heart and finds herself gasping. Caught. The vision of Chege leaning in, the feel of his lips, the sour liquor taste of his mouth—it burns through her just as sure as the *changaa* from his flask.

"Leda, hello." The gray-haired doctor looks up from his chart as he enters the room. "Hey, you okay?"

"Yes," she says, her breath still jagged and darting, uncatchable as rabbits. "No."

Doctor Gordon's face is creased like pillow markings. "No, of course not," he says gently. "These situations are very difficult." He's clutching the chart to his narrow chest.

It's bad news.

"Leda, we'll get the blood test results in a few hours, but I'm afraid…you aren't eligible for donation at this time."

Leda looks away to let the news penetrate. So, then it's settled. She can't save Estella. She will let her mother down, again, in the worst way. Because the doctor's words have a deeper meaning. They mean Estella will die.

"In your condition, I mean." Dr. Gordon is clearing his throat, trying to get her attention. "You are ineligible in your current condition."

Leda looks at him blankly. Her condition?

"Leda, you do know that you're pregnant...don't you?"

Two hours later, Leda knocks at her mother's door. She didn't call ahead, she can't just go barging in.

She rubs her hands together—they're clammy, with a coat of sand. After leaving the doctor's office, she drove along the coast until she screeched to a halt, parked and sat on the beach, shivering under the gray sky. But nothing could slow the avalanche of her thoughts, and no sense could be made of the colliding mess.

So Leda drove here. To tell her mother the bad news.

She knocks again.

No answer, even though Leda knows she's home. She turns around and sits on the doorstep, sure she's going to throw up, but what falls from her mouth instead is a sob, with a line of sobs backing up behind it. The racking intensity scares her. Estella always forbade crying and the conditioning stuck.

Now here she is on her mother's doorstep, bawling like a two-year-old. She almost doesn't hear the click of the door.

Almost. Frantically, she gulps down sobs like they're billiard balls, while swiping her eyes. She wipes her nose on her sleeve.

"Leda?"

She fans her face, begging the red to drain from her cheeks. With a deep breath, she turns. The vision of her mother is a zap of electrical shock. Estella's wrinkles are piled up like the hide of a shar-pei. Her skin without makeup has the wan lumpiness of lard. She looks old. *No,* Leda thinks, *she looks like she is dying.*

"Come inside," Estella says and leaves a gaping black hole in the doorway.

Leda stands and follows into the dark, shuttered house.

"Sit down," her mother says as they enter the kitchen.

That's what I need, Leda thinks. *I need someone to tell me what the hell to do.*

"Where's your team?" Leda asks.

Estella looks at her, clearly annoyed at the sight of her daughter's red, puffy face. "What?"

"Your team. The death squad." She'd meant it as a joke, but seeing Estella wince, Leda wants to smack herself for saying it.

"I sent them away."

Leda sits at the table. Estella continues to the opposite end, the seat farthest away.

"I saw the doctor today," Leda says.

Estella opens her mouth, as if she will speak, then closes it. Neither one of them knows where to begin. Leda picks at her fingers, the nails chewed to the quick, and studies the wood grain of the table.

"Stop picking," Estella says, glaring at Leda's hands.

She stops. "The blood-test results are still to come, but there's a…complication. A condition." When Leda's eyes close, the memories replay, stacking upon one another. First, Chege's marred face leaning into hers, his dreadlocks blotting out the light. But then she sees Ita's face. The day he opened the door, the sun painting his eyes with gold.

Before Leda can stop it, tears well in her eyes. They slip through her eyelashes, make a mad dash for her chin.

"Don't cry," Estella says.

Leda's eyes fly open, the weepiness swinging to sudden

anger. "Why?" She looks at her mother. She truly wants to know. "Why can't I cry? You're dying. And I'm—" more tears spill over her cheeks "—pregnant."

Estella blinks. She blinks again and Leda lowers her chin, anger extinguished by guilt. The look in Estella's eyes—it is the realization that her daughter will fail her, one last time. She gets up from the table, wobbles, then sets course for the refrigerator, her slippers sanding across the floor. She begins a process as familiar to Leda as the sound of the sea. The clink of the ice. The sloshing pour of the vodka.

But, Leda thinks foggily, *there's still a chance.* "I don't have to keep it." Her throat closes off when she says it. She puts a hand to her neck, against the sensation of a phantom vise. "Awful things happened in Kenya…"

As she trails off, the silence looms around her. Her mother's silence. Her mother's lack of interest, her complete lack of concern. Leda feels the chill in her bones, heightened by the gaping emptiness of the cold house. Soon, when Estella isn't here anymore, she realizes for the first time how truly alone she will be. She imagines giving birth alone, trying to be a good mother, all alone. *I can't. I can't do it.* Now, no way the tears will stop. She wipes at them one by one, but they spring up like leaks in a crumbling dam.

"Goddammit!" Estella whips around and smashes her glass to the ground. The shatter is like the earth cracking, splitting through Leda as though she herself is a mirror shattering into a million pieces.

Estella looks at what she's done, heaving, her hands trembling in the air. Leda's heart pounds in her chest, but her trunk is petrified wood.

"I'm dying," Estella says. "I'm as good as dead." She touches her hairline, shakily smoothes back a curl. "The oncologist called. It's everywhere. It's over." Leaving the glass where it fell, Estella trudges back to the table. She takes her faraway seat and stares at the wood. In a voice so quiet, Leda wonders if she's imagining it, she says, "It's her fault. She's the cancer in me."

"Who?" Leda asks.

But Estella only wrings her hands. They're still shaking. She mutters something else, unintelligible, to herself, as if she's forgotten Leda's in the room.

"Whose fault?" Leda tries again.

Estella sighs, irritated. "Your *grandmother's*." The word sounds like a curse.

"Oh," Leda says. Her grandmother died when she was four, and that comprised the entirety of what Estella ever revealed about her. Leda may have seen her a couple of times but she had no memory of it. "I don't remember her."

"Lucky you," Estella says, and turns her head. She studies the shattered glass with an intensity Leda finds disconcerting. But Estella doesn't elaborate. She's far away somewhere, as if her daughter doesn't exist.

Leda slips her hands into her lap. She pinches the skin on her wrist and twists hard. She has a sudden powerful urge she hasn't had in many, many years—to make a cut, just a nick, but big enough to bleed…

Estella's fiddling with something in the pocket of her robe. Even though she knows better, Leda asks, "What is it? What do you have—"

"None of your business," Estella snaps. Another hook from Leda's childhood sound track.

But obviously she's gripping something in her pocket. Leda suddenly imagines a gun. She takes a closer look at her mother's appearance. Estella's face is moist, like she's sweating. Her skin hangs slack, but flushed. "Mother—" Leda says, starting to feel nervous.

Estella sees her worried face. "Oh, for Christ's sake," she hisses and yanks the thing from her pocket. She smacks it on the table and Leda flinches.

It's a stack of photos. Leda stares in surprise. Then shivers wind up her arms. The photo on top is in black-and-white. A pretty young woman holding an infant. "Us?" she asks.

Estella snorts. She rolls her eyes. "No, me. And my mother. The bitch."

Leda recoils.

But Estella hardly seems to notice. She stares at the photo, her lips pursed into a thin steel line. She stares for a long, long time.

Finally Leda whispers, "What did she do to you?"

Estella shakes her head. She wrings her hands some more, notices the habit, hides them her lap.

By the time Leda has stopped expecting an answer, Estella says, "What didn't you do to me?" She's addressing the photo, in disgust. "You needed a mother, not a child." Estella's eyes veer back to the smashed cocktail. "Gave me my first drink at ten. To keep her company."

Leda stands, goes for the mop.

"Leave it," Estella says. "Just leave it alone," she adds and Leda suspects she's not talking about the mess. She flips to another photograph, one Leda's seen before—a sepia glamour photo of Estella, her hair shining like waves of silk. "No wonder I ruined my life."

It stabs Leda in the stomach—her mother's crystal clear regret. She slumps back into the chair, only because she's worried she's going to faint.

A mean glint enters Estella's eye as she turns her head toward Leda. "Guess now it's your turn."

Leda's stunned. She puts a hand over her stomach. *No. I would never be like that. Like you.*

Estella's eyes are trained on Leda like an attack dog. "You know I don't even know if your father was...your father," she sneers. "He was rich. Rich and old." She looks around the house purposefully. "Can you imagine what I had to do to give you all of this?"

Flip. A photo of an old man holding an infant Leda. Her mother smirks at the image. Leda stares at the photograph, too. The man's smile is genuine and wide-open. A smile like Ita's.

"Should have known there was a reason he went along with everything so easy—"

The man in the photo smiles at Leda, his wasted arms wrapped tight around the swaddled baby.

"He was sick. He didn't want to die alone."

Leda can't pry her eyes from the photo. Estella notices.

"Yes, he wanted you." Estella squashes her thumb on the edge of the fading photo. "But he died, left me alone with you."

Leda touches her scar out of habit, caressing it while she stares at the photograph. Now she feels her mother's eyes on her scar. "I tried, you know. But, God, it was awful—"

Leda tries not to listen. She wills her soul to remember the man in the photo somehow. Oh, how she wishes she had known him.

Estella pushes her chair back from the table with a loud screech across the floor. She takes two stormy steps, fumbling with her robe again. From her pocket, she takes out something small, closed in her fist. When she opens her palm, Leda gasps.

It's a necklace. A platinum chain with a diamond fixed in the middle.

Estella coils it atop the photo, like a snake. "He gave it to me the day you were born. I never wore it." Estella drops the necklace and doubles over to cough, an awful sound like a death rattle. Leda puts out her hand, but Estella waves her off. When she recovers, she gives the necklace one last look, then forcibly straightens herself and turns away.

Leda watches her mother go, puts her hand to her throat, envisions Ita clasping the sparrow necklace around her neck, his perfect smile that made her stomach heave. "Little monsters," she says.

"What?" Estella says from the hall.

For the first time in her adult life, Leda feels sorry for her mother.

"Nothing."

CHAPTER 26

January 10, 2008, Kibera—Ita

WHEN MARY SHOWS UP AT THE ORPHANAGE A week later, Ita stares across the threshold as if she's an apparition. Since Chege's death, every day has been a waking nightmare full of ghosts.

"Good morning," Mary says.

She's real, Ita realizes, noting the deep lines on her face and her hair, normally neatly plaited, puffing out from beneath a soiled handkerchief.

Ita lets her inside. "How is Paul? How's Grace?"

"Alive," Mary says. When he locks the door and walks past her, she says, with heavy feeling, "Thank you. I can never repay you—" She spots Kioni over Ita's shoulder.

"A friend," Ita says. "An old friend. Kioni."

Mary and Ita stare at each other, unspoken words piling up between them. He decides not to tell her about Chege, and she decides not to reveal the shadowy thoughts crossing her face.

But now the boys have caught sight of her. They bolt from the mat where Kioni had been giving them a lesson, and swarm around Mary like bees to fruit juice. Mary opens her matronly arms and hugs them fiercely with her eyes squeezed shut. The desperate joy on the children's faces makes Ita realize how they've been suffering, from fear and worry, but also from his silence.

It is Kioni that has cared for them this long week.

Ita sees her crouched like a blown-out lightbulb. Without the children occupying her thoughts, she is the same as him, nothing but a shell in the wake of Chege's death.

Since that night, they've barely spoken. Kioni took over Mary's role—cleaning and cooking, caring for the orphans. The schools are closed indefinitely, so she set up a classroom in the courtyard. She sings to the children, smiles at them, nuzzles them, but around Ita—she tiptoes. It's as if there is an imaginary boundary between them. They skirt all mention of Chege, of the dwindling supplies, of the never-ceasing violence, of the past hurt that slices them every time they pass too close to each other.

Ita's heart sinks. Kioni came here for help, not to witness Chege's murder, not to mother seven orphans while Ita broods over a foreign woman who never belonged here.

She turns as if she can hear his thoughts. Her big brown eyes fill with concern. Ita smiles, Kioni looks unconvinced, and he smiles bigger, this time it's nearly genuine. She raises an eyebrow and grins, tiredly. She waves him over. Mary's still catching up with the boys, asking them about their studies and what they've had to eat and whether they've washed behind their ears. Ita sidles over to Kioni.

"We should go out," she says. "With her here. To look for supplies."

He nods. "Yes, but I should go alone. It's not safe for you."

Kioni gives Ita a long look. He hears her silent words in his head. *It's never been safe for me.*

"We'll go together," she says.

★ ★ ★

Kibera looks like a bomb-testing site. "I don't want to go too far," Ita says, eyeing the path nervously.

The streets are still far too empty. That fact alone keeps his defenses up.

"Okay, you lead," Kioni says.

Around the first corner, the phone-charging cart lies empty, abandoned. "Your phone is dead?" she asks when he stops before it.

"I'm out of card, out of money. So it doesn't matter." Staring at the empty shelves, he's thinking about Leda. Has she tried to call him? Is she okay? The desire to know burns through him.

"Maybe she's emailed," Kioni says softly. "Maybe she has sent money. The boys say—"

"No," Ita says. "You don't understand."

"What happened, Ita? What happened to her? To you."

Ita looks farther on down the road. "There's a general store, Nelson's, around the corner. He might have something left to sell. He knows the boys."

When they arrive, however, the little kiosk is shuttered up with scraps of cardboard and metal. Ita frowns and stops, but Kioni moves ahead.

"Call to them. What did you think, they would put things on display, nice and pretty, for looters?" She goes around the side of the little structure and waves him along.

Ita raps on a section of metal. "*Habari,* Nelson. It's Ita."

There's a moment where nothing happens and Ita glances to the street, realizing how exposed they are here. But then a tiny crack appears between two sheets of cardboard and through the slit of darkness comes a feeble voice.

"Ita?" It's a woman—Nelson's wife.

"Joyce, are you okay? May I enter?"

Her hesitation is clear, but she tells Ita to come around to the other side, where the family lives.

When the door opens, both Kioni and Ita stumble back in shock. There are so many people inside the room, there's hardly space to put a single foot. Twelve pairs of eyes—women and children—fix on the visitors. Ita looks at Kioni, sees her eyes fill with tears.

He reaches into his pocket, pulls out a wad of shillings and presses it into Joyce's trembling hands.

"Nelson?" he asks as gently as he can.

But Joyce looks away and doesn't answer. She tiptoes a careful path through the silent crowd. As she rummages in the corner, Ita digests the fact that he's the only man in the room, feels the weight of it.

Joyce is making her way back, carrying a plastic bag. When Ita sees that it holds two tins of tomato paste, three withered onions, and a lump of dried peas, he feels ashamed. "I cannot take this, Mama. You keep the money. For them."

Joyce presses the bag into his hands. "For your boys. Please." Her eyes find Ita's. "Kenya will need good men now, God help us."

"What will happen to them?" Ita asks back at the orphanage. Mary has the children with her in the kitchen, leaving him and Kioni alone in his room.

"They will persevere. As women do," Kioni says. "You don't have to save them."

His skin prickles at her words. "I can't save anyone. None of the women I love."

Kioni's head jerks in response.

"I am a curse," he says, and leans his head against the dusty wall.

"Is that really how you see it?"

He hears the kindness in her voice. But she doesn't know what happened most recently. He closes his eyes to avoid looking at her, knowing it will only break him if he is finally going to tell her. "The night the violence broke out, Leda was swept away in a mob and Chege found her. He—" Ita doesn't think he can say it, the word is a piece of glass slicing his tongue. "He *raped* her." He hears Kioni's sharp intake of breath. "I found them, but not in time. I hit Chege and he ran off. The police took Leda away." Ita opens his eyes. "She isn't coming back, Kioni. She will never bear to look at me again. I would remind her only of…" *Of how I failed her. Same as I failed you.*

"Oh, Ita." Kioni sighs. "Is that what you think?"

She knows it is not only Leda he thinks of now. The story will not be silent. It begins to tell itself in the still room—the day when Ita was very sick. When his body shook so hard it knocked his teeth together like a dropped box of nails. When his skin grew so hot and he scratched so hard, trying to peel it off.

"Sometimes things happen to people," Kioni says softly. "Bad things. And sometimes people make choices. Bad ones. But the choices belong to them. Not you."

Her words are distant, less real than the memory rising in the space between them.

Kioni was thirteen, her spindly arms holding Ita, trying to keep him still, to calm his shivering. Chege paced circles around them, beside himself.

"You don't remember how sick you were," she says. "You would have—"

"Died," he finishes. "I do remember. I remember the day I should have died." He squeezes his eyes shut. "I remember better than anyone."

"No," Kioni says, "you don't."

She gets up off the bed, crosses to the wooden stool and sits, allotting space for the truth to be told. He feels dread bubble up like acid in his stomach.

"You were in death's embrace. I could see her icy fingers clawing at you, making you tremble like that. Chege could see it, too. God was planning to take you from us, clear as day. If we were going to keep you, we couldn't ask God for help anymore. We were going to have to take it up with the devil."

June 28, 1992, Kibera—Kioni

Chege's eyes are wild, so wild they frighten Kioni. Instinctively, she backs away from him.

"It is the only way we can get that kind of money," he says. The kind of money they need to take Ita to a hospital, he means. The kind of money that can buy medicine.

"Please," she says. She knows that, before, she offered this bravely, but now that it has come down to it she begs for some other way. Something terrible that Chege can do, instead of her. She has a desperate thought. "The necklace?" she squeaks. But she knows they won't—can't.

In her heart, she knows it's too late anyway. They need a sure thing. In Kibera, if you have drugs, you sell them. If you have guns, you rob. If you are a woman…

She tries to keep from crying. She is a woman, now, isn't she? Thirteen. Same age as Ita, same as Chege.

"He'll die," Chege says. "And we'll die, too, if that happens."

She can hear Ita moaning. He's calling for her. She lifts her chin to meet Chege's eyes fully. She nods her head, once, and it is decided.

She goes to Ita, pulls him into her arms again while Chege goes to make arrangements.

A half hour later, he returns.

Kioni nestles Ita best she can into a halved cardboard box. It will hide him, if not exactly shelter him. She makes a pillow out of plastic bags and winds others over his feet to insulate any warmth that remains in them. He is barely conscious. His eyes roll back to the whites, fluttering, while he mumbles and groans.

Chege whispers that they must leave now. Kioni rises. She kisses Ita's forehead, tastes the salt of his fever on her lips. "I'll be back soon," she whispers to him. "Very soon."

As they walk away, Chege stops so that Kioni nearly runs into him. "He will never forgive me, will he?" he asks.

"Nor me," she replies.

It doesn't occur to either one of them that Ita will blame himself.

Kioni follows Chege as best she can, but she's already weak from fear. Chege turns back often, but never catches her eye. He knows what is coming as well as she does.

When they arrive, a man sits on a stool outside the shack. He looks Kioni over and nods, reaches back and knocks on the slatted wood door. Kioni looks at the slits of light peeking through and feels her knees knock together.

Chege puts his hand across the door frame, blocking her. "*Ganji*," he says to the man, making his voice deeper than it really is. *Money*.

The man looks Chege up and down and laughs. He laughs

hard enough that she can smell his rotten breath. And see his brown teeth.

The man takes some money from his pocket and puts it in Chege's hand. Chege counts it with his eyes, his head jerking up sharply.

"More," he says. "She a virgin. And pretty."

Kioni's stomach heaves at the words. So much hatred swells in her, she hopes Chege feels it like a knife in his back.

The man's eyes roam over her body, sizing her up, licking his lips, making her skin crawl. He thrusts more money into Chege's hand, then raps loudly on the door.

The door swings open. A man takes up the whole doorway, the light behind him, so Kioni can't see his silhouetted face.

Chege's skinny arm is still blocking the doorway, looking ridiculous across the man's wide midsection. As if he sees that himself, Chege lowers his arm.

Now that nothing stands between Kioni and the towering man, she feels as if she might wet herself in fear. She bites her lip. *It's done,* she tells herself. *Chege has the money. Ita will get the medicine. It is already done.*

The man steps back and the room shines a spotlight on Kioni. All eyes on her as she steps inside.

The door slams behind her and she looks around the room, trying not to meet the man's eyes roving over her body. She wonders if he will be kind. Maybe he thinks she is pretty and he will be kind.

"There," the man says, pointing at the mattress on the floor.

Kioni bites her lip, harder this time, and sits down on the thin mattress, her tailbone hitting the dirt beneath. When she looks up at the man now, her breath catches in her throat. He looks like a giant about to burst through the ceiling.

He looks down on her silently like he is waiting for something. Maybe she is supposed to do something? Undress, she guesses.

Trying not to cry right away, Kioni tugs at her sleeve, notices that her fingers are trembling. When she's pulled one arm through, she hears Chege yell. She freezes. Now the man watches her with his arms spread, his knees bent like he will pounce if she tries to run.

The door bangs open and three men storm through. Chege is behind them, screaming, clawing at their backs, but the man on the stool by the door yanks him out of view and shuts the door again.

Chege screams and screams and Kioni opens her mouth and screams like the devil is stabbing her with his pitchfork.

Looking back, Kioni would always weigh that one decision—the decision to scream. Always, she would wonder if it would have been better to seal her lips shut and let the men do what men do to whores they've paid.

Because it is her wail that turns the look on the men's faces from hunger to fury. And it is then that they rip off all her clothes and take turns on her body, jabbing into any hole they can find, one by one and then even at the same time, splitting her skin at the seams and bloodying them all. All the while beating her to within inches of her life as the man outside knocks Chege unconscious.

January 10, 2008, Kibera—Ita

"Stop!" Ita screams. "Please stop. Why are you telling me this?" He claps his hands over his ears. "Don't you think I've imagined it every day since Chege dropped you bleeding into my arms? I would have stopped you, don't you see? I would have saved you! I would rather have died than for you to—"

"No, Ita," Kioni says. "You don't see. You don't understand, after all this time." She peels his hands from his ears. "You don't always get to save us. Sometimes we get to save you. Sometimes we get to save *you*."

"No. No." His sobs catch in his throat, choking him. "You should have let me die."

Kioni folds him into her arms. They hug each other tight, as they did that terrible night. The night Chege carried her half a mile and collapsed at Ita's feet, handing over her broken body like a sacrificial lamb.

"After...the way you looked at me—" She burrows into his neck. "The way you tortured yourself. It was worse than what happened. I knew then that you would never have peace, never forget. Never love me."

Ita pulls away and grabs her wrists, forces her to look at him. "I *did* love you. Even if we were kids. I loved you more than I loved myself or anything in the world."

Kioni leans forward and presses her forehead against his. He lets go of her wrists and slips his hands into hers.

"Ita, do you still love me? Like I have always loved you?" She doesn't wait for an answer. She presses her lips hard against his mouth.

Ita mashes his chest against Kioni's breasts. He wraps his arm around her lower back. He feels the blood rush to his hands, to his groin. He squeezes her tighter. Harder.

But.

But.

But his heart doesn't soar alongside hers. He feels a surge of emotion, but it is one of regret and hurt, of grief. His stomach doesn't flutter, rather it sinks. Kissing Kioni feels like spiraling down a bottomless hole.

Ita's mind races, chastising his heart. *Here is your chance. Your chance to make it right. The boys will have a mother. You will have a home. She deserves it. You deserve—*

But then suddenly Ita finds his lips hovering alone in the air and Kioni staring at him with her wide brown eyes. They peer into his, searching, then suspicious, then hurt.

She knows. She knows the truth just as he does.

"You're not, are you?" she says in monotone words. "You're not in love with me."

Ita considers lying. His mind jolts back and forth, knowing what this is about to cost him. One small lie and he will not be alone. Three words to create a family for the boys, a haven in the violence. And for himself an absolution. Wouldn't the words be true, in a sense? Of course he loves Kioni. He always has. He loves Kioni as he loves breathing.

Ita blinks. That's it. He loves Kioni as one loves breathing, automatically and unconsciously, and nothing more. And she knows it. Sadness rises in his belly like floodwaters.

Kioni's eyes spill over like two ponds on a rainy morning. "You are in love with *her.*"

CHAPTER 27

December 27, 2007, Kibera—Leda

CHEGE'S LIPS, CLOSED OVER HERS, WERE SOFTER than she would have imagined. He stroked her tongue with his, gently, like he knew her, understood her, knew what she wanted. He tasted like smoke, like a bonfire, he tasted like the air that safari night when Ita told stories around the fire.

Ita.

Leda's heart dove into her throat and began to thunder. The effects of the *changaa* evaporated like dew in a desert. As she jerked free, air pricked her wet lips and her mind picked up speed. What had she done?

Chege watched her implode, smiling like a Cheshire cat, his lips spreading wider by the second, enjoying Leda's collapse. His smile curdled her stomach, sour vomit rose in her throat. She scuttled away from his grin, struggling to get her brittle legs beneath her.

As she staggered to her feet, she looked around at the world caving in like a crumbling cliff. In the distance, in the kitchen, she registered the clinking and clattering of the boys. The thought of facing them made her ill. She looked to the door behind her, imagined she heard Ita returning with Mary.

Flashes of the fallout whipped through her mind. Chege telling him what happened. Ita's eyes turning on her. He wouldn't believe it at first. But then he would look into her guilty face and he would see. He would see her for the monster she really was.

The whole time, Chege's eyes never left her. Leda felt his gaze crawling over her skin, enjoying himself. When she dared to look at him, he met her dead-on, yellow eyes glittering like a cat in the darkness. "Run," he whispered.

Leda staggered backward, her mind reeling. What should she do? What *could* she do?

She had to think. She had to get away from Chege.

Leda dashed to her room. Inside, she panted, her mind whirring like a blender, thoughts whipped into madness. She would say that Chege tricked her. That it was all a mistake. He took advantage. She was drunk—

Her heart sank. It was hopeless. She'd taken the drink. She'd let him kiss her.

With tears blurring her vision, Leda started to pack her things. She snatched up items and stuffed them into her suitcases—medicine, toiletries, cameras, clothes. Suddenly she stopped.

She looked at all her things. She took the memory card out of the camera and set the camera back down. Then she reached for her money belt, and stood up. She fastened the carrier under her waistband, lowered her shirt, and left the room.

The courtyard was empty. She could hear Chege with the boys in the kitchen, clearing her an exit ramp to the gate. Her heart was still torn, thinking of leaving the children like this, but the second she pictured anew Ita coming home, Chege rushing to meet him, telling him—

Leda hurried across the courtyard, slid open the door, and left.

As soon as Leda checked back into the hotel, she stumbled into the room of white walls and mahogany furniture and collapsed onto the bed.

She watched the ceiling spin. She imagined she could smell Chege's scent on her, like smoke, and taste the liquor on her breath. She ran to the bathroom and threw up, three times in a row. She realized she hadn't even left a note for Ita.

But Chege would tell him. Wasn't that why he'd done it—to kill their relationship and send her away? Leda clawed at her face, climbed back into bed and smothered her head under a pillow. She was a monster.

Chege hadn't tricked her. What he'd done was demonstrate his point. She didn't deserve Ita. He was right.

And now Chege could tell him as much, with proof. Throw it in Ita's face.

God, she was such a fool. Her little speech on Christmas. She shuddered, remembering his face. He does so much every day, mending souls and climbing mountains. Then she comes in with a trust-fund checkbook and a self-satisfied smile.

All the hopes and good intentions she'd brought to Kenya sucked out of her, she wrapped herself in guilt and slept. And as she drifted off, she dreamed of sparrows.

Two sparrows, soaring and dipping, weaving in the sky.

Sometimes the sparrows were black, dripping paint. Sometimes they looked real. Sometimes they were made of gold.

Leda woke up, gasping for air, her hand on the necklace still linked around her neck, burning into her flesh like the henna had. She could still feel Ita's hands rubbing her skin with cool cream and the warmth of his smile—a memory a million miles away.

As she drifted back off, she went in and out of a twisted dreamworld. Sparrows soaring over the rusted rooftops of Kibera, carving figure eights in the clouds.

Soul mates in the sky.

CHAPTER 28

January 11, 2008, Kibera—Ita

KIONI LEAVES AT DAWN. ITA TRIES TO STOP HER, it isn't safe for her to go, but she doesn't care. She takes a knife from the kitchen and heads straight for the front gate. Ita convinces her to accept the rest of their money, for bus fare.

After she's gone, he stares at the door, his mind fissuring like concrete after an earthquake.

He turns and staggers across the courtyard. He wakes Mary in a rushing whisper, with just enough lucidity left to hear how crazed and off-kilter he sounds. He implores her to wake the boys and take them to a neighbor. Her eyes show confusion and outrage at the command, and her mouth rattles off baffled questions that Ita answers automatically. Yes, without breakfast. Yes, now. Right now. Right this second, so he can be alone, so he can think before his mind turns to mush.

Mary's up, rising quickly, pulling open the sheet. Her eyes dig into Ita's, her brow knotted with worry. She opens her mouth to protest, but something she sees in his eyes stops her. She dresses in a flash, crosses the courtyard and collects the children.

Ita hears them whispering, startled, then scared. He knows he is behaving strangely, sending them outside as if it's a regular day and not the end of the world, but he can't stop it. They have to go. They have to leave, like everyone else.

When they're gone, Ita paces the orphanage, kicking up dust. He has to think of a solution.

There has to be a solution.

He's trying, reaching, but one thought finally trumps all the others. *I have nothing left to give. Nothing.*

What can he do? It's over. They're out of money, out of food. The schools are closed, indefinitely. It isn't safe here or anywhere in Kibera. What can he do? He can go to the missionaries—see if they can take the boys. Then he can close the orphanage and wait out the violence.

Life is war, Chege would snarl into Ita's face, standing on his toes for effect. *Why pretend otherwise?*

Ita goes into his room and lets the stillness of the orphanage steel him. The boys will cry, they will lash out. Everything he has tried to teach them will be lost.

All he has to do is start the process, say it aloud. No one will blame him in these times. There will be no more safaris. The world will tell its citizens not to come to Kenya, where the tourist industry has been murdered by the violence, the same as all its victims—with no thought to consequences.

He leaves his room, goes to the space near the washing area. He stares at the leftover cans of paint. He lugs the cans into the courtyard, two at a time, then sits down on one of them to rest. All around him dance the murals he painted with Leda and the children. Was it really such a short time ago?

He looks at the yellow sun, remembers Leda laughing in his ear. Then he looks at the sparrows, and his mind shakes free of the last grip of reason. He stands up on shaky legs.

With trembling fingers, he picks up the brush atop one of the cans. With its handle, he pries open the colors.

Ita begins to paint, to paint over every mural in the orphanage. Over the animals the boys painted with Leda, he paints black columns of smoke. He paints the truth. No rainbows or yellow suns exist here anymore. Kenya's underbelly is exposed. Exteriors always hide something. Messy human anatomy underneath smooth taut skin. Evil intentions behind friendly handshakes. Genocide behind slick election-poster slogans.

Ita paints Raila and Kibaki as two black clouds, raining down fire on shadowy stick figures below. He paints their hands reaching up like bare tree branches, outstretched and empty. Ita paints stormy seas with ships carrying slaves. He paints Chege dancing, his dreads arcing from his head as if he's been struck by lightning.

Sweat runs down Ita's arms in rivulets. His hot, moist skin makes him think of Leda spread out on the bed, her white skin glistening, her hair curling in the heat. He hears her laugh in his ear, feels her breath on his neck. He paints her as an angel with broken wings.

All the paintings are rough, outlines, but the colors speak clearly—black slashes and red everywhere. Darkness and death.

All of a sudden, Ita stops. He staggers back from the wall, a sound gurgling in his throat like a clogged drain. His sandals make two long continuous tracks as he backs his way toward his room. He pushes the door open with his back, his eyes fixed on what he's done. His vision reels, he feels like he's falling. He has to lie down or the paintings will swallow him up. He can hear them. The billowing smoke, the ships at sea. The fluttering sound of the wounded angel, scuttling away from him. Chege's feet, dancing with the devil.

But there is another sound. Outside, growing louder, cutting through his raging thoughts. A scraping sound. Scrambling.

His mind jolts back to reality.

Someone is trying to break in. Climbing over the metal wall.

Ita reaches for his rifle.

CHAPTER 29

December 30, 2007, Nairobi—Leda

AFTER DREAMING OF SPARROWS FOR TWO DAYS in her hotel bed, Leda jolted awake the morning of her flight, with one thought burning clear as a torch in the shuttered room. She had to return to the orphanage.

Oh, how she wished the dreams were an omen, a sign that Ita wanted her to come back. But she knew they weren't. She didn't deserve his forgiveness. She didn't deserve his love. The dreams were meant to torture her, to make her see what she had destroyed, what she was giving up. Leda didn't deserve anything from Ita, ever again.

But lying there in the spacious room, Leda knew what Ita deserved. He deserved an apology. He deserved his mother's necklace back. And he—and the boys—deserved an investor.

You no angel. Chege's words rang in her ears, but she pushed them aside and got out of bed.

After she packed and dressed, she took an envelope from the hotel desk. She wrote out a short note, biting her lip as she did. She tucked all the cash she had into the envelope, but it wasn't enough. With her heart racing, Leda dug in her suitcase for her checkbook.

Once she'd tucked the check into the envelope in her money belt and gathered all her things, she stood by the door, feeling better, feeling as if she could at least do *something* to make up for—

Who am I kidding? She wanted to see Ita again. Yearned to see him. Nothing—not guilt or self-loathing—could stop her from wanting what she knew she didn't deserve. She was returning because she wanted to see him, to say goodbye. She could only hope he would grace her with that.

Leda's ankles twisted and bent as she scurried down the dirt path, crossing the sewage pond and skirting through the refuse.

Over the waterfall of her thoughts she could still see how Kibera had changed. She had watched the news at the hotel, she knew what was happening—the protests. The election results still hadn't been announced. There were accusations of fraud, people were angry. She shouldn't be here and she knew it.

It will be fast and then I'll go. Her flight was in four hours. She just had to get to the orphanage quickly. The streets were quiet. The beauty shops and music stores didn't have the usual crowds out front. At a row of *dukas,* a lone seller stood nervously. And the children—where were all the children?

Leda squeezed the envelope against her stomach. She looked over her shoulder. If anyone knew how much money she carried…

The road opened up before her. At the far end, she spotted a gang of men huddled together, holding signs in the air. Leda squinted to read them. Black marker on cardboard, scrawled by hand. *No Raila. No peace.*

No peace. Leda's skin went cold.

Two men stepped apart and she saw what they circled—a bonfire of rubbish. The men tossed metal onto the pile, hooting and laughing.

Leda darted across the dirt path quick as a rabbit, not looking to check if they'd seen her. Her breath came shorter.

She made it to the orphanage door. She couldn't help but remember the first day she'd arrived, how she'd stood there with Samuel, no idea the turn her life was about to take. No idea she would be offered a chance at happiness, and that she would ruin it.

She knocked, before she lost her nerve. After it received no response, she knocked again.

"Ita?"

The name stood there in the street with her. This would be last time she saw him, wouldn't it? If he opened the door at all. With tears in her eyes, she stood and waited, hearing the men around the bend, their voices like clanking metal.

Finally there came a jangling and a welcome but awful scraping noise on the other side of the gate. Leda's heart waited in her throat.

"Jomo," she said when a face appeared in the crack.

When the corrugated metal inched back another tiny bit, Leda smiled big as she could manage, fifty different emotions stewing in her stomach.

Jomo's expression, which wasn't exactly a smile but definitely not a frown, slid off his face. He looked over his shoulder. Ita would not be happy to see her.

"It's okay. *Hakuna matata.* Let me in." Leda wedged her toe into the opening.

Jomo's eyes met hers before he looked down at her foot in the doorway. He opened the gate the rest of the way and she stepped over the threshold.

Leda put out her hand as she scanned the courtyard. Jomo's slender hand slipped into hers at the same moment her eyes met Ita's.

A moment passed before Jomo's fingers slithered away.

Leda expected to fall at Ita's feet, repentant. But she felt something else entirely. Under his gaze, she became a ball of rising bread, music cresting. Her skin tingled. She yearned to be caressed, to feel his hands waltz over her skin in that sweeping way of his. The hairs on the crown of her head stood up like wire coils and then—

He turned off his eyes. Like closing the shutters on a midnight serenade, they went dark. And cold.

Leda's first instinct was to run. To run out of that place. Not just out of the orphanage where children's futures balanced on a seesaw. Not just out of Kibera, where the seesaw had tipped long ago. No, her first instinct was to run out of Kenya and away forever.

But as she shifted her weight, she felt the envelope in her money belt, pressing against her stomach. She owed him this. The truth, an apology. And the money.

"What are you doing here?" Ita growled. "Are you here to get your things?"

"No." *God, no.* "I want you to have my things, keep it all. There's medicine in there, and—" The wince in Ita's eyes stopped her. She was bungling it already. "I came to explain."

"You disappeared. Now you come back, only to leave again. Why?"

"Ita. Please—" She stepped closer.

"You left," he said three octaves higher than his growl, near the whimper of a child. "Chege said—"

Leda inhaled.

"—you left early, that you didn't want to hurt my feelings, admit you would never return. You told him you had fun, but you could never be with someone like me, could never stay in a place like Kibera."

Chege didn't tell him about the kiss.

Leda felt the dust at her feet turn to quicksand. She was sinking, about to be buried alive by her guilt. Chege didn't tell him. *But it still happened.*

She saw the falling look on Ita's face. He was confused, hurt. He wanted her to deny it.

"No. It isn't like that. It wasn't like that. I'm so sorry—" How to start? How to say it? The pain in Ita's eyes was already too much. Telling him about Chege would double it. Would it be cowardly not to tell him, or merciful? And the children, gathered around, listening, watching—Chege had told them lies, too. Was the truth better than the lies? Leda's heart sank. Did it matter at all? The truth was she was leaving them. "I came to say goodbye. And to give you something."

"Will you come back?"

There it was. The question. Leda had always planned to leave. The question was what happened next. Ita's face was changing back into itself, smoothing, calming. He was processing her reappearance, hoping—

"Do you want me to?" Leda wanted to hear him say it. Instantly, she was ashamed of herself. She was a terrible person. Ita had to know. He had to know who she really was. "I want to come back," she said. "Desperately. But I have to tell you something first, and you will hate me for it. You won't want me to come back."

Ita frowned. "How could I ever hate you?"

The look on his face, gentle and concerned—it sliced through her insides. She would never be good, so unconditionally, absolutely good like that.

The weight of the words in her mouth sawed through the rope that had tugged her there. Determination, courage—they fell from her like bricks. The thought of leaving felt like cutting off a limb to escape. The thought of staying was impossible. But the pain of losing Ita suddenly weighed the most of all and it fell on top of her as if the sky had turned to cement.

"Please—" Leda squeaked and her knees wobbled.

"Please—" she whispered and her cheeks were drawn with tears.

"Please—" she mouthed and Ita caught her in his arms.

He stroked back her hair so he could kiss her forehead three, four, five times in a row, slow as a summer afternoon.

His lips found hers and stopped the world from breathing, stopped the earth spinning, stopped the trees swaying. There were no words for those moments outside time and space. Leda and Ita existed only in and of and for each other.

When their lips parted, Leda took a few seconds to open her eyes. His were waiting.

The children started clapping. They hooted and laughed.

"I'm yours," Leda whispered. "Yours." Ita leaned in to kiss her again, but she pulled back and lowered her eyes. "But you don't know what I am, what I did—"

"Come," he said, taking her hand and leading her to his room. "Tell me."

Inside, he pulled her to him again, kissed her deep enough to take her breath away. But this time, kissing him made Leda think of Chege and she yanked herself apart, gasping, and dropped to the bed. He sat beside her, concerned, a tenderness that tore her in two. With tears stinging her eyes, she reached into her money belt and took the envelope out. She pressed it into his hands. "Take this."

But Ita barely looked at it, he put it aside, on the desk next to his bed. His eyes were locked on Leda—full of compassion, pained to see her pain, eager to listen and comfort her. It broke her heart once and for all.

She took a deep breath. "Voting day, when you were gone—"

"*Ita!*"

It was Michael, just outside the door. He pounded with both fists. "Ita! *Kibaki alishinda!*" he shouted. Leda struggled to translate, tried to process the frantic words. The election results had been announced. Kibaki won.

"Outside," Michael cried. "Look!"

Ita sprung from the bed, turning back to look at her, just long enough to thrust out his palm. "Stay here."

He left and shut the door.

The wall behind Leda's head connected to the outside. The roar that rose in the street grew so loud she felt as if people were stampeding through Ita's bedroom. Men chanting. Women screaming. Children howling. Destruction, as if Kibera were being trampled by a giant. Leda listened with her heart in her throat—people and houses being crushed to the ground, by men bent on avenging all they had been denied, everything they'd had to endure.

Leda sat on the bed and listened until she could stand it no longer. When she opened the door, she could see an orange glow and pillars of smoke billowing into the air beyond the orphanage walls. When she took a breath, ash clogged her mouth and she doubled over, coughing.

Everyone was huddled by the gate. Walter bawled on the

ground, no one picking him up, his little face scrunched up so tight, his wailing mouth was all she could see.

She rushed over and picked him up, pressed him to her heart and stroked his hair. Ita looked up in surprise and barked, "Leda, go back inside! Everyone, go with Leda. Now, *kwenda*—"

But with Ita's back turned for just that one moment, Jomo had time to open the gate.

The gate to hell.

Through the crack, Leda saw the mob storming past. Machetes thrust into the sky—glinting in the firelight—feet pounding the dirt, howling mouths agape and foaming.

Without warning, Jomo dashed into the mass of men. He was immediately engulfed, swallowed by the roiling froth of limbs and torsos.

"No!" Ita screamed.

For seconds that felt like eternity, they all peered into the chaos.

Then Leda spotted him. Jomo was on the ground, bleeding, men with machetes trampling over him. They would kill him.

Without thinking, Leda ran out into the mob after him.

CHAPTER 30

January 11, 2008, Kibera—Ita

ITA CROUCHES, THE RIFLE AIMED IN FRONT OF him, ready.

He scans the inside perimeter of the courtyard, trying to pin down the sound's origin. He hears the loud clang of someone throwing himself at the metal wall, trying to clear the top.

Then he sees it—two sets of fingers and a foot in a sandal. Clutching. Clinging to the wall straight ahead. Ita aims the rifle. But the disembodied fingers and foot vanish with a thud behind the wall.

They didn't make it, but they will try again.

There's a pause, a deafening silence that claws at Ita's ears. He waits, ready.

The same sequence again—Ita hears the scrambling in the dirt, the determination of body and mind. Then the thump, the clang of body on metal.

And now Ita has to decide. Morality doesn't always allow for deliberation, it happens in instants. Which is the choice that will save him and which is the choice that will kill him slowly, for the rest of his life?

When the fingers appear, Ita doesn't fire.

When the foot appears, he takes a breath.

When the foot becomes half a leg in jeans and a knee, Ita squeezes the trigger.

The choice is made. The sound of the bullet pinging off the metal rings through the air. He missed on purpose. The foot and fingers vanish with a thud and a yelp.

It takes a few seconds for Ita to realize that the yelp was not a man's, but a boy's. And that the sandal was blue. Familiar. Jomo.

The rifle in Ita's hands is a hose turned into a serpent. He casts it to the ground. Then he drags a stool over to the wall, climbs atop it and peers over.

Jomo is heaped on the ground, clutching his ankle and rocking himself. He's hurt.

"Stay there!" Ita says and Jomo looks up at him, terrified. "I'm coming to get you."

Ita runs around the side of the orphanage, scoops Jomo up into his arms. His heart races as he carries him inside, disgusted with himself for what could have happened. Jomo doesn't say a word. Ita wishes he would yell at him, but no, the boy bites down on his lip to quell his tears, tucked silently in Ita's arms as he speeds through the courtyard into the medical room.

Ita sits the shaking boy down on the metal table. "Are you okay? Is it your ankle?"

Jomo nods, clutching his right calf. Ita slides his jeans up and sees that already the ankle is hideously swollen. *Please don't let it be broken.*

"Okay," he says, "I'm going to turn it around, very carefully. You tell me when to stop." He slips off Jomo's sandal and straightens his leg. He proceeds to turn the wounded ankle slowly, 360 degrees. Jomo sucks in a wincing breath, but Ita makes it the full circle without him calling out. A sprain then, most likely. Ita sighs.

"What were you doing?" he snaps. "Why didn't you knock? Where's Mary? Jomo, I almost—"

But Jomo's face is like a beaten puppy's. Something is very wrong, not just the ankle. His long fingers grip the edge of the metal operating table, the rest of his body is quivering.

"Jomo, what is it?" Ita is aware he's making it worse, scaring the boy by his tone. He tries to soften his voice, imitate how Mary talks to them, soothingly. "You can tell me. What is it, angel?"

This was the wrong thing to say. Jomo's silent whimpers switch to muted sobs. His shoulders shake so violently Ita worries he will make himself sick. Not knowing what else to do, Ita takes the boy into his arms and hugs him tight.

Miraculously, Jomo allows it. His dusty head tucks underneath Ita's chin. Ita feels his dread start to fade away.

Then suddenly Jomo recoils. He scoots to the other side of the table, leaving a cold hard space between them.

"Jomo." Ita gives him a long look. "Tell me."

Jomo's eyes dart to Ita's hands. "The necklace," he says.

The necklace? Ita looks at the boy in confusion.

"Necklace," Jomo repeats.

He wants to see the necklace? Ita reaches inside his pocket and takes out the broken sparrow necklace. The severed links of chain dangle from his fingers. Jomo's eyes fix on the necklace and grow wide, wider.

"Where did you find it?" Ita asks, watching the boy's tear-smeared face. But maybe that is the wrong question. "When?"

"That night," Jomo whispers.

Ita feels a drumbeat in his stomach, the heartbeat of a monster growing within. "Tell me, Jomo. Tell me now."

"I saw—" Jomo halts.

"You saw what?"

"Everything," he answers, looking at the floor. "I saw everything."

CHAPTER 31

December 30, 2007, Kibera—Leda

AS LEDA RAN TOWARD THE MOB, SHE FIXED HER eyes on Jomo, on the flickering glimpse of him between ankles and legs. But once she dove into the crowd, all clarity vanished.

The pain was shocking enough. Elbows jarred, feet kicked, weapons nicked her flesh. Instead of falling, she was lifted and carried forward, her toes dragging in the dirt. Men growled and screamed in her ears, spit peppered her face. A shoulder jabbed her in the jugular. They chanted, they bobbed in unison, they shoved each other in fervor. They were a train she'd climbed aboard, speeding down the dirt artery of the slum.

Leda lost sight of Jomo and couldn't hear if Ita had come after her. She couldn't see or hear anything clearly at all. Shadowy glimpses of sweat, blood and metal flashed before her as she squinted, trying to form an exit plan.

When a man to her right shoved another man to the left, creating a pocket, Leda's feet hit firm ground and the crowd spit her out on a corner.

Leda flattened herself against a storefront, the sheet of corrugated metal cool against her shoulders. She looked down at her arms and saw they were scrawled with bleeding scratches. In the street, the mob started to circle, thrusting their fists in the air. *No Raila, no peace,* they chanted. *No Raila, no peace!* Someone hurled a burning stick, set two men aflame. A man shoved his neighbor crashing through a front door. A woman inside screamed, children ran out, wailing.

She had to move. She had to get back to the orphanage. But she was so disoriented, she had no way to get her bearings. And she had to find Jomo.

A man in the crowd stood still suddenly. He looked at Leda, his squinty yellow eyes glittering. He nudged the man beside him, pointed.

Move. Now.

Her back to the metal, Leda edged the way she thought she'd come, eyes down, praying for invisibility.

Suddenly she pitched backward into empty space, a narrow path between a row of shacks. She turned and ran as fast as she could. Her feet sloshed through a stream of sewage and debris, until one of her shoes slipped off. Leda cursed under her breath as her toe sliced down on something sharp. The stumble brought her to her knees, her skirt soaking up the mud, adding weight.

As she struggled to her feet, she heard voices enter the alley. And footsteps. She didn't look back. She ran.

Until someone grabbed her elbow and yanked her backward.

Leda careened into the man's chest hard enough to topple them both. She landed sitting on his stomach, bewildered and terrified. The man wrapped his arms around her middle so she couldn't get up. Her feet pawed in the mud while her hands grasped at air. A river of urine and filth coursed over them both.

His friends caught up, skidded to a stop, and for a second they were silent, as if they were as shocked as she. The man let go and Leda scooted as far away as she could. Her breath came in sharp fragments. When she tried to stand, her feet snagged her skirt and she fell back down. Sobs tore through her throat and snot poured from her nose.

The men stared at her. "No Raila, no peace!" one of them yelled suddenly and thrust his machete into the air. Short, spiky dreadlocks stuck out of his skull like nails.

The other three teenagers followed suit, one holding a hammer, one a kitchen knife.

For a second, Leda thought they would move on. She scuttled away, close to the ground, like a crab. But as they plucked their friend from the mud, one of the men turned sharply to Leda and pointed.

"Kisasi!"

That word Leda knew. *Revenge.*

The men looked around the empty alley, out of sight of the mob. They looked at their weapons, their thoughts uniting as plainly as rain falling into the sea.

The kid closest to her reached out.

Leda clawed the ground, trying to rise, trying to run away. But her elbow was caught in rough fingers that gripped hard enough to pull her shoulder from its socket.

No. Please. Please, world, God, fate, don't let this happen.

CHAPTER 32

January 11, 2008, Kibera—Ita

ITA LISTENS IN TERROR AS JOMO SPEAKS, stringing together more words in his first rushed sentences than Ita has heard him utter in the months since he arrived at the orphanage.

"I was scared. I was hurt. I ran through the streets. I hid in a shack." The words dart from Jomo's pinched mouth.

As a horror show takes shape in Ita's mind, he begins to understand, get a glimmer of what happened that awful night.

December 30, 2007, Kibera—Jomo

Jomo crawled out from beneath the mob. He ducked into the closest alley, sure he'd broken every bone in his body. As he surveyed his bleeding skin, his swollen limbs, he heard men's voices approaching. He was petrified, there was no time to escape. The way back to the orphanage was in the direction of the voices. Peering through the darkness and the smoke, Jomo searched for a place to hide. He tried one door—locked. At the next, a woman's voice hissed for him to go away. Mercifully, a third door gave way when he pushed it open. Inside, the shack was empty. Jomo dashed in as the voices came closer, more of them now—a gang.

He looked around, there was a low bed frame that he could maybe fit beneath. He tucked himself under and pulled in rumpled clothes to hide himself from view. Jomo braced himself. He could hear the men, louder, taunting. When Jomo peeked, he could see through the open door. He cursed himself for not shutting it, locking it.

But then there came another noise, whimpering. A woman. Jomo saw her, a shadow running past, just as a man's hand reached out and grabbed her arm.

Jomo peeled aside the clothes, started clawing his way out.

The men had Leda.

CHAPTER 33

EACH MAN'S HANDS ON LEDA'S SKIN FELT LIKE desert sand. Hot. Gritty. Rough as splinters of glass.

She ricocheted around their circle, a lotto ball in the air mix machine, fate holding its breath. Behind the lunging silhouettes of the men, the slum exploded—fire licking and climbing, spitting at the world. There was another sound, too, mixed with the whooshing sound of the inferno. Wood, metal, bodies, children—all crumbling, cracking, hissing and screaming in the flames. A symphony of loss.

The men, who were boys really, yelled incomprehensibly, but Leda knew their intentions.

They ripped the buttons on her shirt.

They yanked the hem of her skirt.

A cloud of reddish dust rose from their feet, as though trying to hide her. But the dust dashed away as Leda was flung to the ground.

For a moment nothing happened.

Then it was like vampires at the sight of a wound. The men converged—kicking, poking, laughing. They tugged at all

her protruding parts. Leda was a centipede in the dust, trying to fold in one hundred legs. Trying to protect the things
that mattered, the things that could not be undone.

*Maybe they will just beat me and go away. This is not my fight. I
came to help.* Leda wanted to shout in their faces. *I came to help.*

But then she heard it, jumbled with the clatter of their
words. *Ita.* Another one said it. *Ita.*

So they knew who she was.

She was a fish flopping, a tree fallen. A spider in the wind.
She was Ita's love.

For an instant, Leda thought it would save her. But as their
voices rose, she knew it had doomed her instead.

When the boy dropped down on top of her, the force of it
was like a metal roof pinning her in a hurricane.

Instantly, all Leda could smell was him—sweat and dirt,
but rancid, like musk and cheese rusted over with blood. He
used his trunk to flatten her into the ground, his rib bones
stabbing into her sternum, her bare skin ground into the rocks
and trash. His legs and hands scrambled for Leda's flailing
limbs. The man-boys above laughed and hollered.

All she could do was flail and scream.

Leda called out for the man she loved, the only person
who'd ever really loved her.

CHAPTER 34

December 30, 2007, Kibera—Jomo

WHEN HE HEARD HER SCREAM FOR ITA, JOMO knew what he had to do. He would have to run faster than the wind. Once he got out that door, he would circle around. He would jump over houses if he had to. He would make it to Ita in time to come save Leda. It was up to him.

Jomo dug forward, until his head then his shoulders poked out from under the bed. His fingers scratched at the dirt, he was stuck, trying to wriggle himself free.

But then Jomo heard a new voice, and allowed himself a sigh of relief. It was a welcome voice. Chege.

CHAPTER 35

December 30, 2007, Kibera—Leda

LEDA CALLED FOR ITA WITH ALL HER SOUL.

But it was the devil who arrived instead.

Ita's beloved monster, Chege.

Chege's voice arrived first—a low growl, a familiar snarl. It was the battle cry of an unchained wolf, at home in the darkest of times.

Chege was above her. His dreads closed over Leda and her attacker, a curtain of night.

"Help me," Leda said. *Did Ita send him?*

As Leda tried to decipher Chege's spitting words, he yanked the man off and her body took a breath. The rancid smell, his clawing zipper, the pain in her lungs—it all disappeared into the racket above and for one second Leda felt light as a sparrow in the sky. She allowed herself to breathe. There was mercy in Chege's heart after all. He would save her. At least for Ita's sake.

But then Chege's eye flickered, a flap of emotion like blinds shuttering the daylight. His hand shot down and wrapped around her throat, a coiled python, and her breath was lost.

His other snapped the necklace from her neck. The gold necklace Ita had given her, the sacred chain that was everything to him.

This, Chege knew better than anyone.

He stared at the necklace in his fingers, his eyes bulging, and Leda knew the truth. Chege's heart wasn't merciful, it was a furnace of coal that burned only with rage. When both his hands pulled Leda up by the throat, the glint of the gold chain taunted her, the shiny sparrow charm a spark in her peripheral vision as the necklace dropped to the dirt.

Up, up through the dust, Chege brandished her like a chunk of meat.

He'd claimed her. Head wolf gets the kill.

His eyes darted about. Leda saw it when he did—a door ajar. He smiled, baring his brown teeth.

Faster than Leda could scream, Chege kicked her feet to knock her off balance, then dragged her across the alley, to the open door. The boys lapped at their heels, eyes ravenous. Behind them, the fire rolled atop the mud shacks like a river of exploding stars.

Maybe they will burn for this. Maybe we all will.

Chege yanked her into the dark room, kicked the door shut, and all light went out in the world.

Leda screamed and punched and hit. She bit and clawed and shouted Chege's best friend's name into the darkness. To remind him. To rebuke him. To make him see himself: an abomination.

And as she fought, like a cat under a crocodile, he thrust his hot, wet mouth over her ear, stubble slicing her skin, his arms pinning her sure as shackles, as he hissed, in a voice that would never leave her again—

"Stop! Stop! Leda, you are safe. I not gunna hurt you. Shhh. You are safe."

When the words finally penetrated, cut through Leda's screams and pierced her heart, she went limp beneath him.

A sob formed in her belly and swelled until it was born between them, shaking them both like trees in a tempest.

Relief flooded her veins until she swam in it, tears adding to the torrent. She opened her eyes like an owl in the night, and found herself on a dirt floor, in a one-room shack in a slum on the other side of the world, somehow miraculously, astoundingly alive. Then she found Chege's almond-shaped eyes looking into hers.

A cry paused on its way up her throat and changed into a sigh that fluttered from her like snow. A fire, kindled by naked flesh pressed together, by the scent of skin and sweat, by the swell of emotion overtaking them both, erupted between them. It was all too much—the terror-filled night brewing past with future, stewing all human feeling into a tidal wave no one could outrun. Too late. Too late to go back. Too late to escape.

Chege's mouth clamped down over Leda's—hot, hungry, desperate—and Leda opened her lips, letting his tongue inside. She let the little monsters win.

CHAPTER 36

January 11, 2008, Malibu, CA—Leda

IT'S JUST AFTER MIDNIGHT. THE CLOCK IN Estella's dining room is ticking. It's telling Leda, Time does not erase your sins.

The nurses put Estella to bed tonight, her breath dragging in and out of her body like the sea over jagged rocks.

Now that they've gone, Leda is alone in the kitchen. She puts her hand on her stomach. Not entirely alone.

Too late. Too late to go back. Too late to escape what happened.

Leda jumps at a sound overhead, a thud that landed directly above where she sits at the kitchen table.

"Mother?" Leda calls, the chair scraping the floor as she finds her feet, heads for the stairs. "Mother," she calls again at Estella's door. "I'm coming in." As she opens the door to the pitch-black room, light from the hallway filters in. The bed is empty.

She runs in to find Estella facedown, sprawled at an odd angle, a few feet away. She crouches beside her, rolls over her mother's limp body. Her eyes flutter. She's conscious.

"I'm calling 911."

Estella tries to speak, but her voice is slippery, bubbling.

"Shhh, it's okay. You're okay. Don't talk." Leda's hand fumbles across the nightstand for her mother's cell.

She dials 911 and returns to Estella's side. As Leda recites the address for the ambulance, Estella groans, a distorted rumble of agony that makes Leda's blood run cold.

She studies her mother's face. One side of her lip is curled down, the other limp. A stroke? "Please hurry," Leda says and hangs up the phone. She pulls Estella into her lap and remembers how she did the same with Ita, how her hair draped over his broken face as she pleaded with God not to make him suffer for what she had done. Not to make him suffer for her sins.

CHAPTER 37

December 30, 2007, Kibera—Leda

THEIR LIPS SLAMMED INTO EACH OTHER, seeking, licking, sucking. While Chege cupped one hand behind Leda's head, protecting it from touching the ground, the other roved over her skin, her breasts, grasped the curve of her hip, smeared orange dust across her thighs. Her back arched as Chege kissed her throat, sucked at her nipples.

It wasn't like the searing happiness when Ita kissed her. It wasn't the enveloping sense of safety. No, the heat between Chege and her was dark and licked at her like fire, flooded through her like a drug, dangerous but addictive.

She heard the undoing of Chege's pants, felt his bare thighs, felt him hard against her underwear. Then he tugged them down, pulled her panties off.

No, wait, Leda heard a little voice say somewhere inside her soul.

But the fire paid no mind, and it climbed and climbed through her limbs, unfurling and curling like a vine, exploding between her legs, wrapping tight around her hips, setting her stomach aflame—

"Stop."

She wasn't sure she said it aloud, until Chege's head rose from her neck like a lion pausing as it devours its kill. His hands stopped pawing, his nakedness pulled away. With inches between them, Chege panted, waiting. Waiting for what Leda would say next.

"No, Chege. I can't do this to him."

The door banged open and fell from its hinges. Chege dropped down on top of Leda like a shield, his head in her neck and dust everywhere.

Over his shoulder, silhouetted in the doorway, Leda saw Ita's face, carved by horror.

CHAPTER 38

January 11, 2008, Malibu, CA—Leda

LEDA GRASPS HER MOTHER'S HAND IN THE ambulance as the paramedics whir over her like vultures, picking and pricking, clawing and cawing. They're giving her medicine, they're trying to save her, but the beeping of the machines, combined with the siren of the ambulance—it's all Leda can do to keep from screaming.

Estella's eyes have lost some of their fog, her head lolls in Leda's direction.

"Mother? Can you see me? Can you hear me?" Leda peers into her face, leaning in close amidst the roar. The paramedics pause in their mad dash to listen, too.

But the sound that comes from Estella's mouth is an awful, muffled slur. She's staring at something. Leda realizes her mother's eyes are focused on her throat. She puts a hand to her chest. The diamond necklace. Estella left it on the table that day. Looking at the photos of her father, Leda had slipped it on. She'd done it for comfort, imagining the old man's kind heart, believing he would want her to. She'd even let herself imagine Estella wanted her to have it, too.

"Want me take it off?" Leda asks, feeling her cheeks burn. *So stupid.* She should have considered Estella's feelings, the symbol of her sins and regrets the necklace must seem to her. Leda moves to remove it, both hands on the clasp.

But Estella's head lolls slowly left to right, her face pained. Leda stops fumbling with the clasp, brings her hands back down to her lap, and Estella's eyelids flutter. With great effort, she nods her head. Once. Then her eyes close and the beep becomes a scream and the paramedics push Leda aside.

Leda's breath is heaving. She fingers the necklace.

I will wear it, she promises. *I will remember. I will try to do better.*

CHAPTER 39

January 11, 2008, Kibera—Ita

JOMO SPITS THE WORDS FROM HIS MOUTH AS if he's choking on fish bones.

Ita hears the torment, a young boy's confusion, disgust over what he witnessed in that room. Ita feels for him, even as his blood starts to boil and he grips the edge of the metal table as if he will tip off the edge of the earth.

At the part of his story where Ita came barreling through the door, Jomo's voice nearly drops off completely. Jomo admits in a strangled whisper to watching the men beat Ita and drag him outside, confesses he stayed hidden under the bed and did nothing, scared to death.

Finally, after the police came and went, Jomo emerged. He found the sparrow necklace squashed into the mud in the alley and pocketed it before ducking around the corner and running back to the orphanage. The slum was engulfed in chaos, a roar like lions in the clouds.

Finally, Jomo can say no more. His thin shoulders cave in on him and he slides off the table, ashamed to even look at Ita.

Ita is amazed that his heart continues to beat, though it's

in four pieces. One for himself. One for Jomo. One for Leda, one for Chege. His thoughts are a pack of wild dogs, tearing each other apart. He can observe, he can listen, but he can do nothing to stop the battle.

Chege's death.

Leda's betrayal.

Kioni.

The violence.

The fires.

That night. Ita is back in that night, his feet pounding the dirt, searching, pushing through the mobs, calling out Leda's name. Finding Chege's men crowded outside the door, cheering. Bursting inside. Seeing their bodies pressed together. Naked flesh, the red scratches on her skin, the blood and bruises. The dust curling around them. The look in Chege's eye. Guilt. Guilt so sharp he couldn't see past it to Leda's mirror-image eyes.

Ita's mind wanders into a seething cloud, a swarm of locusts eating his insides. There is no escaping the horde of emotions. Hatred, jealousy, love, regret—one by one and at all at once they swirl up through his guts until he wants to cry out.

When Jomo tugs on Ita's pant leg, he lets the cry escape. Jomo jumps back, as if expecting to get hit. Steps forward again, as if wanting to.

"There is more," Jomo says. "In your room, on your desk, I found something. I stole it." He holds an envelope out to Ita. A cream-colored envelope, thick and folded, worn at the edges. Ita's name is written across the front. He feels a shiver go up his spine as its familiarity settles upon him. Leda gave it to him, that night, but in the chaos, he'd forgotten about it until just now.

"I'm sorry," Jomo is saying, near tears. "I was going to

take a little and give the rest back. I was going to run away. I'm sorry."

Ita takes the envelope, feels how fat it is, how heavy.

"I understand if you hate me," Jomo says, "if you don't want me here anymore."

Ita opens the flap of the envelope. It's stuffed with money, layers and layers of cash, flattened together. And there's a letter.

"I'll go now," Jomo whispers.

But Ita is transfixed by the letter. Only when Jomo turns and hobbles to the door, wincing at the pain of his ankle but forcing himself to step on it as punishment, only then does Ita feel a flutter in his stomach, rising like birds taking flight. Jomo means to leave for good. He doesn't expect to be forgiven, doesn't expect to be loved. Doesn't feel he deserves it.

"Jomo, wait—"

The boy doesn't turn. But he stops. Halfway through the door, he stops.

"Jomo, look at me."

He turns around, his eyes flitter up to Ita's and then drop. He looks just off to the side, face blank, mind racing. It is such an exact replica of Leda's stance, Ita wants to cry. To hug him tight.

"Sometimes, we can't help it," Ita says. "Sometimes, we can't outrun the little monsters inside us that make us do bad things." He sets down the envelope so that his hands are empty, open. "But do you know something?"

"What?" Jomo's voice is the squeak of a mouse, the tiniest squeak of hope.

"We're all like that. Everyone has them."

Jomo doesn't say a word. He's holding his breath.

"Which means we can forgive each other."

Jomo's face is like paper in the fire, curling in on itself. Ita takes a chance—he opens his arms. Jomo considers, lowers his chin, hesitates.

When he tucks into Ita's arms, he cries. His little body shakes like acacia leaves in the rain. But his feet are planted firm as if they're growing roots. He will stay with Ita a long time.

One arm still wrapped around the child, Ita reaches his other for the envelope on the table. When he opens the flap, he feels a chill. He slips the letter free.

Leda.

Her name fills the room as though whispered by the red dust itself.

He unfolds the paper.

Ita,
You deserve better, in every way.
  Take this money. And please cash the check. I want to help more, too, as much as you'll let me.
  I'm sorry. But I don't expect you to forgive me. I don't think you should. I tried to warn you—I'm no good at love. Even if I love you more than you can ever know.
Leda

Ita stares at the page. He reads it three more times. *And please cash the check.*

Jomo's stopped crying. He gently pulls away and looks at Ita with big, full eyes. He watches as he nudges the cash aside in the envelope. Tucked in at the back is a check wearing Leda's name and address and a number with four zeros to follow.

Jomo watches, curious. Ita thanks God Jomo didn't throw it away, not knowing what it is.

Because Ita does. It is a small piece of paper big enough to save them.

Big enough to save them all.

CHAPTER 40

LEDA WATCHES THE MOUNTAIN AND THE mountain watches her. The nearby tree continues to cheerlead. Everything in its place.

Including me.

Amadeus jumps up into Leda's lap and curls into a furry ball to be petted.

"Hey, there," Leda says and scratches his Mohawk.

She reaches beneath the little dog and pulls out the stack of photos on her lap. She flips through them one by one, her new ritual. She sees the photos differently now. In Estella's glamour shots, she sees the vulnerability in her mother's sultry gaze. She sees the sadness in the old man's, her father's, happy eyes—the acceptance of the short time they will have together. She lingers over the photo of her mother holding her as an infant, still unable to sort out the complicated mix of emotions it brings.

Next, Leda flips through to the newer, shinier photos, the ones she finally got printed. She finds the one she is looking for—a picture of Ita, his smile jumping out at her in its brilliance.

Amadeus lifts his head. He sniffs the picture.

"Nope," Leda whispers. "Still no word."

Nearby, on a small table, sits Leda's laptop. She opens it and the website, already up in the browser, jumps into view. That smile. Leda's heart still skips every time she sees it.

It's comforting somehow that the website is still up, even though she knows it doesn't mean anything necessarily. She reads the papers—she knows how terrible things still are in Kibera.

But the check was cashed.

She closes her eyes. *Ita is alive.*

She's left phone messages. She's emailed. She's even sent a letter.

Leda watches the goose bumps fan out across her forearms at the thought. She wrote the letter at the hospital, in the early morning hours before Estella died. It was as if her mother's passing gave her courage. The courage to tell the truth.

But she didn't tell him about the baby—his baby—not yet.

He had to be allowed to hate her first, if he wanted.

Leda looks at his smile, on the computer and in the picture in her fingers. *He is too good.* If he knew about the baby he would sacrifice his feelings to do the right thing.

Leda wants to do the right thing for once. For him.

Ita has the money now, for the boys, for his dreams. If he wants to forget her, she will let him.

Because for the first time, staring at the mountain, Leda feels strong. She can do it alone.

The rare sound of the doorbell sends Amadeus yelping and jumping off her lap, the photos slapping the deck and shuffling themselves. Amadeus heads for the door, barking loud enough to put Paul Revere to shame.

Leda picks up the photos and shuts the laptop, placing the pictures gently on top. She pads barefoot after Amadeus, wondering who on earth could be ringing her bell—who even knows she's here?

When she opens the door, the sound that leaves her lips is scratchy, like a sparrow taking off from a branch. The smile she finds on her doorstep brings tears to her eyes.

"Ita," she breathes.

"Leda," Ita says.

Sunlight streams in from behind his head, illuminating him like an angel, and Leda feels its warmth wrap around her, blanket her with happiness.

"You're here," Leda says.

He reaches out, his fingers touch the diamond necklace at Leda's throat. He cocks his head.

"My mother's," she says.

Ita nods, his face saturated with emotion. He reaches gingerly into his pocket. In a move that's been planned, rehearsed, dreamed out, Leda can tell, he takes out the sparrow necklace. He clasps it around her neck, the sparrow finding its place just below the diamond sparkling in the sun.

"I'm here," he says.

Leda takes a deep breath. "You got my letter?"

Ita's brow knots into a question. "No." He scoops up his bag and takes a step forward. To come inside.

But Leda doesn't budge. Her stomach heaves and her skin feels hot.

"What is it?" he says, his smile slipping into a frown.

"You don't know." Leda feels sick, her hand shoots out for

the support of the doorjamb. Amadeus barks at her feet, sensing her stumble. "Chege didn't tell you?"

"Leda, I know everything. Jomo saw it. He was under the bed in the shanty that night."

"Oh my God." Leda hides her face in her hands. Horrific, for a child to see such a thing. "I'm sorry, Ita. I'm so, so sorry."

"I know." Ita's fingers encircle her wrists, positioning her two hands like a prayer between them. Leda opens her eyes. "I know everything, Leda. Everything." Ita winds her arms around him, around his waist. "And I am here."

With those words and the buoying realization that they are true, Leda slumps into Ita's embrace, falls into him. When she breathes him in, she imagines she can smell the soap he uses to wash the boys' clothes and faces, hear the little songs he and Mary sing to them. Leda's face burrows into Ita's chest and she feels the warmth fan across and through her, stirring up her heartbeat.

"Chege is dead," Ita says quietly. He says it in such a way that holds ten different meanings at once, for him, for Leda, for them both. But then she can no longer hear her heartbeat, because of the sobs that have overtaken her body.

The news of Chege's death combines with Estella's passing, two gaping holes allowing for so much possibility. Leda cries with her eyes squeezed shut, and the force of it shakes them both. When the sobs turn to gasps, she pulls an inch away. When she meets Ita's eyes, she finds his quiet, accepting gaze unfaltered.

"You don't know everything," Leda says.

Ita looks at her with so much tenderness, she hopes she will never have to leave that gaze again. She hopes with all her heart her child will know that love.

"We're going to have a baby."

★ ★ ★

That night, Ita pulls the mattress onto the back porch. He and Leda lie under the stars, their fingers twining and untwining in the night air, stroking each other, knowing each other, loving each other.

"Or we could bring the boys here," Ita whispers excitedly.

"Mary, too," Leda says and he laughs. "Okay, maybe not, but I'm going to need help with all those boys while you're in med school."

Ita laughs again. The sound fits in the surroundings as naturally as the trees. He rolls over, reaches across her and scratches Amadeus's ear. "Mary would want to stay behind, I think, with Grace. And to continue with—"

"The orphanage," Leda says. "But we should build a bigger one, hire people to help her, and build a school—"

Ita's lips steal her next words as he leans in to kiss her. He pulls away, his eyes hooded. "I love you, Leda. So much it scares me."

Leda sucks in a breath, thinks of the night they lay in the tent, on safari—the shiny plans they whispered, oblivious of the tidal wave coming to wreck them. But the monsters are quiet for now. "I love you, too. More than fear." She means it, body and soul, but with everything that happened, could they really afford to dream again? Could they believe in such a fluttery thing as hope? Love?

Leda squeezes Ita's fingers, silhouetted under a sea of stars. Of course they could.

★ ★ ★ ★ ★

ACKNOWLEDGMENTS

I AM DEEPLY GRATEFUL AND INDEBTED TO MY agent, Frances Black, who said "You're gonna make it, darling"—and then helped make it happen in every way. My editor, Emily Ohanjanians, whose brilliance at what she does leaves me in awe. All the women (and men) at Harlequin MIRA who work tirelessly for their authors. You are the dream makers. Thank you Mariam, Christopher, Mary and all the people I met in Kenya who inspired and informed this book. Thank you, thank you, thank you, Bianca, for being my best friend for twenty-seven years. Thank you, Clovernookers, Kim, DKH, Lilia, David, Raquel, Gavin, Vivienne, Susan Pottography, JBird crew, Jeanine, Nicole, Tiffany and all the lovely Book Club ladies. Thank you, Megan and Aaron, for your support and encouragement always, and Big Bear! Thank you, Mom and Dad, for...everything. And thank you, Jonathan, for being always there—in the trenches, in my daydreams, in my heart.

We hope you enjoyed Deborah Cloyed's
WHAT TEARS US APART, and that the
following questions for discussion help to enhance the
experience of this story for you and your book club.

Contains spoilers

1. The story is set against the backdrop of the 2007–2008 political uprisings in Nairobi's Kibera slum. What role does setting play in this story, and how would it be different if the setting were elsewhere?

2. The story jumps back and forth in time, and is told from different points of view. Why do you think a story like this would be structured in such a way? How would it be different if it were told linearly?

3. Atonement is a running theme throughout this story. Which characters are atoning and what are their sins, real or perceived? How does each character's atonement manifest itself and what does this say about that person?

4. One of the things Leda most admires in Ita is the way he treats the orphans. Why do you think Leda finds this trait in him so attractive? How do Ita and Estella contrast in their parenting styles?

5. Ita's mother's necklace is a very meaningful item in the story. Why do you think Ita would give it to Leda when he was so adamant that neither Chege nor Kioni could touch it? Why does Chege throw the necklace to the ground during Leda's attack scene, rather than keep it or sell it? What does it symbolize? And how does its significance compare to the necklace from Leda's adoptive father?

6. As with most people, Chege's character is complex. He is both loyal and betraying toward Ita, and both brutal and kind toward Leda. What do you think motivates him?

7. Ita seems to make Leda very happy, and he thinks the world of her. Why do you think she lets Chege kiss her on voting day?

8. Money, opportunity and privilege are running themes in the story. How do the different characters make use of what is available to them? How would their lives be different if they were in others' shoes—Ita in Leda's, for instance, or Leda in Ita's?

9. For much of the story, Leda seems to be motivated by her "little monsters"—the demons within that make her feel as though she doesn't deserve the love of a good man such as Ita. Do you think this is a common insecurity in people in general? Why? And if so, how do you feel it drives people's behaviors?

10. The scene in which Leda is attacked by Chege's gang, and then Chege himself, subverts expectations in the end. Would you have perceived the story and the characters' decisions differently if this scene had played out differently? How?

Where did the idea for *What Tears Us Apart* come from?

On the surface, the idea came directly from my time spent in East Africa, an experience that affected me emotionally more than any of the other places I've lived abroad. While many of my experiences of the landscape and kind, humor-loving people were positive, on the whole my stay felt like riding a roller coaster of identity, my sense of self shifting with every new encounter. Everything I thought I believed about race, class, poverty, religion, violence, charity, government and history was challenged time and time again. I took lots of notes and photographs—I knew I would eventually want to write about it, attempt to make sense of my conflicted reaction. But when I returned to the U.S., I set about writing my first book, The Summer We Came to Life, which was set in Honduras, instead. At that time in my life I was itching to get down Samantha's story, plus I realize now I wasn't ready yet to process the cascade of emotion surrounding my time in East Africa.

The novel is set during the 2007 Kenyan elections, and the resultant uprisings countrywide—particularly the Kibera

A CONVERSATION WITH DEBORAH CLOYED

slum. What about this time and place inspired you to use it as the setting for your story?

I spent the summer of 2007 volunteering in rural Muslim areas of Tanzania and Kenya, assisting women with budding micro-finance initiatives. Many experiences there, positive and negative, inspired and informed the book. In transit before and after, I spent time in cosmopolitan Nairobi. It was difficult to convince friends to take me into Kibera, to visit an orphanage, but that experience was one of the most powerful of all. Meeting children living in the most difficult of circumstances, I found myself asking big questions. What is privilege? Destiny? Justice? Nationality? Even the very nature of personality—would we still be ourselves born and raised under completely different circumstances? Regarding the political end of things, my entire time in Kenya I'd been poking about, asking naive questions about tribal affiliation, reading newspapers and magazines, in eager anticipation of the election. Months later, around Christmastime, I watched in horror from my cozy bedroom in snowy Northern Virginia while unimaginable atrocities swept across many places I'd just been—cities and countryside. It affected me profoundly—the sickening mystery of how human beings turn on each other. I chose to set the story specifically in Kibera, however, because it embodied what the book was about for me—inner demons borne of strife and frustration, dashed hopes and complicated alliances.

We experience this story largely from two distinct points of view—Leda's and Ita's. What were the challenges in writing the voice of a young Kenyan man?

An earlier draft of the novel had Leda written in first person and Ita in a more distant third person, with fewer chapters from his point of view. This was due to nothing more than my trepidation about writing from the perspective of a male from a different culture and world. Even though I'd done months of research, scoured accounts and blogs and interviewed male

Kenyan friends, I was still pinned by apprehension and an awareness of how I might be judged for such an attempt. But as the book progressed and took on its own life, it felt more and more unjust not to give Ita his own equal point of view. I knew him intimately by then, certainly as well as I knew Leda. And truthfully, neither one of them could be any more different than me and my life experience. So one day I said—aloud—Okay, Ita, now is the time. Speak up. And he did. And what he had to say reminded me of something I already knew—the human condition is a singular experience in a variety of flavors, but composed of the same emotional ingredients. We all feel abandonment, hope, despair, humiliation, indignation and the bittersweet ache of love. Therein lies the bridge by which we connect to one another.

All of the characters are both endearing and deeply flawed. Do you have a favorite character among them? If so, who and why?

This is a question I got asked a lot about my first book, with its motley crew of characters. The truth is, I have to be equally passionate about all the characters to create them in the first place. But characters have a way of taking on their own lives, and by then I love them in the same way I love my family—with all their idiosyncrasies, and knowing they are destined to be a part of my life forever.

I spend a lot of time contemplating people. I eavesdrop shamelessly. I have a penchant for staring and an odd tendency to ask strangers uncomfortable questions. Habitually, I create life stories for people on the sidewalk and the subway. A crowded restaurant is a meal of quirks and mannerisms, traveling a crossword puzzle of faces. What I mean is, I'm equally as taken with trying to figure out how someone could be or become Estella as how Leda survives being her daughter or how someone like Ita would feel so many conflicting feelings toward a person like Chege.

Chege is one of the most complex characters of all. Why did you choose not to show any scenes from his point of view?

In the end, this book is a love story. In life or in books, a love story belongs to two people—the story of how they come together, how they grow into one, the times they nearly fall apart, and how they stitch or snip the thread. Of course, in life as in books, it isn't that simple. There will always be peripheral characters in our love stories—in-laws and exes and interlopers— woven into the tapestry. But the weavers—the tellers—are the lovers. This story belongs to Ita and Leda.

The orphans really come to life, right from the beginning. Did you know what their personalities would be from the very beginning or did they unfold as such throughout the course of your writing?

Michael and Ntimi I knew and loved long before I had the story in place. They were modeled loosely on a handful of children I'd gotten to know in Kenya. I lived with a family of six and spent time at three different orphanages. In addition, I grew up with a huge extended family, I teach photography in elementary schools, and am a proud aunt to my young niece and nephew. In short, I adore children and relate to them well. I'm especially fascinated by how personality shapes our lives from such an early age. If I closed my eyes, instantly I could picture Michael's wide, serious eyes and Ntimi's quick smile. I loved the contrast of those two and couldn't wait to get to know them better. But Jomo was a surprise. Crafting his sad history, I came to understand how he mirrored Leda in so many ways, why they were drawn to each other, and how Ita's gentle way with Jomo mirrored his relationship with Leda. Sometimes in life, we miraculously (though I like to think of it as destiny), manage to find the one person who can uniquely help make us into the best version of ourselves. If we let them, of course.

Jomo and Leda share the same struggle—to accept Ita's love. Jomo naturally took on much more prominence in the story, eventually coming to play a lead role in the book's climax.

One of the various takeaways from this story is that morality is profoundly nuanced. Why was this theme important for you to explore?

I'm deeply troubled by things like infidelity and betrayal, even when it's not happening to me. This book is really about inner demons—how one's best intentions get derailed. As I contemplated the violence in Kenya and other world tragedies, I began to consider large-scale events in terms of individual morality. From afar, a thing like genocide seems like a collective monster. But isn't it a collective of individual decisions? I found myself exploring the possibility that life experience coalesces into an individual making immoral choices, an idea I find as unnerving as it is explanatory.

In my thirties, as I contemplate daunting things like marriage, starting a family, seeing my parents age and relationships crumble around me, I find the idea of a gray, sliding scale of morality terrifying. I yearn to deny it, convince myself there is very simply a right and a wrong choice, a way to prevent precious things from being soiled or lost. But it was inescapable, writing about the thing that scares me the most: maybe there are no good or bad people, only people making good or bad decisions. I am interested to see what readers think about this.

Your first book, *The Summer We Came to Life*, is very different from this one. How did you progress to writing a love story from that story about friendship?

A fascinating thing about writing fiction has been seeing it align with the different stages in my life. My teen years were all about angst, my early twenties all about rebellion—separating from my parents and societal expectation and blazing an identity out of sheer, pigheaded obstreperousness (thankfully my writing from these two periods will never see the light of day!). I wrote The Summer We Came to Life when I was traveling the world and couldn't wait to get back to my best friends. After I turned thirty, when I started What Tears Us Apart, I was back in Los Angeles, settled domestically, and wrapped in happy love. I was ready to tackle things outside of myself. The Summer We Came to Life was the right time in my life to write about friendships, finding yourself and standing on your own. What Tears Us Apart was the right time to write about love and war, and the war of love.

Share your thoughts and questions with Deborah Cloyed. Visit her on Facebook, at www.facebook.com/Writer.DeborahCloyed.